BANTER

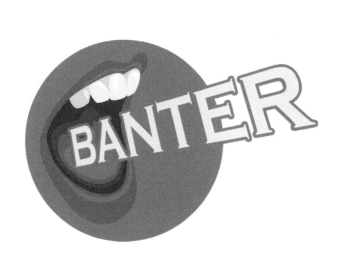

ROCK the BOAT

TRASHED CLASSICS
No. 1

Edited by Lesline James & Tim Lay

ROCK the BOAT

Inspired by the Victorian Classic *Three Men in a Boat*
by Jerome K. Jerome

ILLUSTRATED AND COLOURED BY AUGUSTINE COLL

WRITTEN BY TIM LAY

LETTERED BY PAUL SHINN

Published 2015

© 2010 Banter Publishing Ltd.

www.trashedclassics.com

ISBN: 978-0-9573231-0-0

Adapted by Tim Lay

Illustrated by Augustine Coll

Lettered by Paul Shinn

Cover design Lesline James

Original concept Lesline James

Printed in the UK

Introduction

In the 1880s Jerome K. Jerome took a boat trip down the Thames with his friends George, William Harris and a dog called Montmorency. Three Men in a Boat was Jerome's account of their adventures and became a Victorian era best seller.

Fast forward 120 years…
Rock the Boat mirrors similar scenes and themes with snippets of the original prose embedded in the story, and updates the journey into a modern tale for the Twenty First century.

Along their journey, the band encounter a landscape and social fabric that is startlingly different, yet much the same as Victorian England; wealth and poverty, class and culture, modern gizmos and the traditional English weather.

This is the first in a line of Banter titles from the fiorthcoming *Trashed Classics* series. Taking great works of literature, Banter trashes them (in the best possible way), adding a modern twist for a new audience.

ENJOY!

Day 1

families Suck !

that Sinking feeling

Back in the Game

"ALL ABOARD"

chainsaw MassacRe

keystone CoP

the Stitch-up

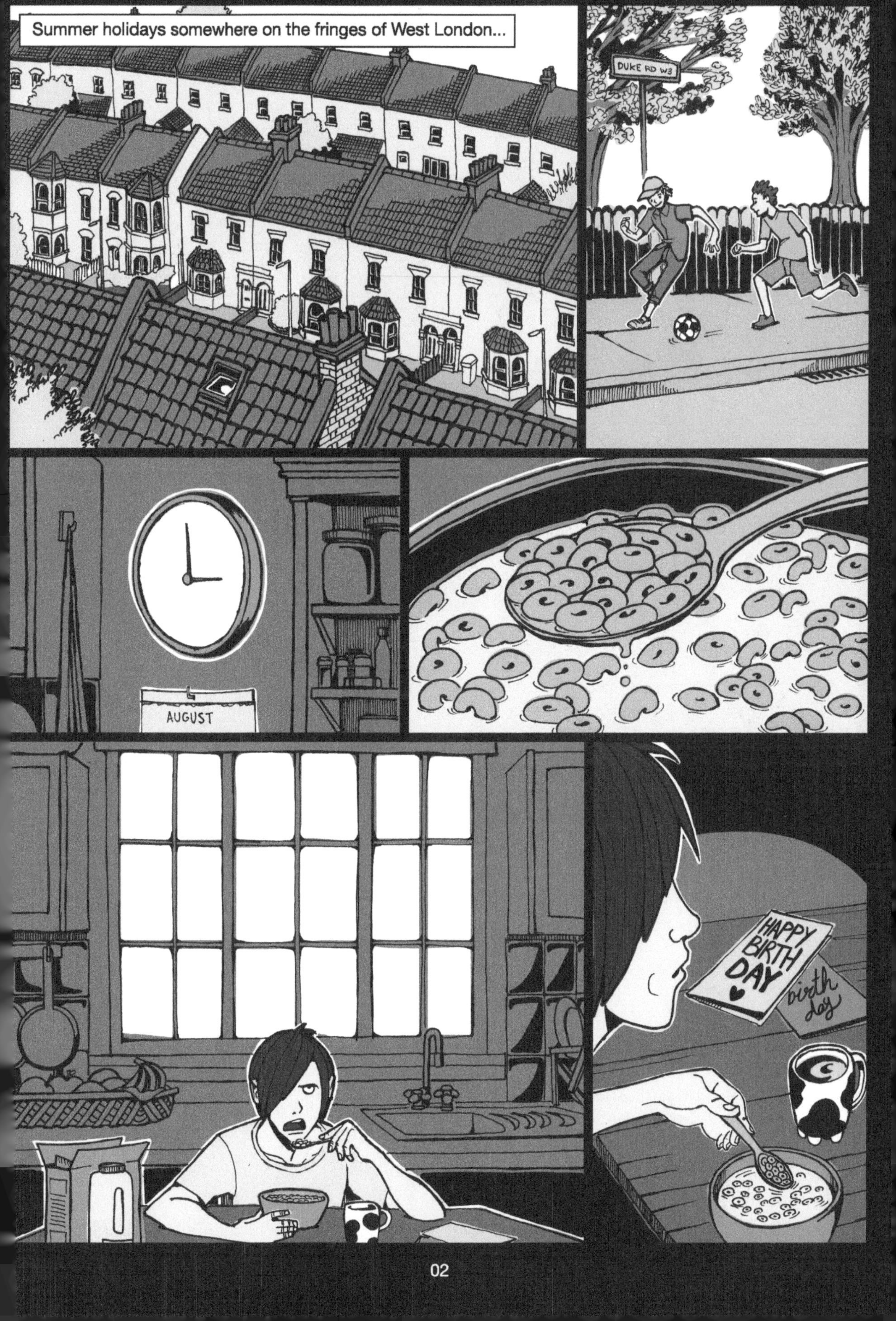
Summer holidays somewhere on the fringes of West London...
DUKE RD W3
AUGUST
HAPPY BIRTH DAY
birth day

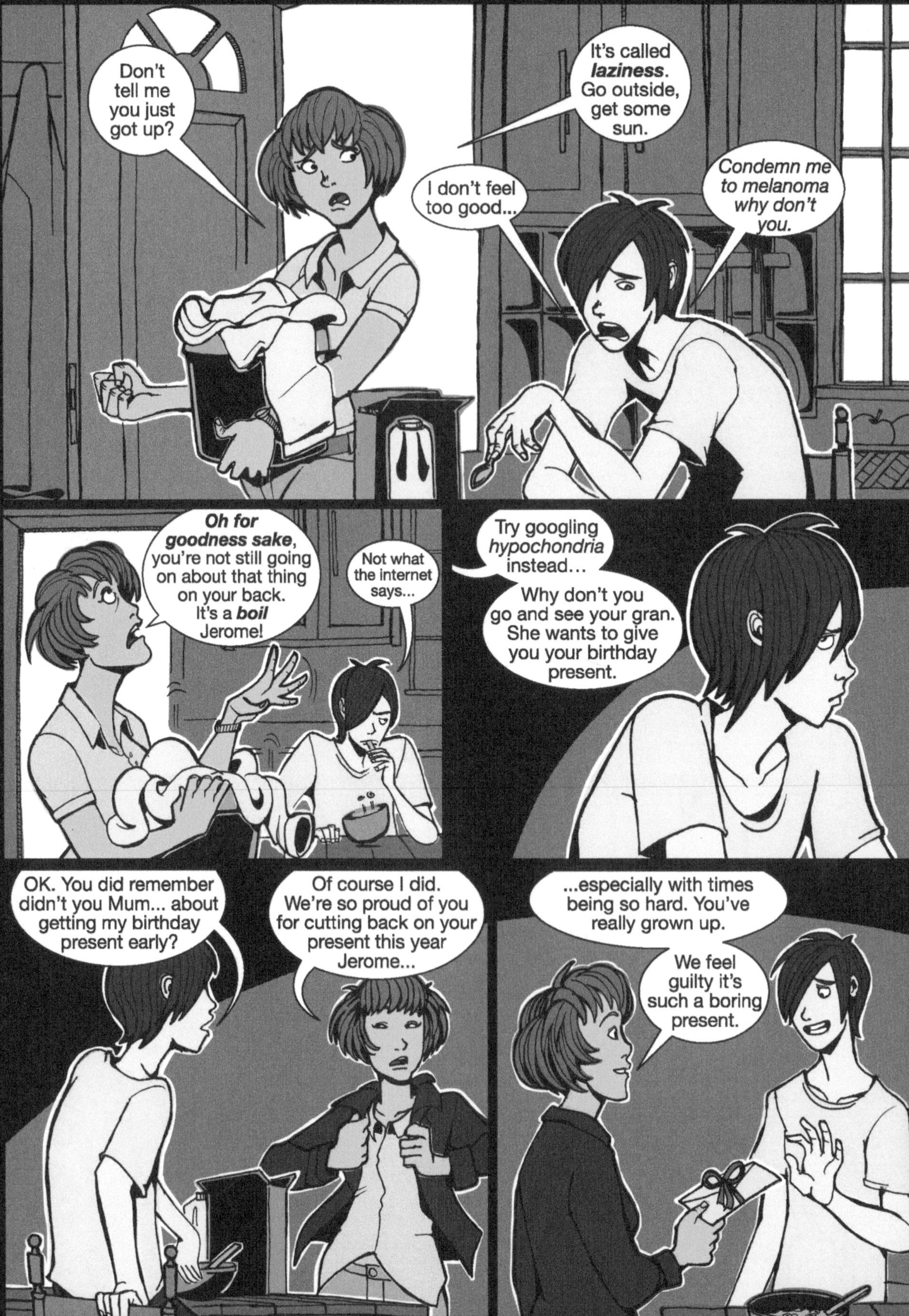
Don't tell me you just got up?
I don't feel too good...
It's called ***laziness***. Go outside, get some sun.
Condemn me to melanoma why don't you.
Oh for goodness sake, you're not still going on about that thing on your back. It's a ***boil*** Jerome!
Not what the internet says...
Try googling *hypochondria* instead...
Why don't you go and see your gran. She wants to give you your birthday present.
OK. You did remember didn't you Mum... about getting my birthday present early?
Of course I did. We're so proud of you for cutting back on your present this year Jerome...
...especially with times being so hard. You've really grown up.
We feel guilty it's such a boring present.

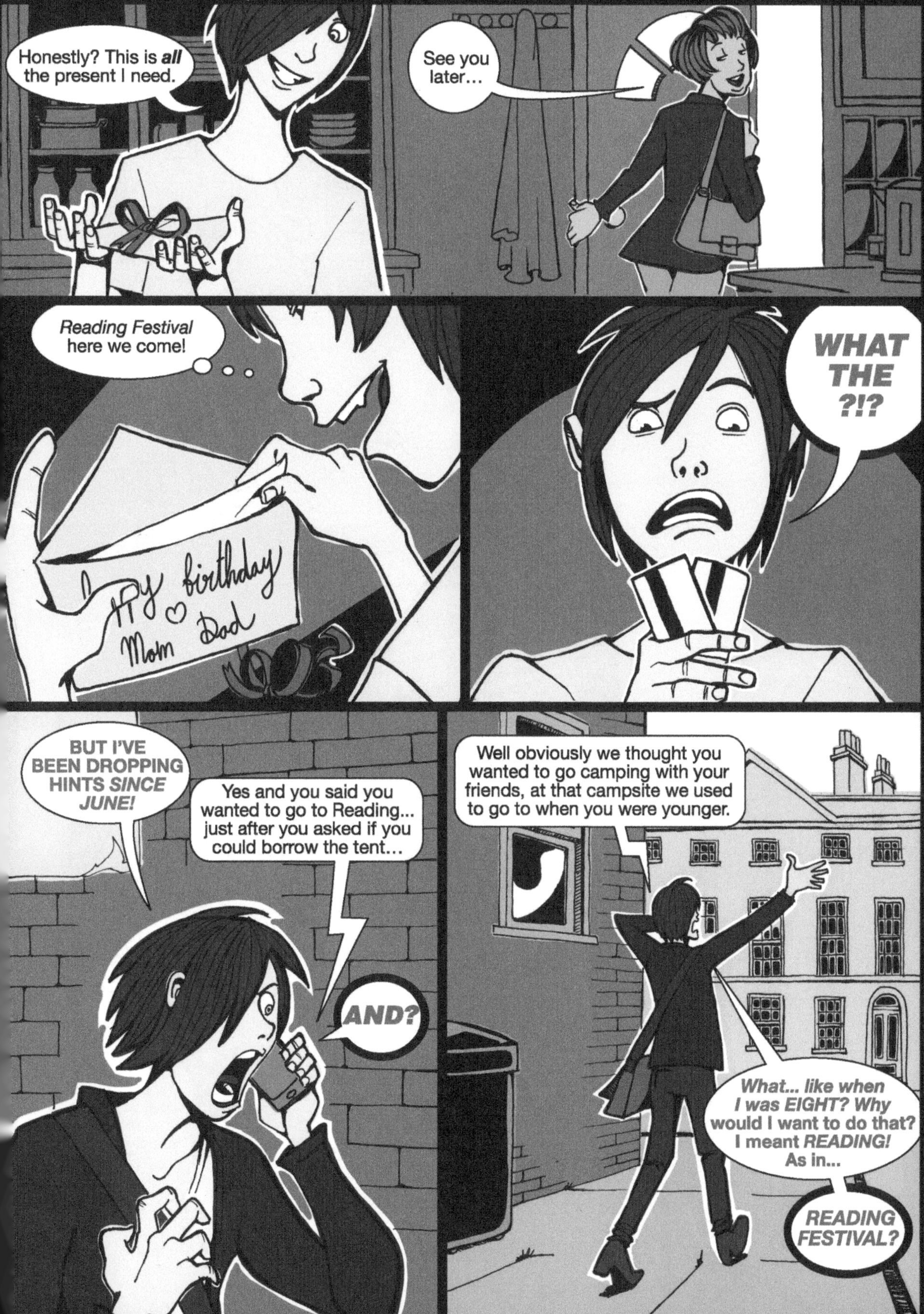
Honestly? This is ***all*** the present I need.
See you later…
Reading Festival here we come!
Hy birthday Mom Dad
WHAT THE ?!?
BUT I'VE BEEN DROPPING HINTS *SINCE JUNE!*
Yes and you said you wanted to go to Reading... just after you asked if you could borrow the tent…
AND?
Well obviously we thought you wanted to go camping with your friends, at that campsite we used to go to when you were younger.
What... like when I was EIGHT? Why would I want to do that? I meant *READING!* As in...
READING FESTIVAL?

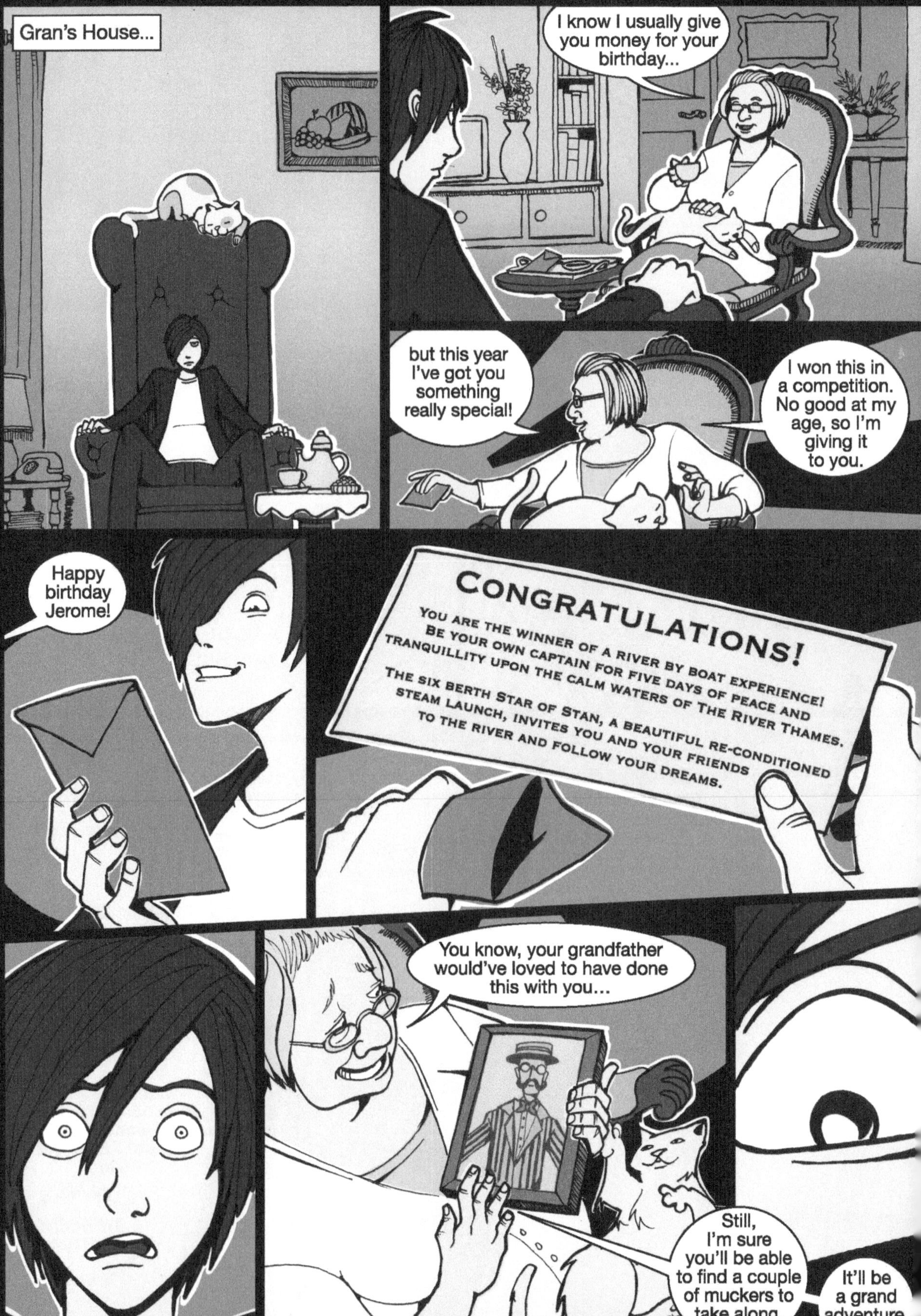
Gran's House...
I know I usually give you money for your birthday...
but this year I've got you something really special!
I won this in a competition. No good at my age, so I'm giving it to you.
Happy birthday Jerome!
CONGRATULATIONS!
YOU ARE THE WINNER OF A RIVER BY BOAT EXPERIENCE! BE YOUR OWN CAPTAIN FOR FIVE DAYS OF PEACE AND TRANQUILLITY UPON THE CALM WATERS OF THE RIVER THAMES.
THE SIX BERTH STAR OF STAN, A BEAUTIFUL RE-CONDITIONED STEAM LAUNCH, INVITES YOU AND YOUR FRIENDS TO THE RIVER AND FOLLOW YOUR DREAMS.
You know, your grandfather would've loved to have done this with you...
Still, I'm sure you'll be able to find a couple of muckers to take along.
It'll be a grand adventure.

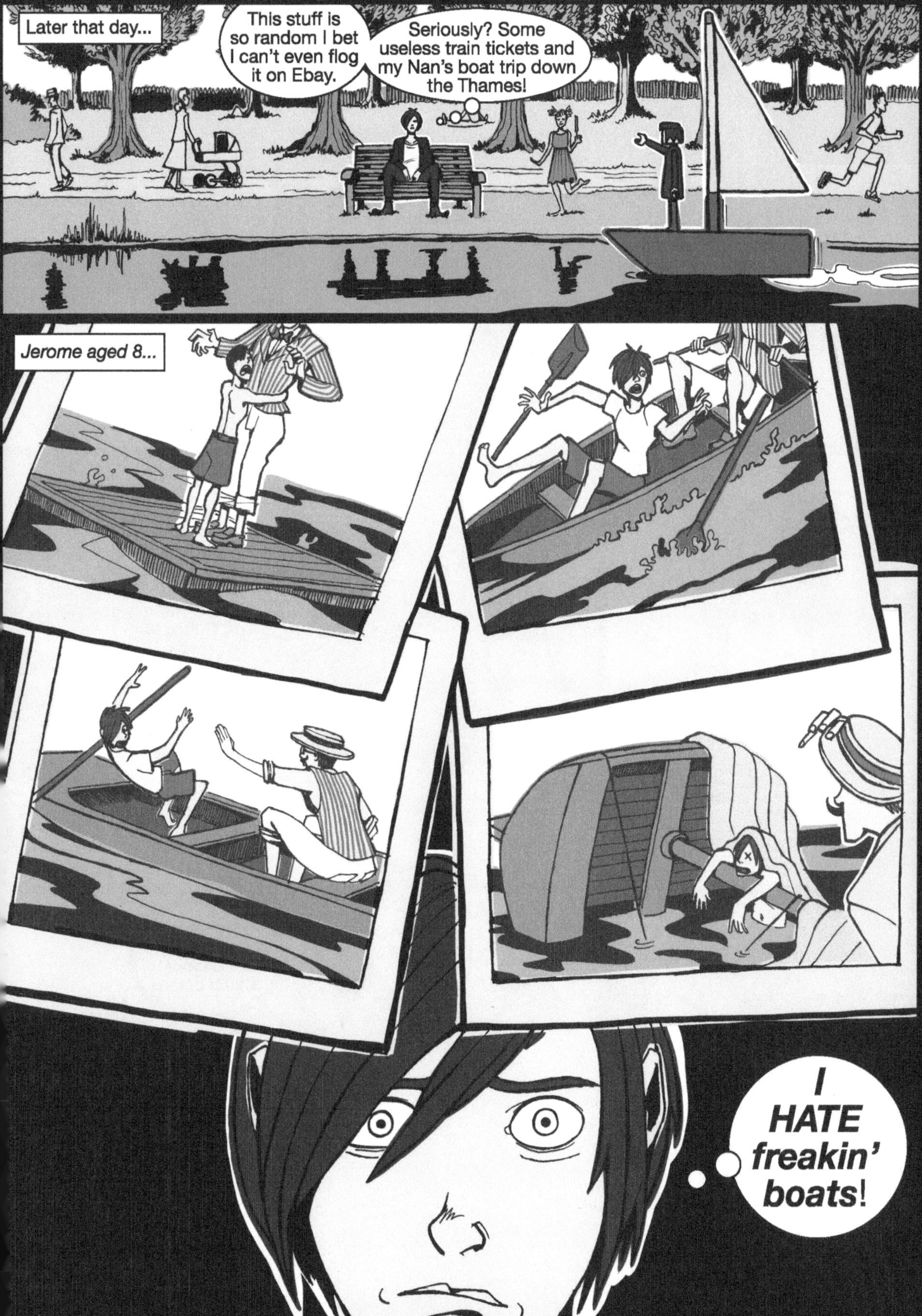
Later that day...
This stuff is so random I bet I can't even flog it on Ebay.
Seriously? Some useless train tickets and my Nan's boat trip down the Thames!
Jerome aged 8...
I HATE freakin' boats!

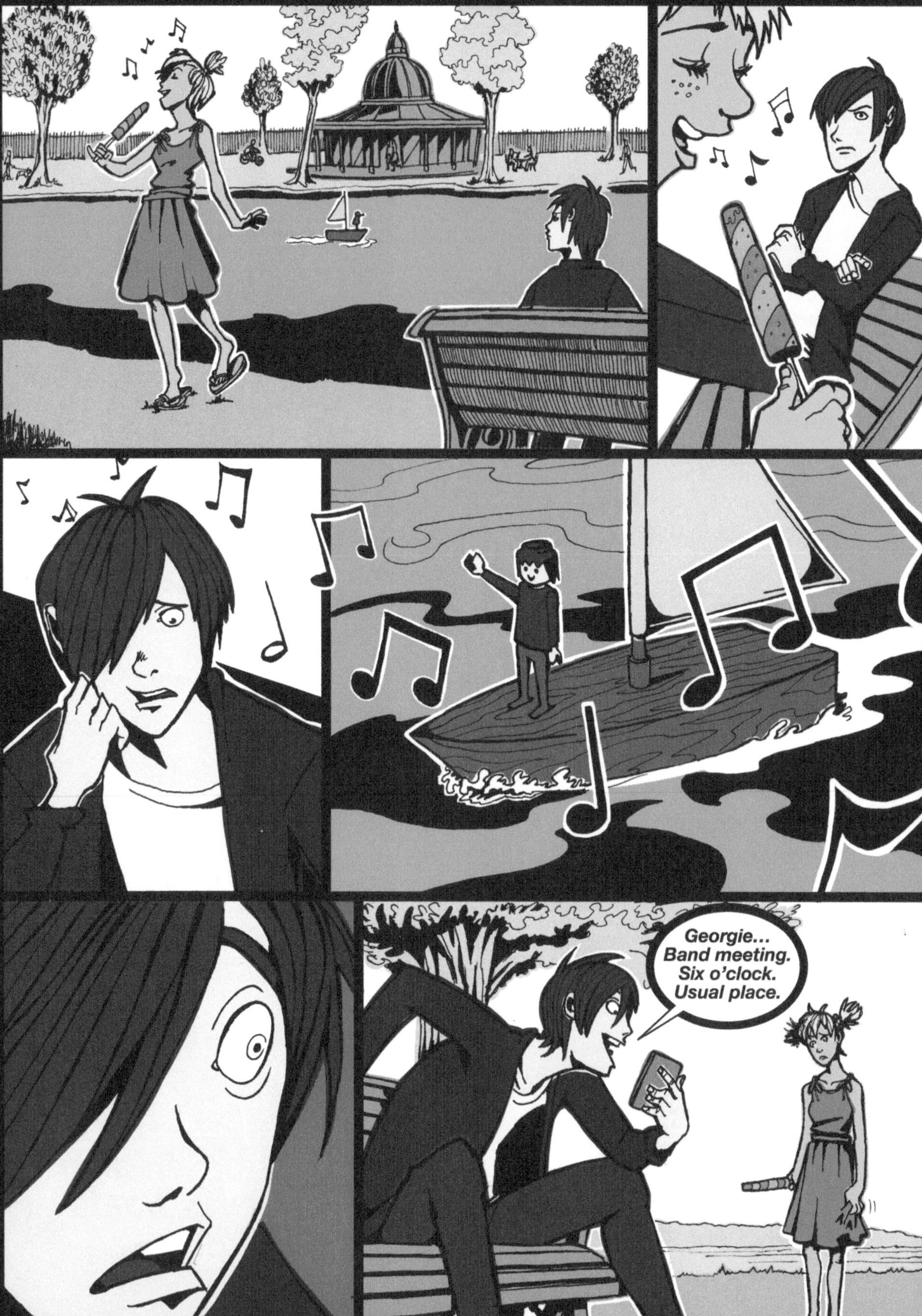
Georgie... Band meeting. Six o'clock. Usual place.

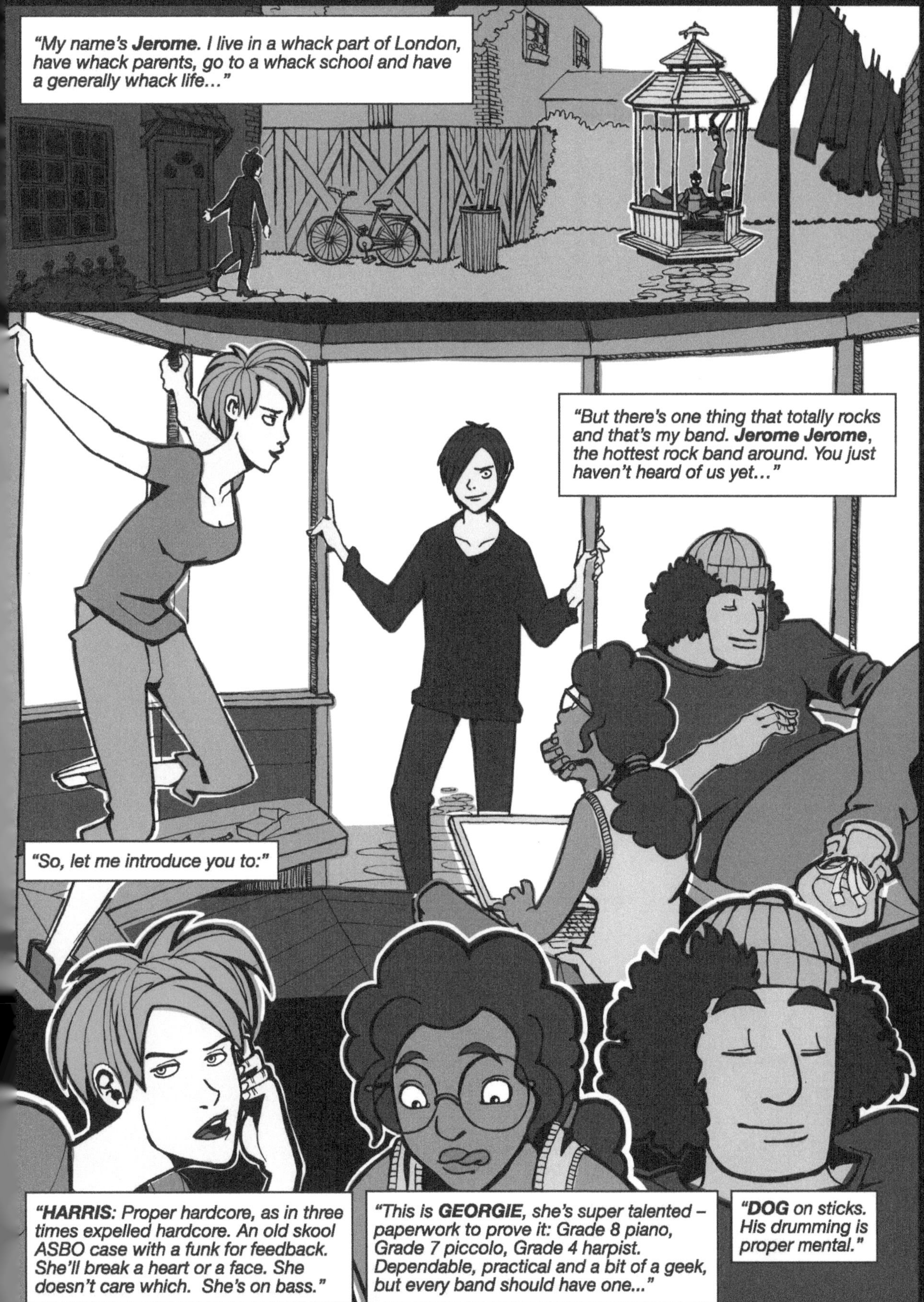
"My name's **Jerome**. I live in a whack part of London, have whack parents, go to a whack school and have a generally whack life..."
"But there's one thing that totally rocks and that's my band. **Jerome Jerome**, the hottest rock band around. You just haven't heard of us yet..."
"So, let me introduce you to:"
"**HARRIS**: Proper hardcore, as in three times expelled hardcore. An old skool ASBO case with a funk for feedback. She'll break a heart or a face. She doesn't care which. She's on bass."
"This is **GEORGIE**, she's super talented – paperwork to prove it: Grade 8 piano, Grade 7 piccolo, Grade 4 harpist. Dependable, practical and a bit of a geek, but every band should have one..."
"**DOG** on sticks. His drumming is proper mental."

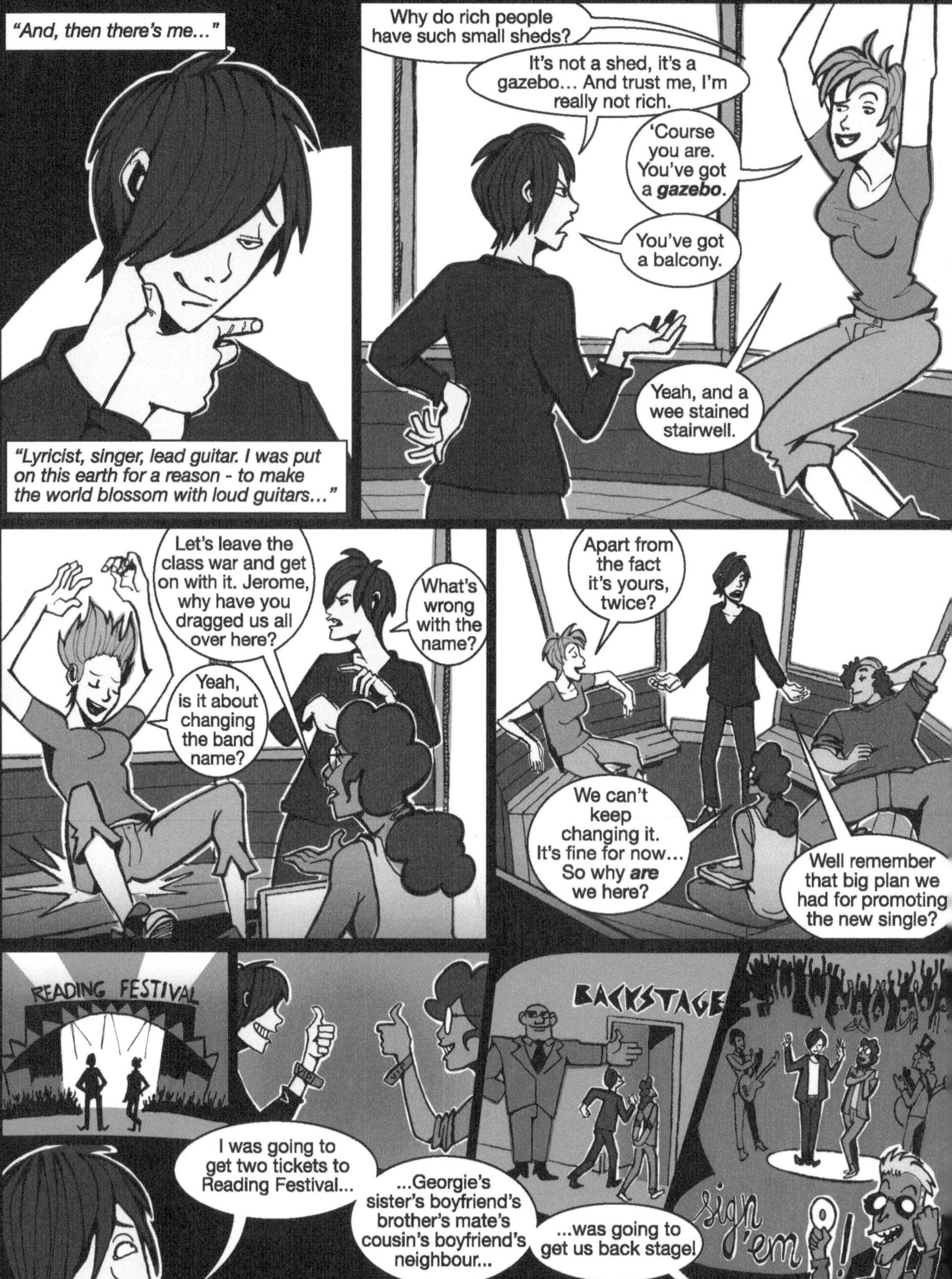
"And, then there's me..."
"Lyricist, singer, lead guitar. I was put on this earth for a reason - to make the world blossom with loud guitars..."
Why do rich people have such small sheds?
It's not a shed, it's a gazebo... And trust me, I'm really not rich.
'Course you are. You've got a ***gazebo.***
You've got a balcony.
Yeah, and a wee stained stairwell.
Let's leave the class war and get on with it. Jerome, why have you dragged us all over here?
Yeah, is it about changing the band name?
What's wrong with the name?
Apart from the fact it's yours, twice?
We can't keep changing it. It's fine for now... So why ***are*** we here?
Well remember that big plan we had for promoting the new single?
READING FESTIVAL
VIP
BACKSTAGE
I was going to get two tickets to Reading Festival...
...Georgie's sister's boyfriend's brother's mate's cousin's boyfriend's neighbour...
...was going to get us back stage!
sign 'em!
Well, that plan's flawed.

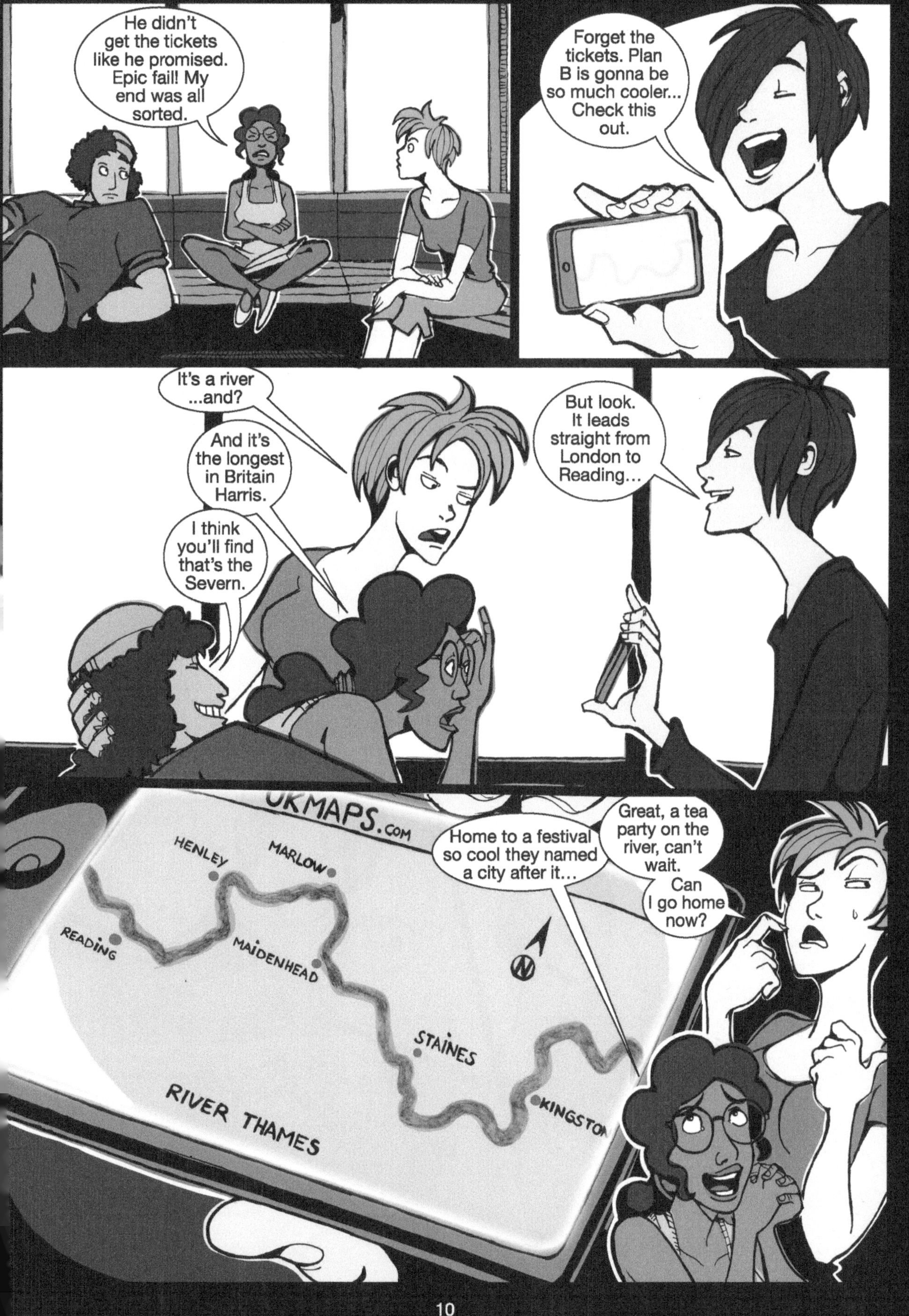

He didn't get the tickets like he promised. Epic fail! My end was all sorted.
Forget the tickets. Plan B is gonna be so much cooler... Check this out.
It's a river ...and?
And it's the longest in Britain Harris.
I think you'll find that's the Severn.
But look. It leads straight from London to Reading...
UKMAPS.com
HENLEY
MARLOW
READING
MAIDENHEAD
STAINES
KINGSTON
RIVER THAMES
N
Home to a festival so cool they named a city after it...
Great, a tea party on the river, can't wait.
Can I go home now?

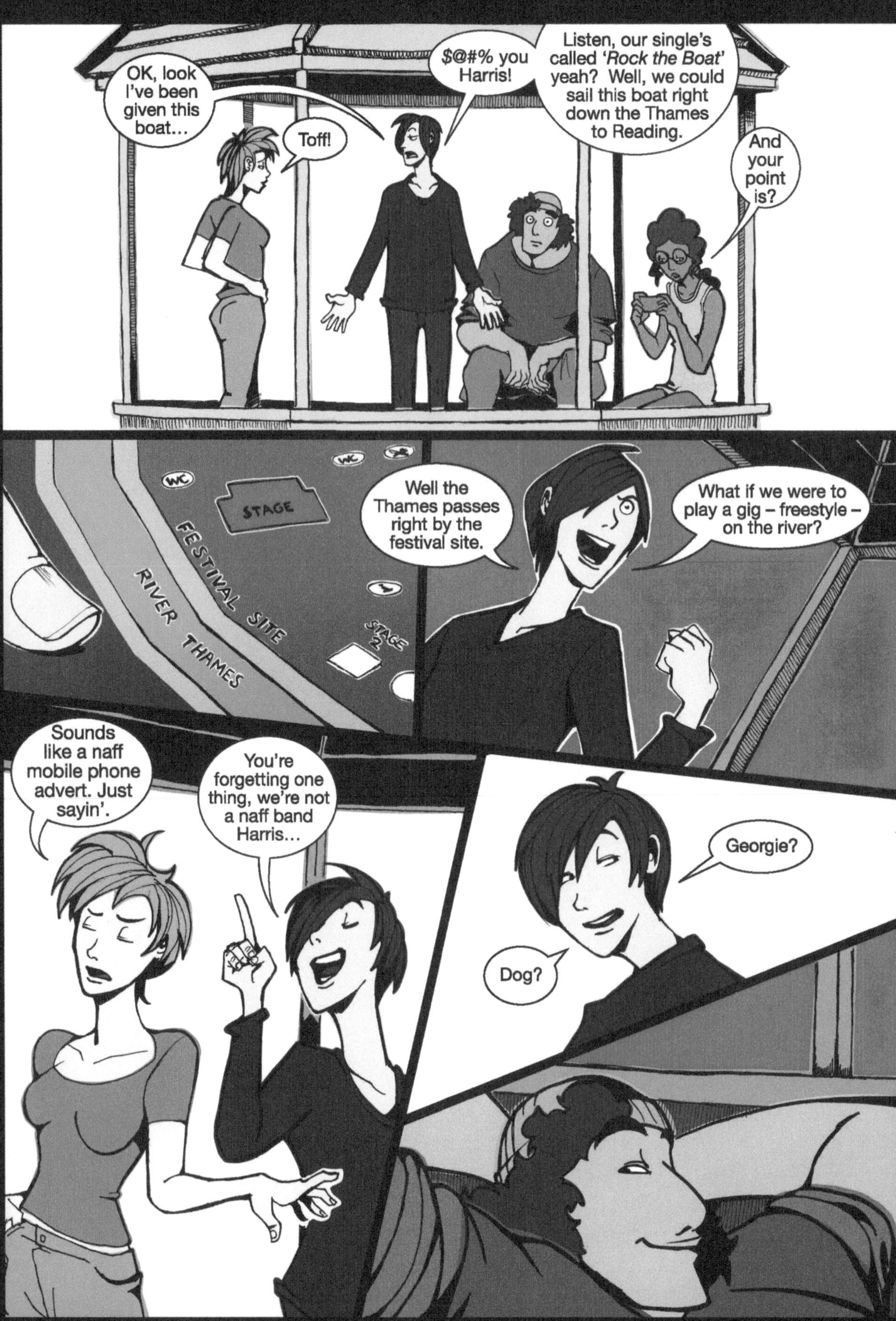
OK, look I've been given this boat...
Toff!
$@#% you Harris!
Listen, our single's called '*Rock the Boat*' yeah? Well, we could sail this boat right down the Thames to Reading.
And your point is?
WC
WC
STAGE
FESTIVAL SITE
RIVER THAMES
STAGE 2
Well the Thames passes right by the festival site.
What if we were to play a gig – freestyle – on the river?
Sounds like a naff mobile phone advert. Just sayin'.
You're forgetting one thing, we're not a naff band Harris...
Georgie?
Dog?

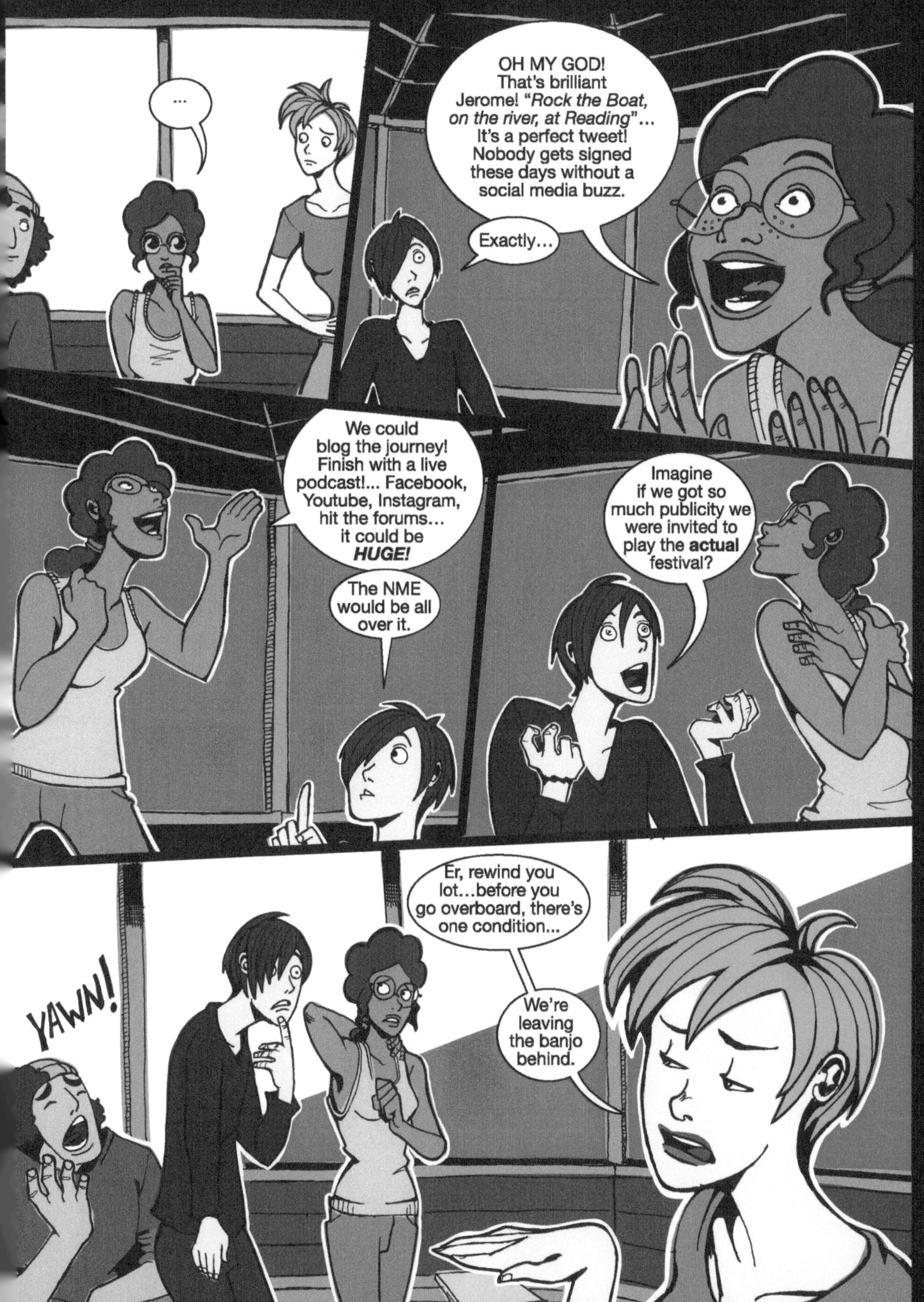
...
OH MY GOD! That's brilliant Jerome! "*Rock the Boat, on the river, at Reading*"... It's a perfect tweet! Nobody gets signed these days without a social media buzz.
Exactly...
We could blog the journey! Finish with a live podcast!... Facebook, Youtube, Instagram, hit the forums... it could be ***HUGE!***
The NME would be all over it.
Imagine if we got so much publicity we were invited to play the **actual** festival?
YAWN!
Er, rewind you lot...before you go overboard, there's one condition...
We're leaving the banjo behind.

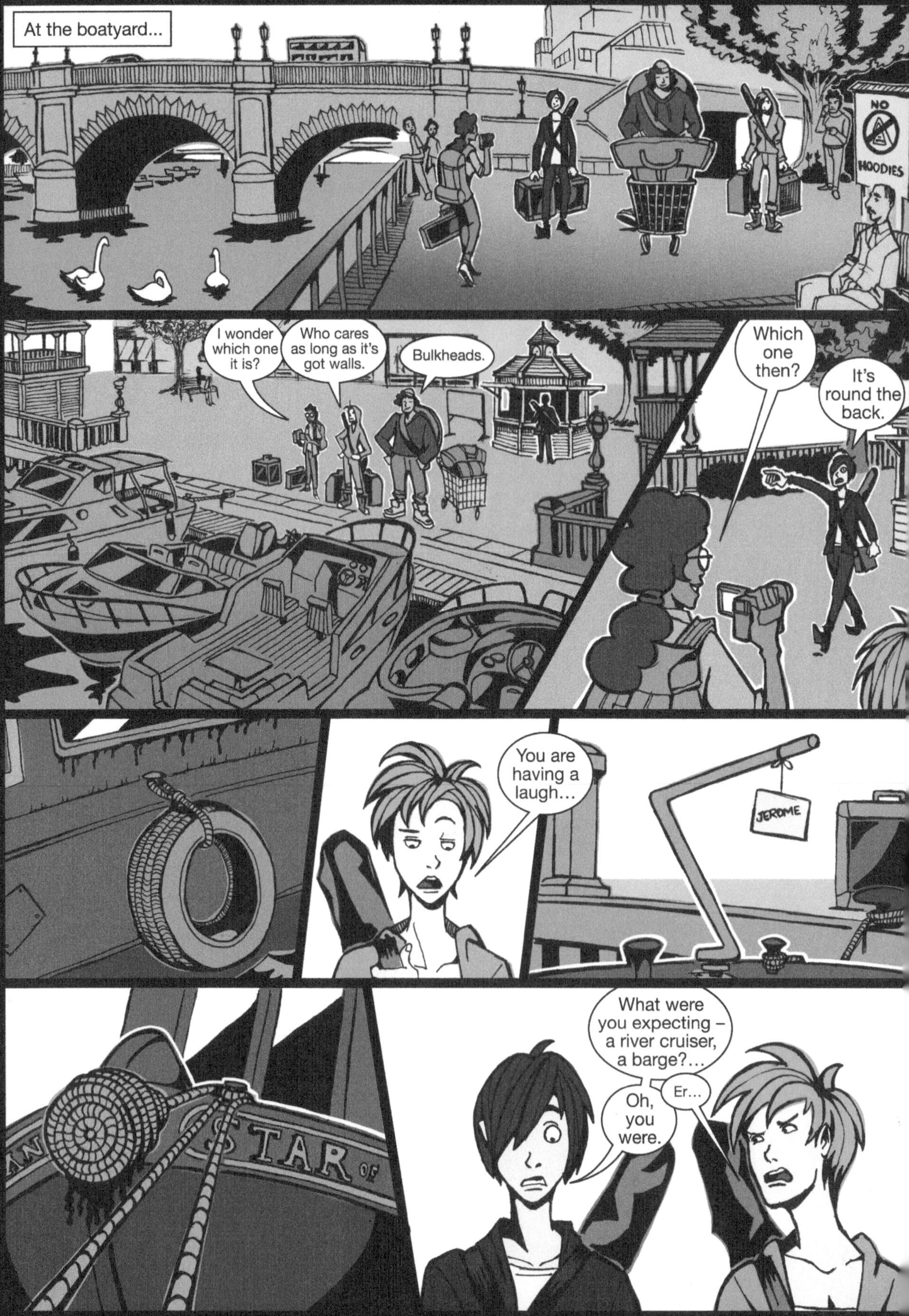
At the boatyard...
NO HOODIES
I wonder which one it is?
Who cares as long as it's got walls.
Bulkheads.
Which one then?
It's round the back.
You are having a laugh…
JEROME
STAR OF
What were you expecting – a river cruiser, a barge?…
Er…
Oh, you were.

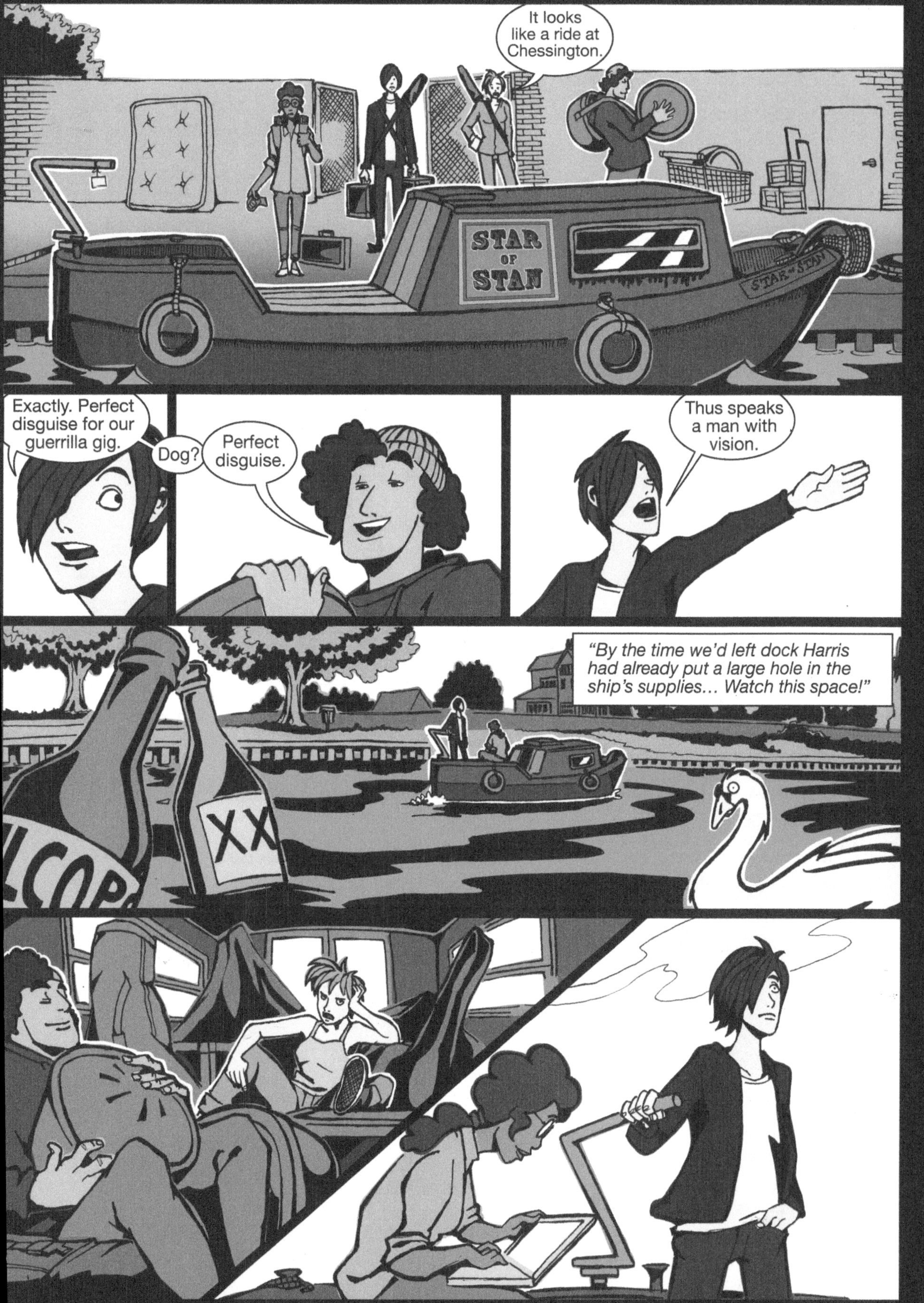
It looks like a ride at Chessington.
STAR OF STAN
STAR OF STAN
Exactly. Perfect disguise for our guerrilla gig.
Dog?
Perfect disguise.
Thus speaks a man with vision.
"By the time we'd left dock Harris had already put a large hole in the ship's supplies… Watch this space!"
XX

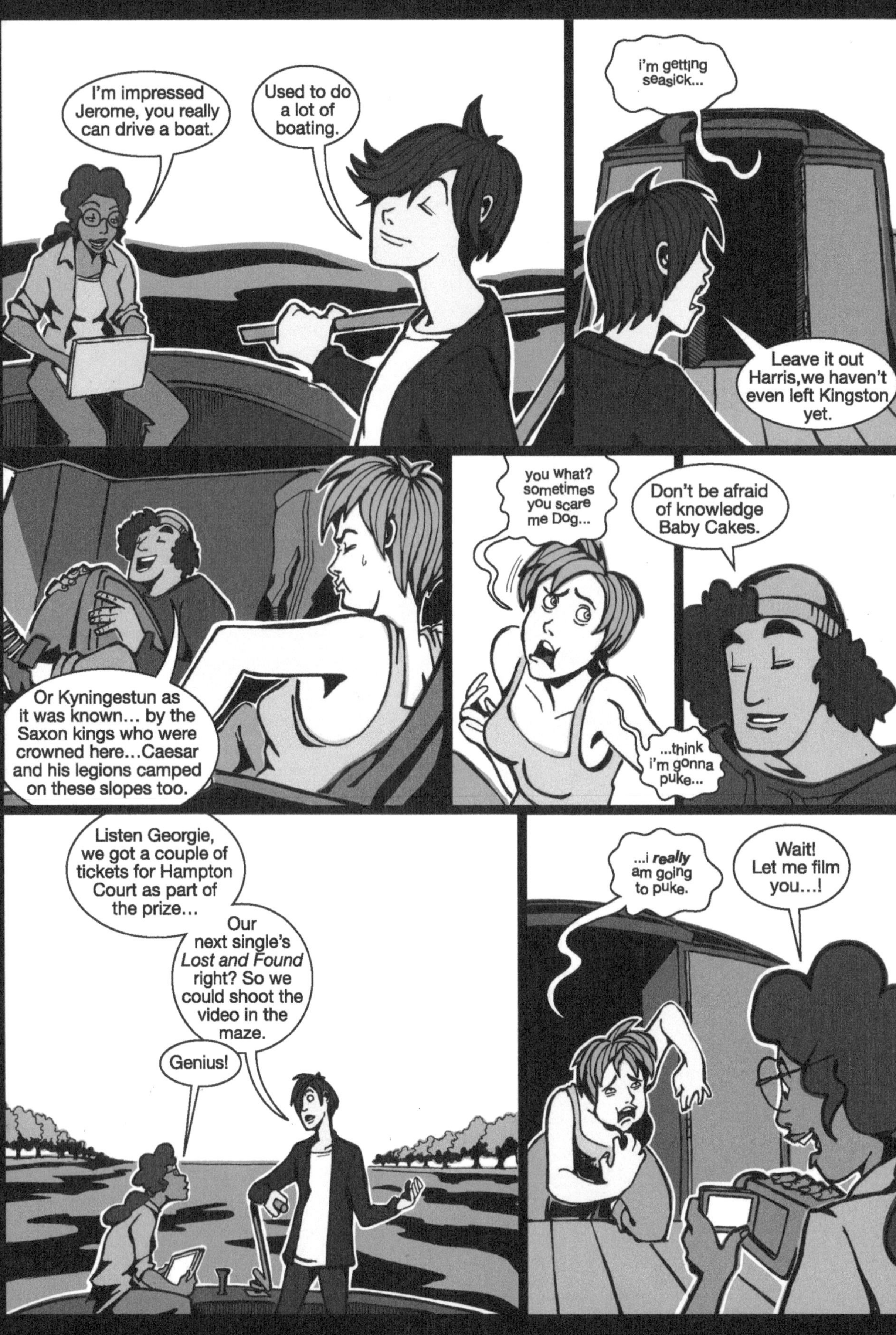
I'm impressed Jerome, you really can drive a boat.
Used to do a lot of boating.
i'm getting seasick...
Leave it out Harris,we haven't even left Kingston yet.
Or Kyningestun as it was known… by the Saxon kings who were crowned here…Caesar and his legions camped on these slopes too.
you what? sometimes you scare me Dog...
...think i'm gonna puke...
Don't be afraid of knowledge Baby Cakes.
Listen Georgie, we got a couple of tickets for Hampton Court as part of the prize…
Our next single's *Lost and Found* right? So we could shoot the video in the maze.
Genius!
...i ***really*** am going to puke.
Wait! Let me film you…!

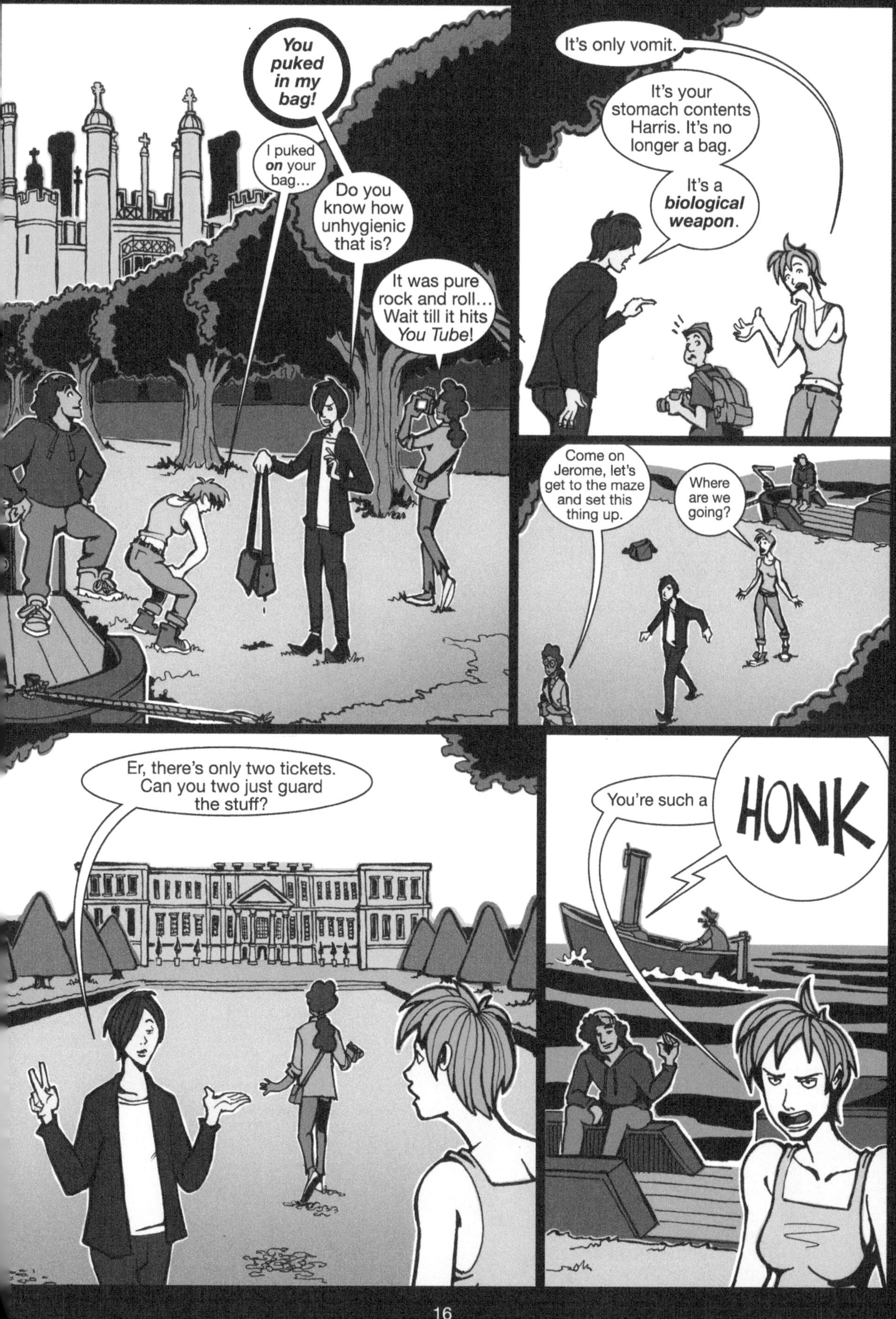
You puked in my bag!
I puked on your bag...
Do you know how unhygienic that is?
It was pure rock and roll... Wait till it hits You Tube!
It's only vomit.
It's your stomach contents Harris. It's no longer a bag.
It's a biological weapon.
Come on Jerome, let's get to the maze and set this thing up.
Where are we going?
Er, there's only two tickets. Can you two just guard the stuff?
You're such a
HONK

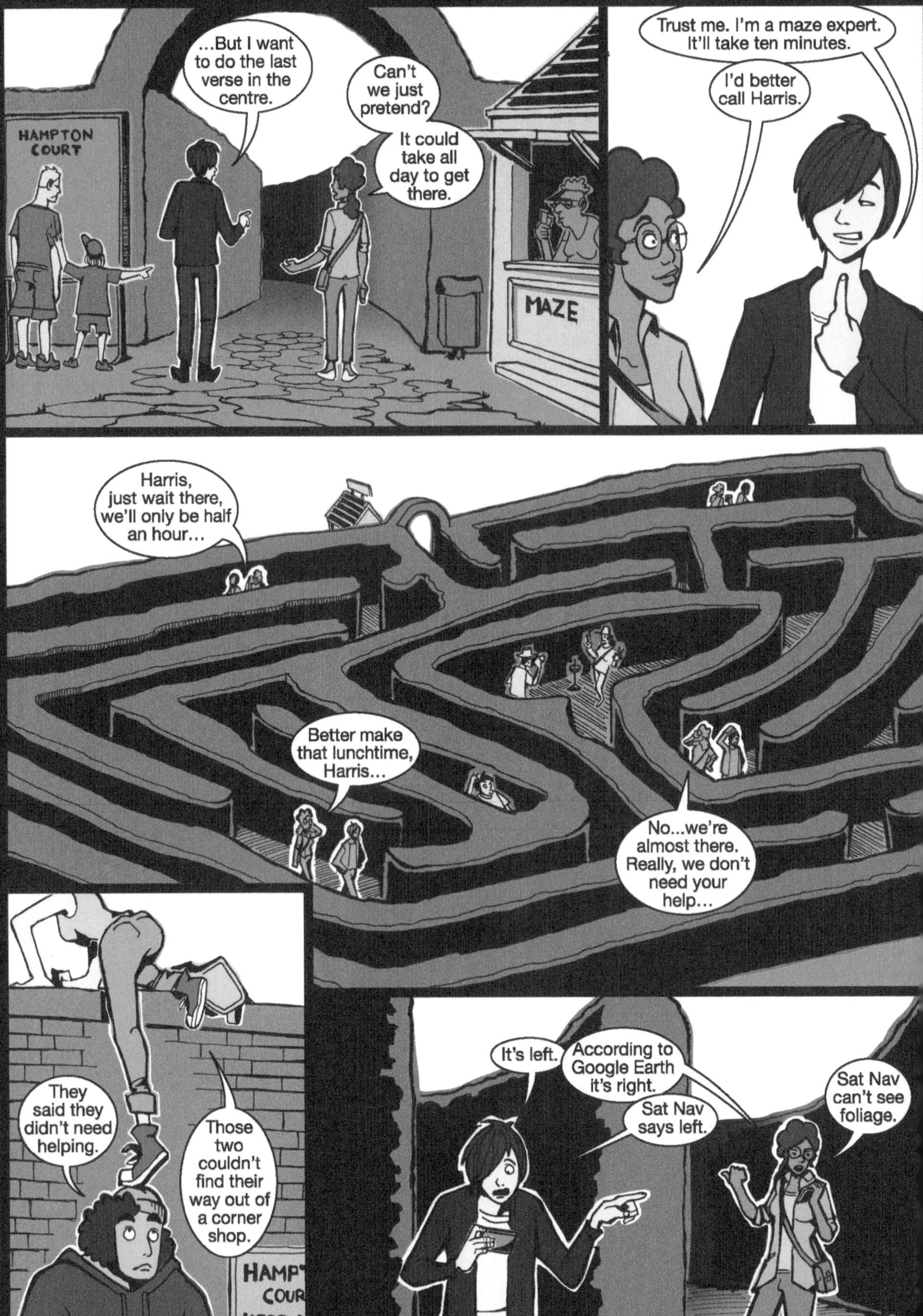
HAMPTON COURT
...But I want to do the last verse in the centre.
Can't we just pretend?
It could take all day to get there.
MAZE
Trust me. I'm a maze expert. It'll take ten minutes.
I'd better call Harris.
Harris, just wait there, we'll only be half an hour...
Better make that lunchtime, Harris...
No...we're almost there. Really, we don't need your help...
They said they didn't need helping.
Those two couldn't find their way out of a corner shop.
It's left.
According to Google Earth it's right.
Sat Nav says left.
Sat Nav can't see foliage.

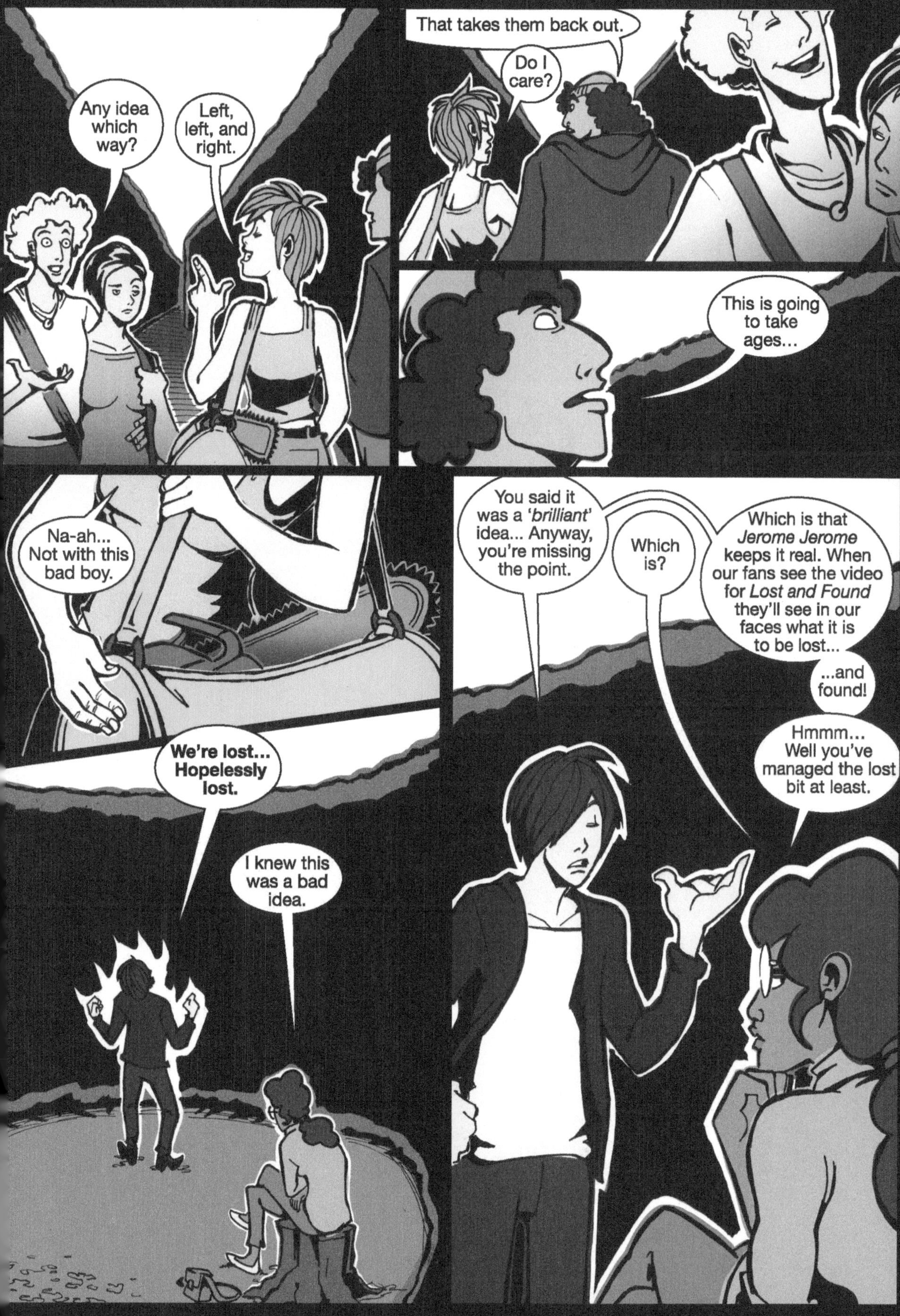
Any idea which way?
Left, left, and right.
That takes them back out.
Do I care?
This is going to take ages...
Na-ah... Not with this bad boy.
We're lost... Hopelessly lost.
I knew this was a bad idea.
You said it was a '*brilliant*' idea... Anyway, you're missing the point.
Which is?
Which is that *Jerome Jerome* keeps it real. When our fans see the video for *Lost and Found* they'll see in our faces what it is to be lost...
...and found!
Hmmm... Well you've managed the lost bit at least.

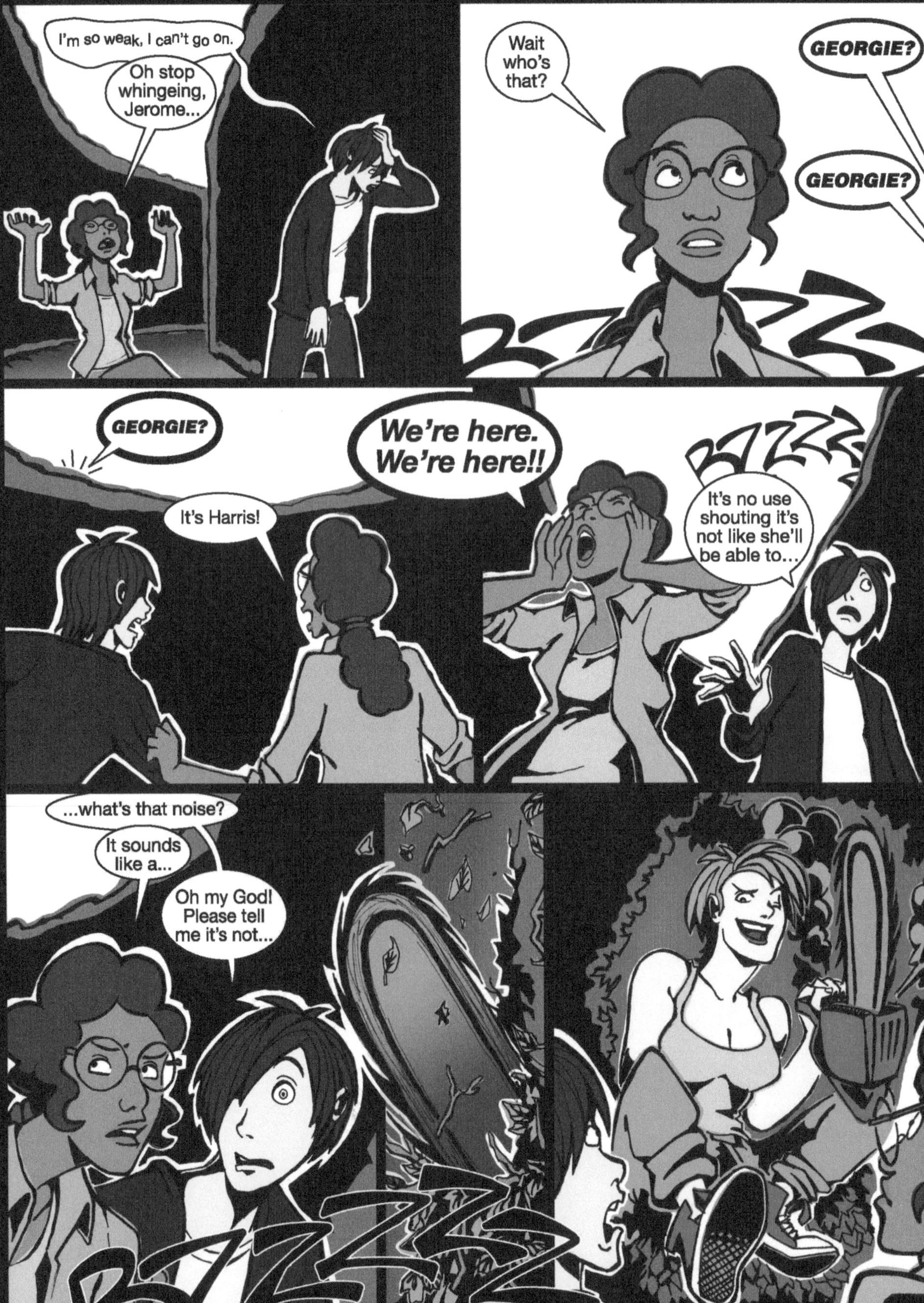
I'm so weak, I can't go on.
Oh stop whingeing, Jerome...
Wait who's that?
GEORGIE?
GEORGIE?
GEORGIE?
It's Harris!
We're here. We're here!!
BZZZZZ
It's no use shouting it's not like she'll be able to...
...what's that noise?
It sounds like a...
Oh my God! Please tell me it's not...
BZZZZZ

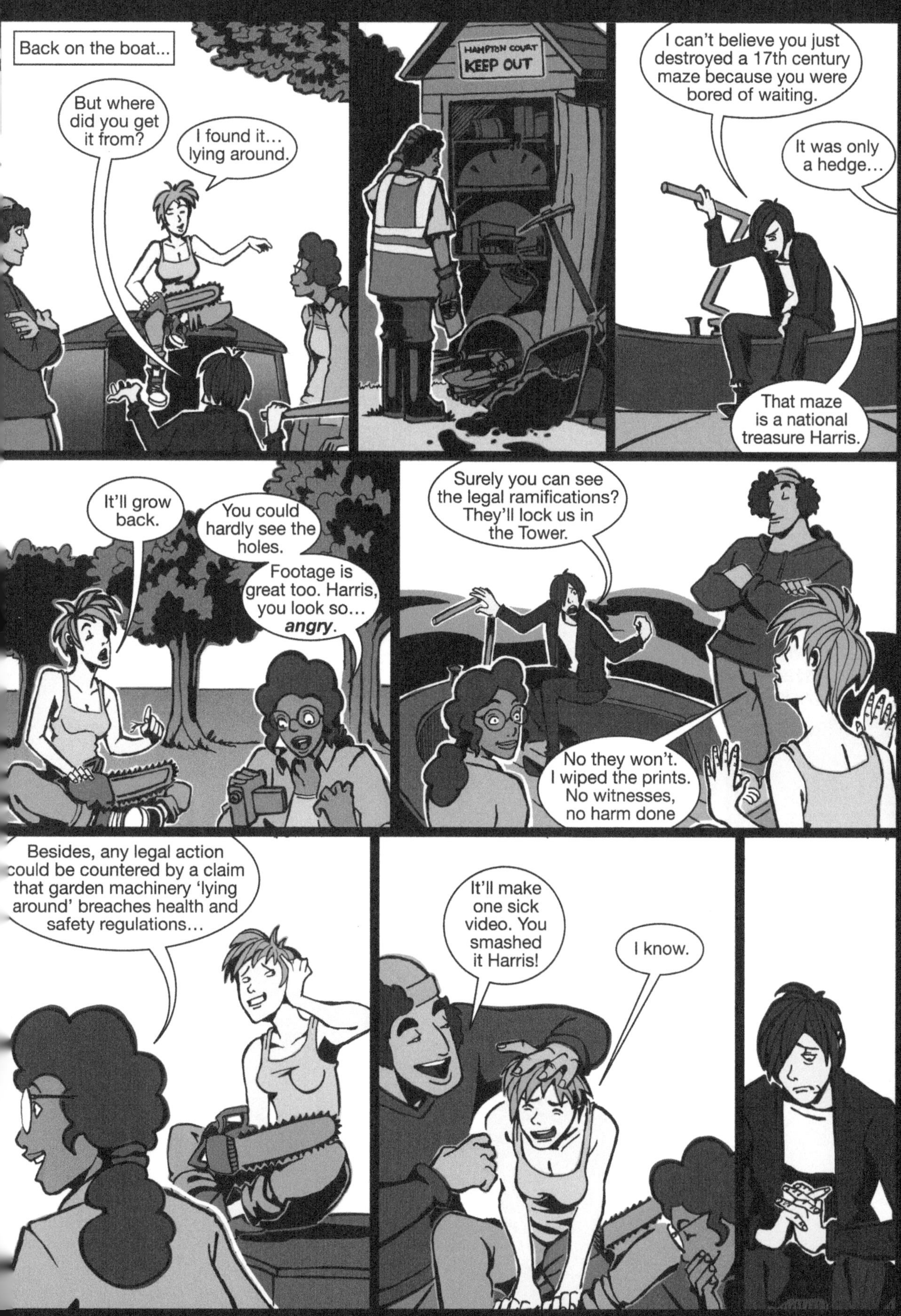

Back on the boat...
But where did you get it from?
I found it… lying around.
HAMPTON COURT
KEEP OUT
I can't believe you just destroyed a 17th century maze because you were bored of waiting.
It was only a hedge…
That maze is a national treasure Harris.
It'll grow back.
You could hardly see the holes.
Footage is great too. Harris, you look so… ***angry***.
Surely you can see the legal ramifications? They'll lock us in the Tower.
No they won't. I wiped the prints. No witnesses, no harm done
Besides, any legal action could be countered by a claim that garden machinery 'lying around' breaches health and safety regulations…
It'll make one sick video. You smashed it Harris!
I know.

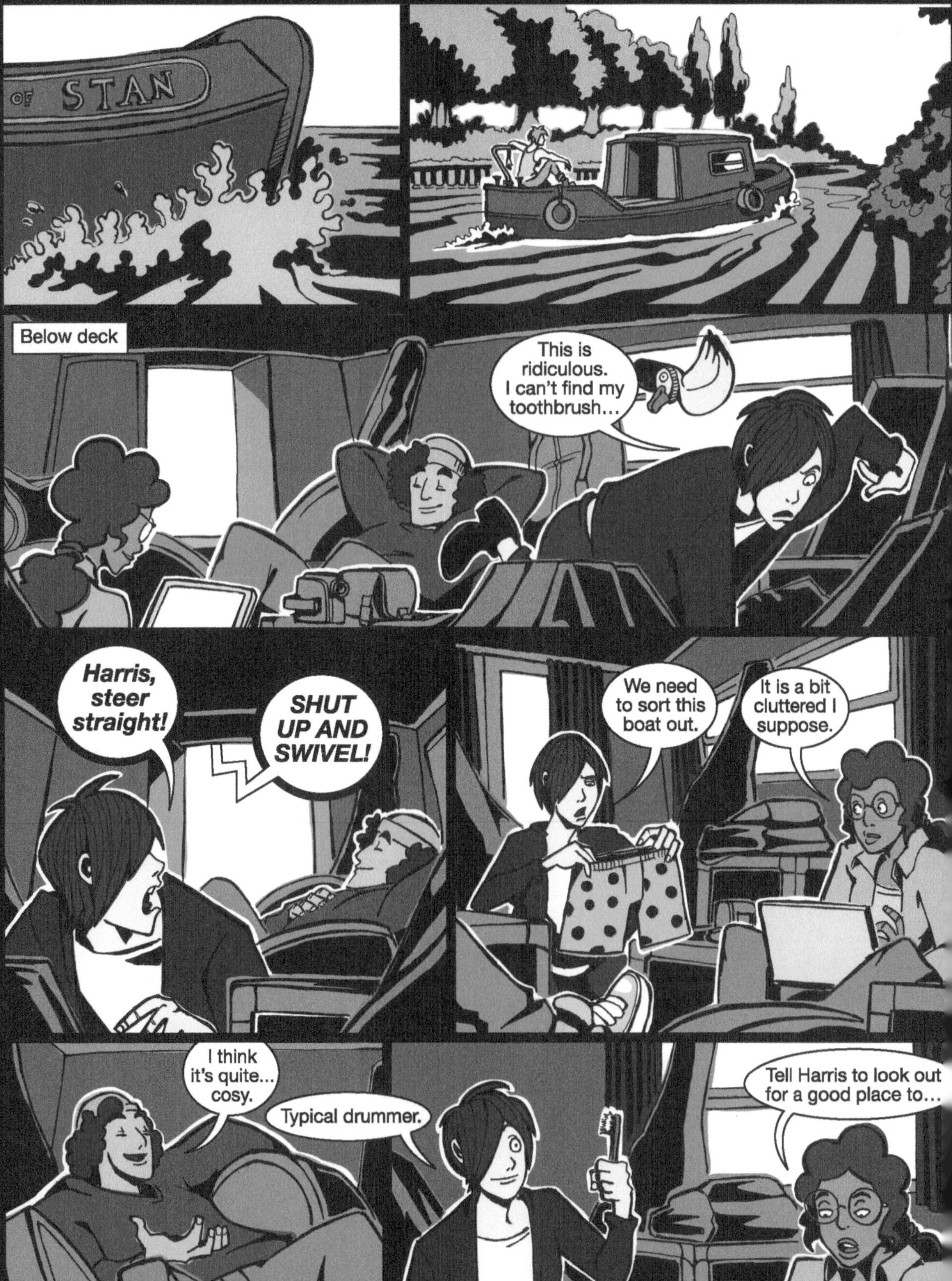
OF STAN
Below deck
This is ridiculous. I can't find my toothbrush...
Harris, steer straight!
SHUT UP AND SWIVEL!
We need to sort this boat out.
It is a bit cluttered I suppose.
I think it's quite... cosy.
Typical drummer.
Tell Harris to look out for a good place to...

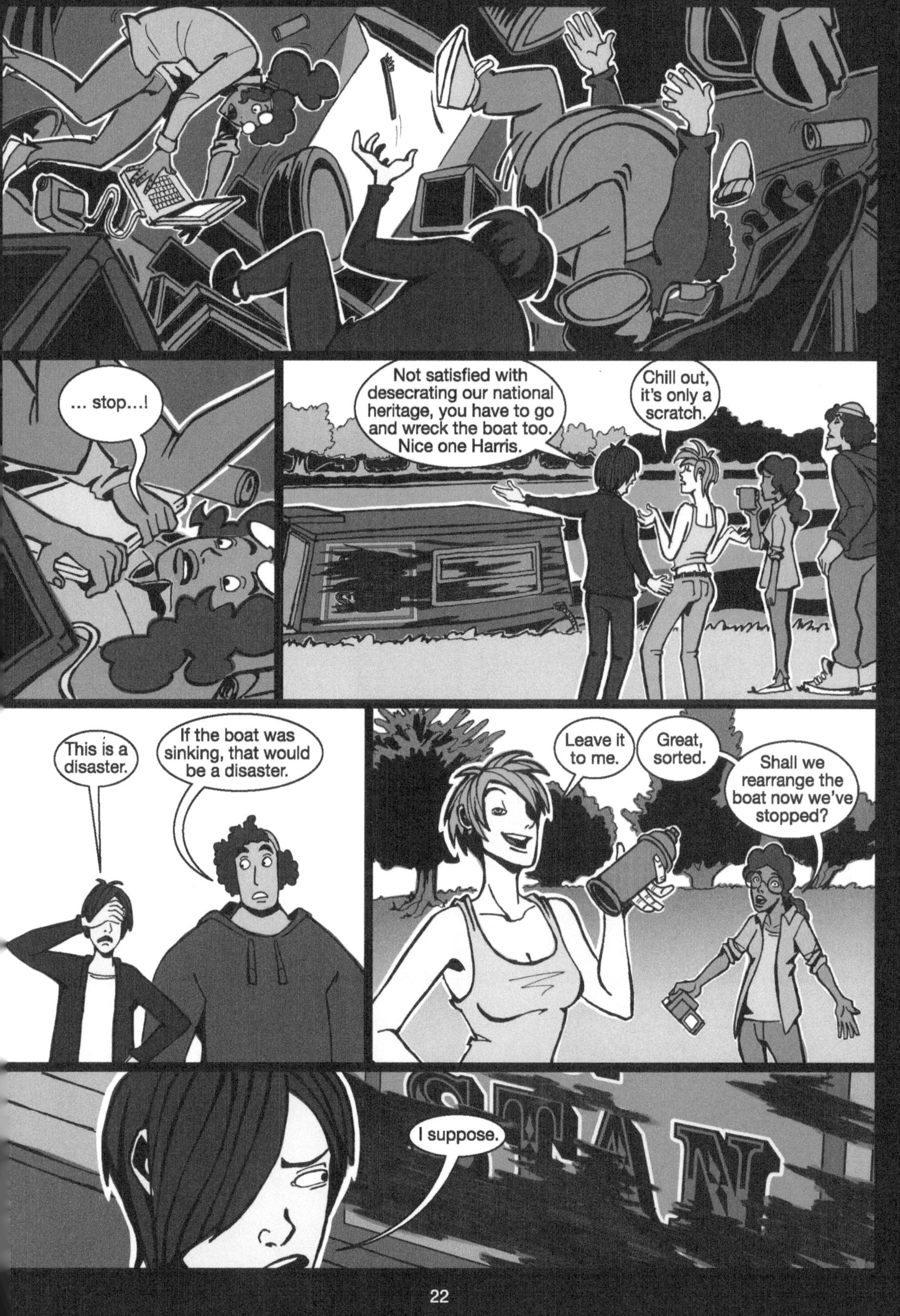
... stop...!
Not satisfied with desecrating our national heritage, you have to go and wreck the boat too. Nice one Harris.
Chill out, it's only a scratch.
This is a disaster.
If the boat was sinking, that would be a disaster.
Leave it to me.
Great, sorted.
Shall we rearrange the boat now we've stopped?
I suppose.

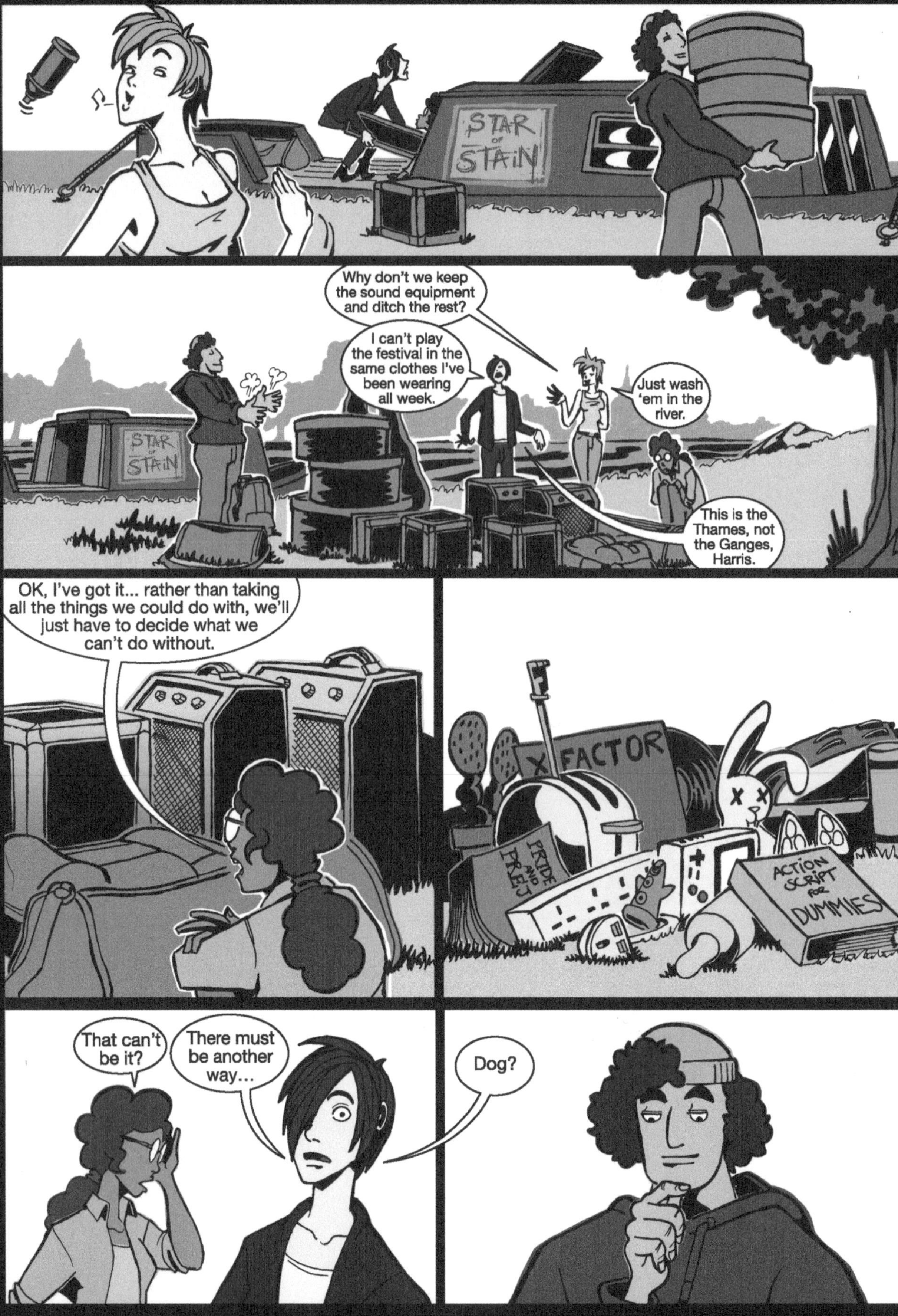
STAR of STAIN
Why don't we keep the sound equipment and ditch the rest?
I can't play the festival in the same clothes I've been wearing all week.
Just wash 'em in the river.
This is the Thames, not the Ganges, Harris.
OK, I've got it... rather than taking all the things we could do with, we'll just have to decide what we can't do without.
X FACTOR
PRIDE AND PREJ
ACTION SCRIPT FOR DUMMIES
That can't be it?
There must be another way...
Dog?

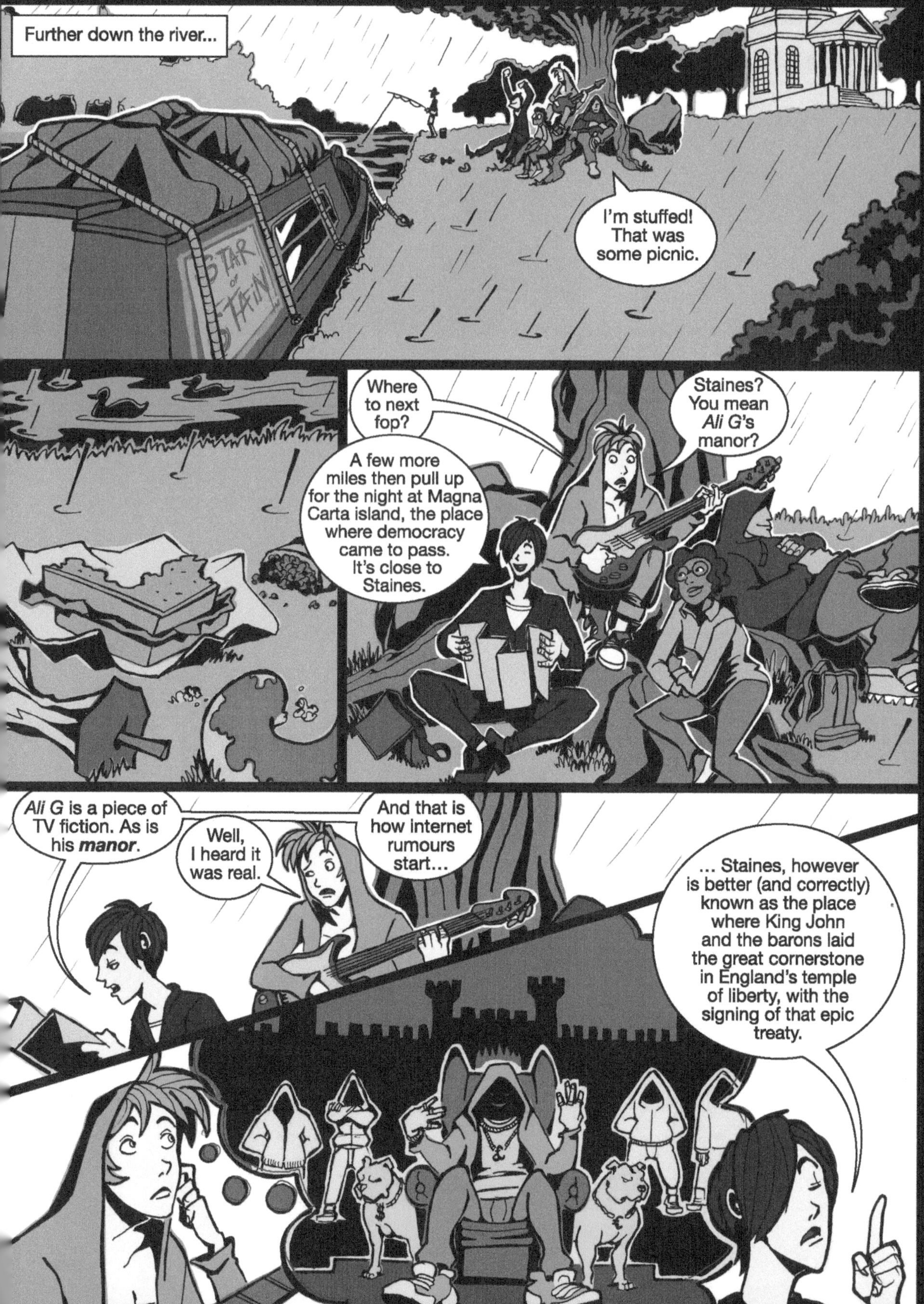
Further down the river...
STAR of STAIN
I'm stuffed! That was some picnic.
Where to next fop?
A few more miles then pull up for the night at Magna Carta island, the place where democracy came to pass. It's close to Staines.
Staines? You mean *Ali G*'s manor?
Ali G is a piece of TV fiction. As is his ***manor***.
Well, I heard it was real.
And that is how internet rumours start...
... Staines, however is better (and correctly) known as the place where King John and the barons laid the great cornerstone in England's temple of liberty, with the signing of that epic treaty.

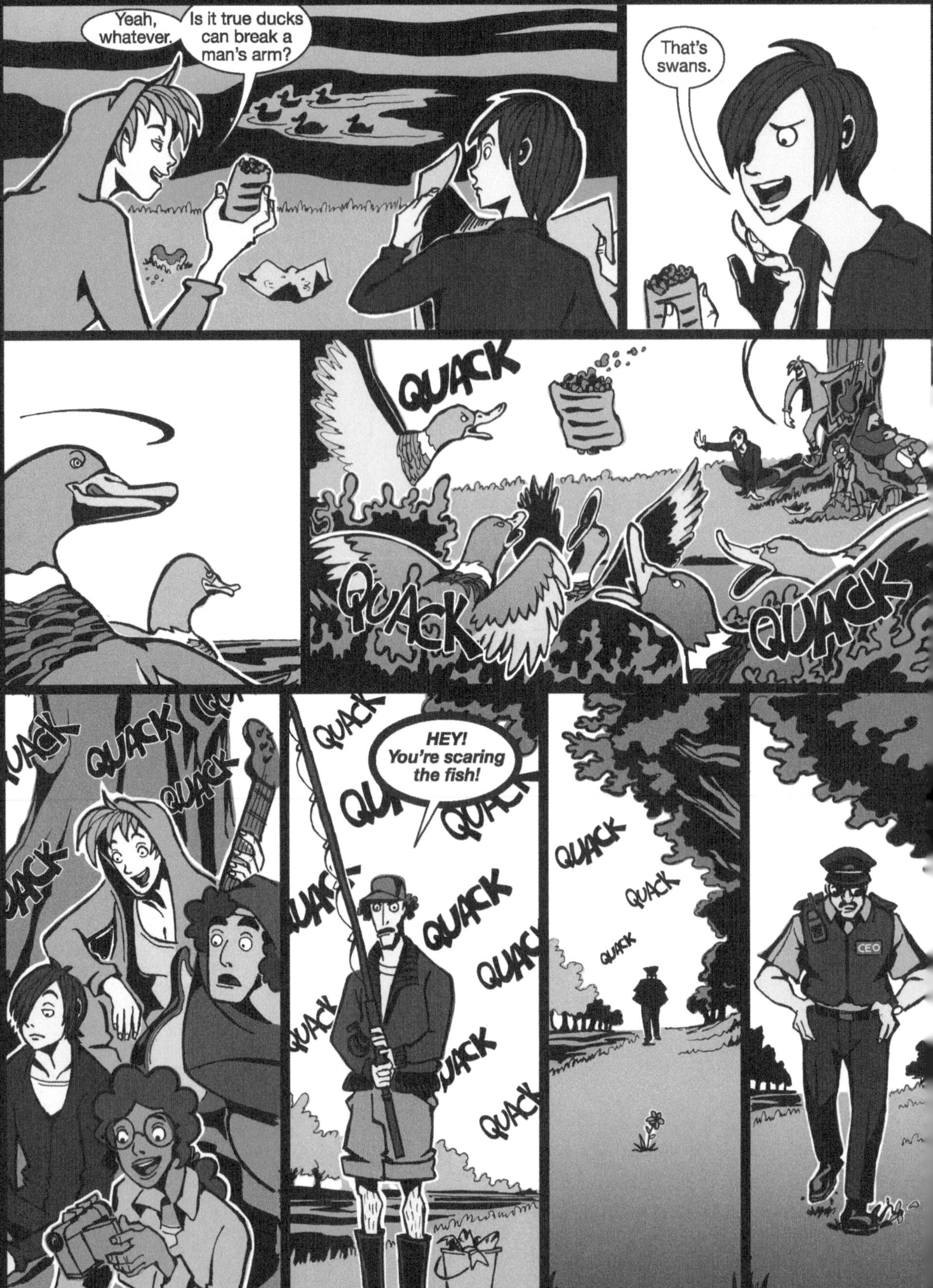
Yeah, whatever.
Is it true ducks can break a man's arm?
That's swans.
QUACK
QUACK
QUACK
QUACK
QUACK
QUACK
QUACK
QUACK
QUACK
HEY! You're scaring the fish!
QUACK
QUACK
QUACK
QUACK
QUACK
QUACK
QUACK
QUACK
QUACK
CEO

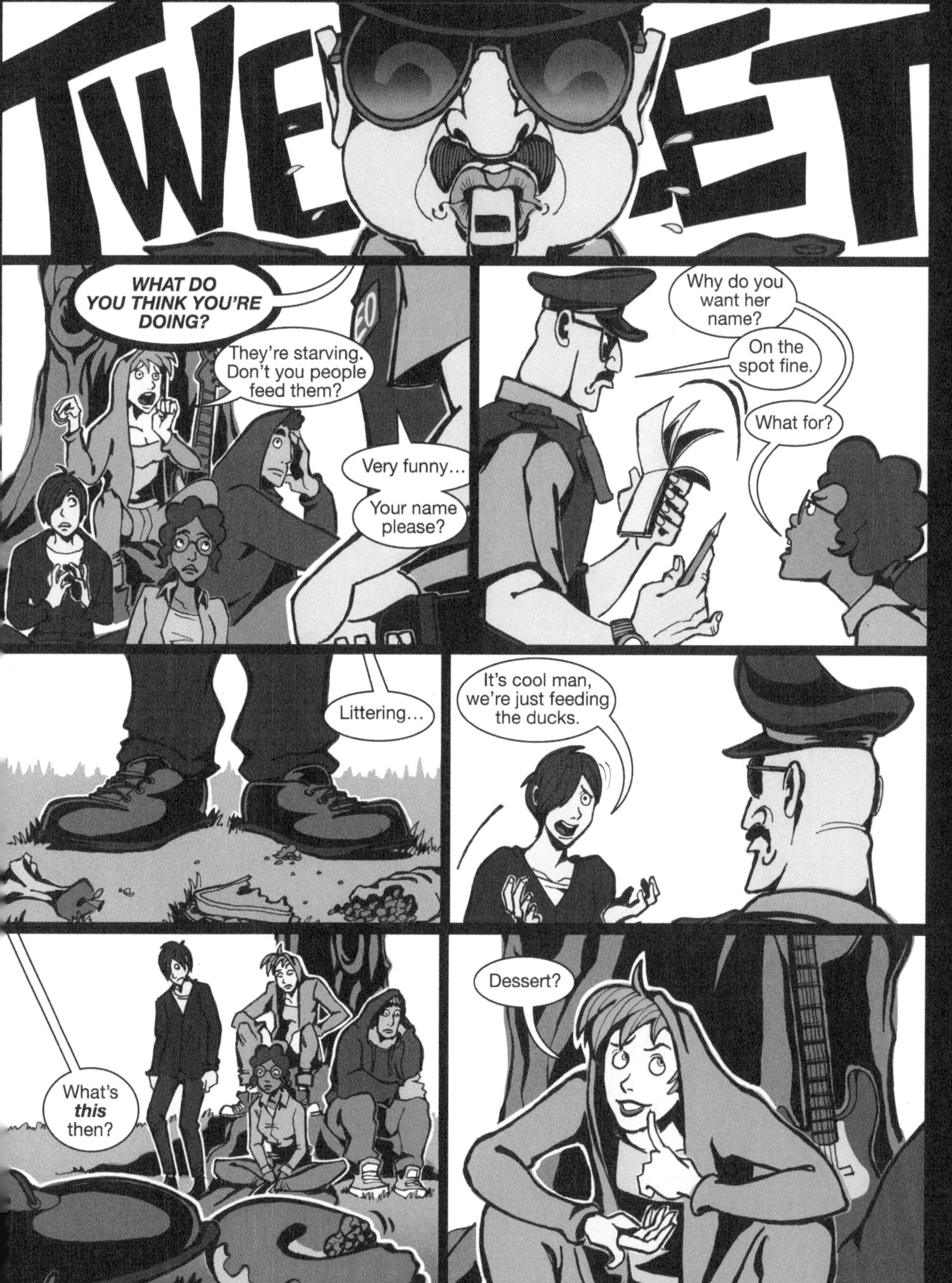
TWEEEEST
WHAT DO YOU THINK YOU'RE DOING?
They're starving. Don't you people feed them?
Very funny...
Your name please?
Why do you want her name?
On the spot fine.
What for?
Littering...
It's cool man, we're just feeding the ducks.
What's **this** then?
Dessert?

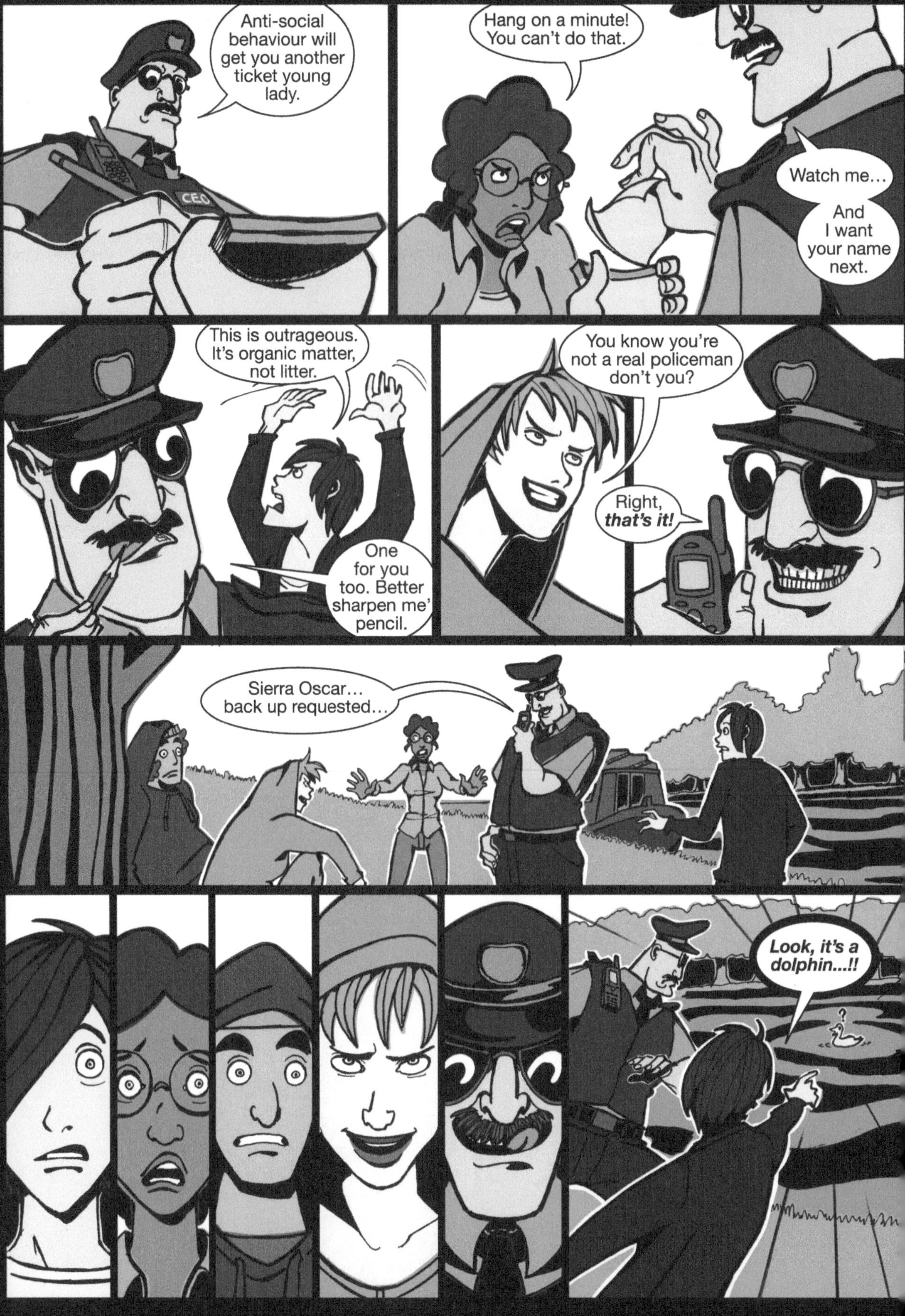

Anti-social behaviour will get you another ticket young lady.
Hang on a minute! You can't do that.
Watch me…
And I want your name next.
This is outrageous. It's organic matter, not litter.
One for you too. Better sharpen me' pencil.
You know you're not a real policeman don't you?
Right, ***that's it!***
Sierra Oscar… back up requested…
CEO
Look, it's a dolphin...!!
?

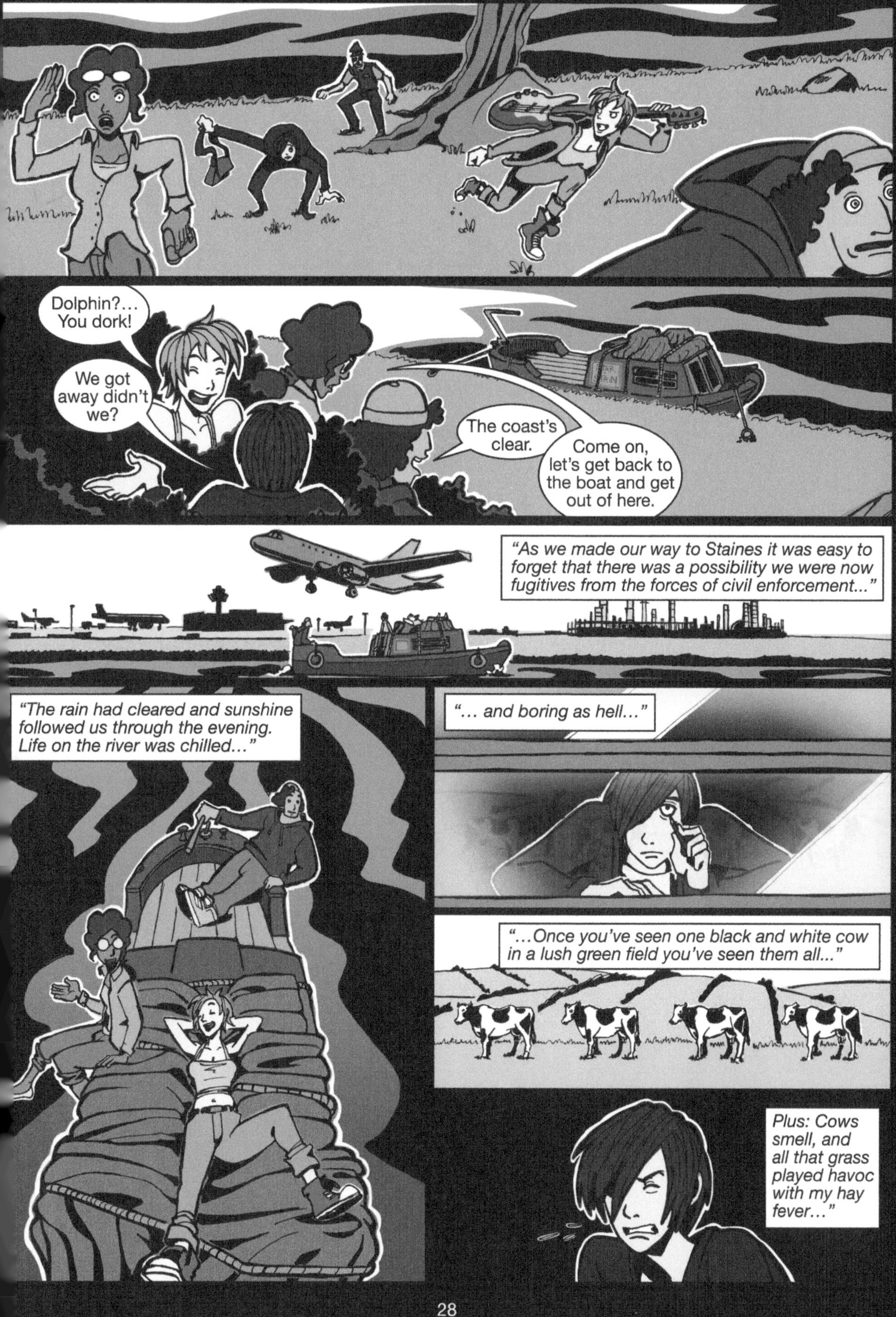
Dolphin?... You dork!
We got away didn't we?
The coast's clear.
Come on, let's get back to the boat and get out of here.
"As we made our way to Staines it was easy to forget that there was a possibility we were now fugitives from the forces of civil enforcement..."
"The rain had cleared and sunshine followed us through the evening. Life on the river was chilled..."
"... and boring as hell..."
"...Once you've seen one black and white cow in a lush green field you've seen them all..."
Plus: Cows smell, and all that grass played havoc with my hay fever..."

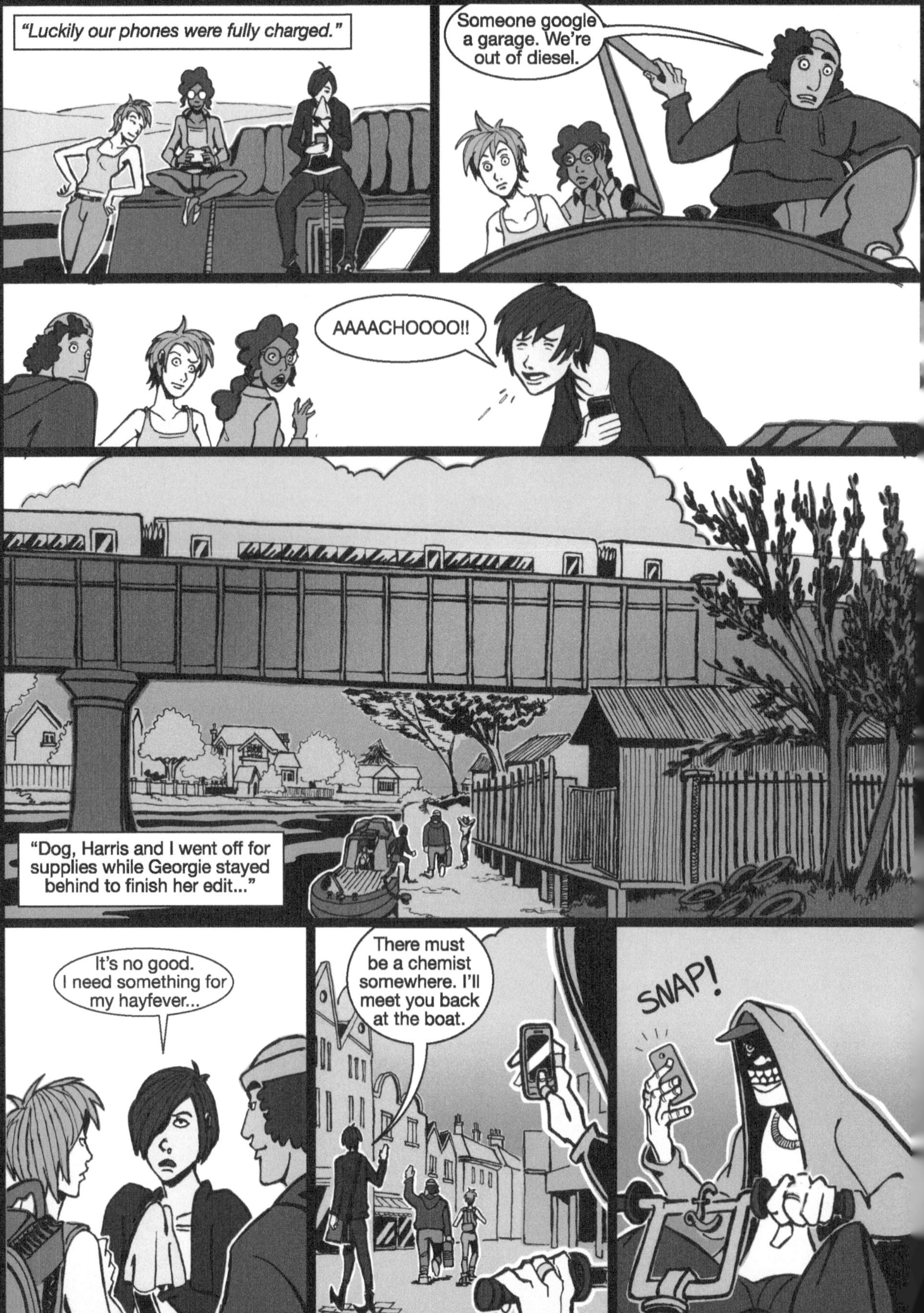
"Luckily our phones were fully charged."
Someone google a garage. We're out of diesel.
AAAACHOOOO!!
"Dog, Harris and I went off for supplies while Georgie stayed behind to finish her edit..."
It's no good. I need something for my hayfever...
There must be a chemist somewhere. I'll meet you back at the boat.
SNAP!

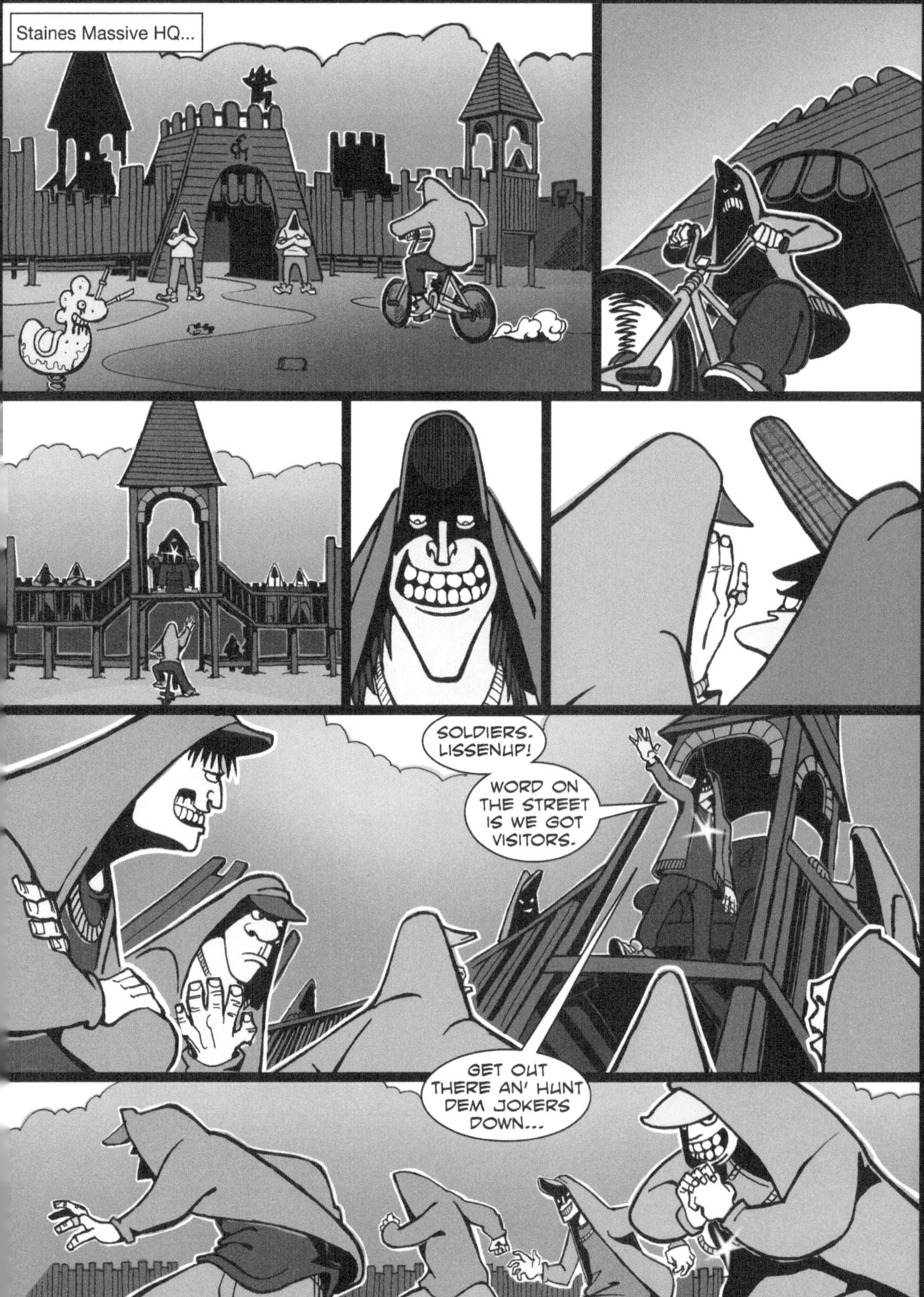
Staines Massive HQ...
SOLDIERS. LISSENUP!
WORD ON THE STREET IS WE GOT VISITORS.
GET OUT THERE AN' HUNT DEM JOKERS DOWN...

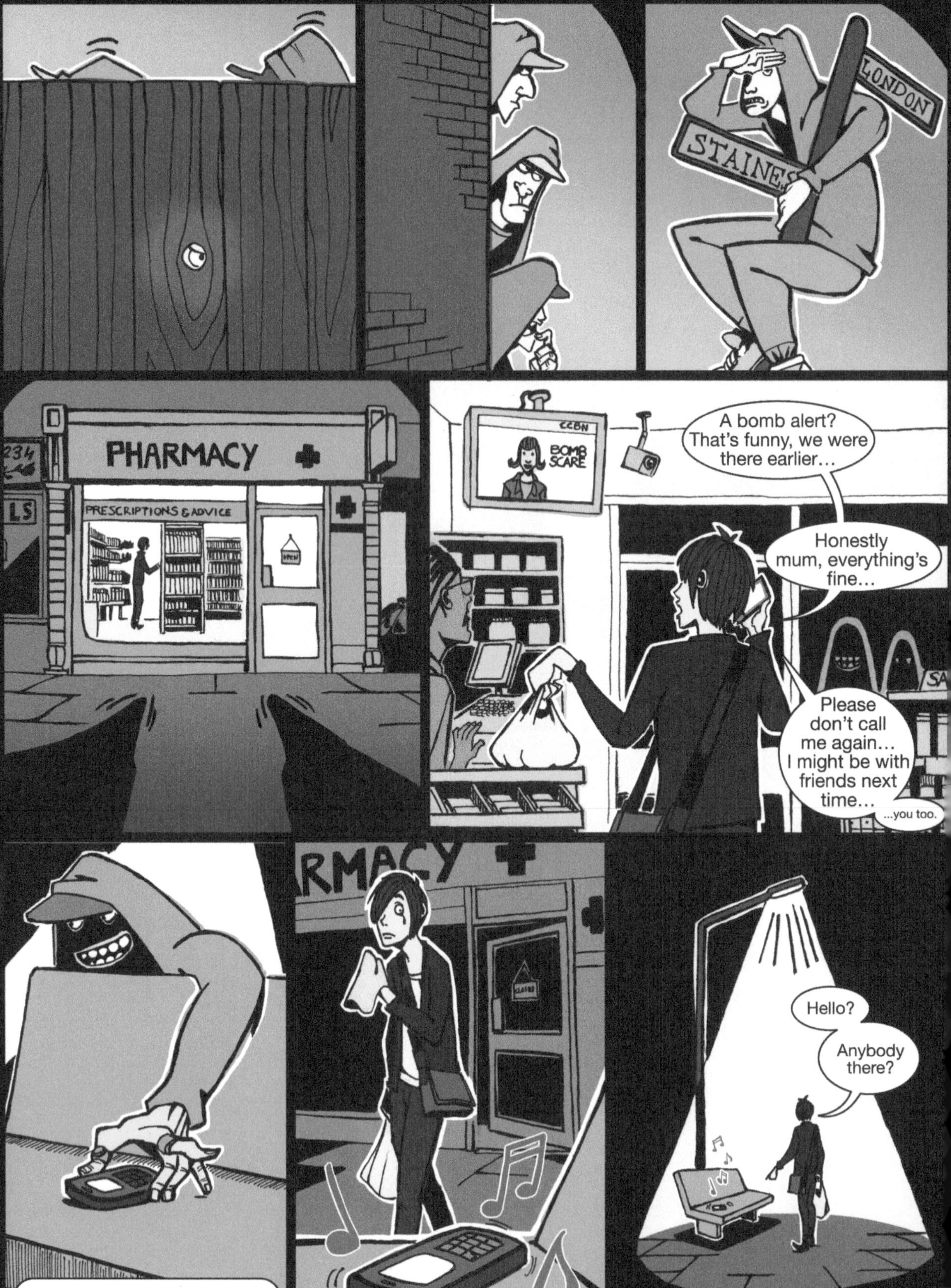
LONDON
STAINES
PHARMACY
PRESCRIPTIONS & ADVICE
1234
CCBN
BOMB SCARE
A bomb alert? That's funny, we were there earlier…
Honestly mum, everything's fine…
Please don't call me again… I might be with friends next time…
...you too.
Lame Excuse for Random Violence Number 33…
RMACY
Hello?
Anybody there?

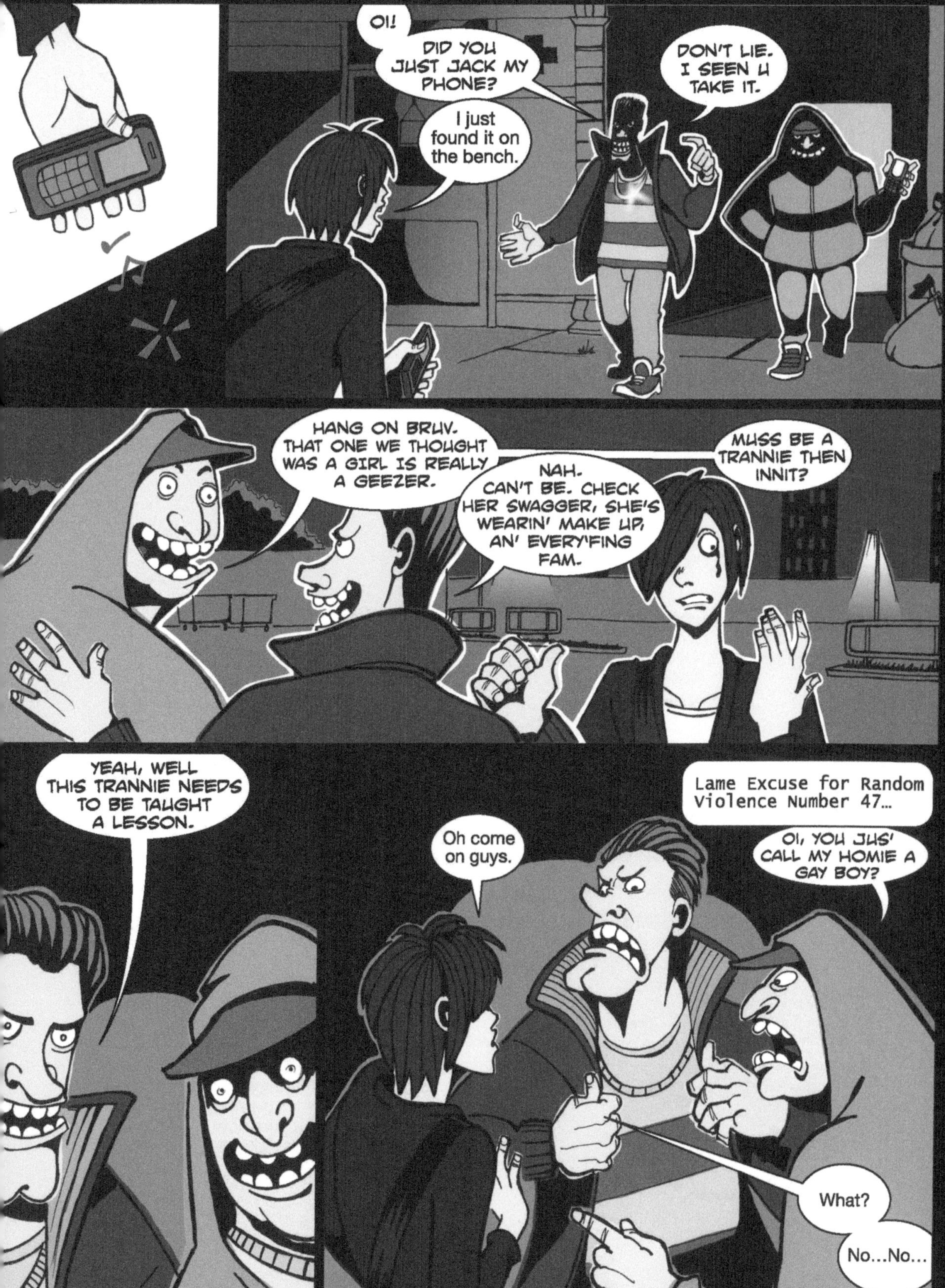
OI!
DID YOU JUST JACK MY PHONE?
I just found it on the bench.
DON'T LIE. I SEEN U TAKE IT.
HANG ON BRUV. THAT ONE WE THOUGHT WAS A GIRL IS REALLY A GEEZER.
MUSS BE A TRANNIE THEN INNIT?
NAH. CAN'T BE. CHECK HER SWAGGER, SHE'S WEARIN' MAKE UP, AN' EVERY'FING FAM.
YEAH, WELL THIS TRANNIE NEEDS TO BE TAUGHT A LESSON.
Lame Excuse for Random Violence Number 47...
Oh come on guys.
OI, YOU JUS' CALL MY HOMIE A GAY BOY?
What?
No...No...

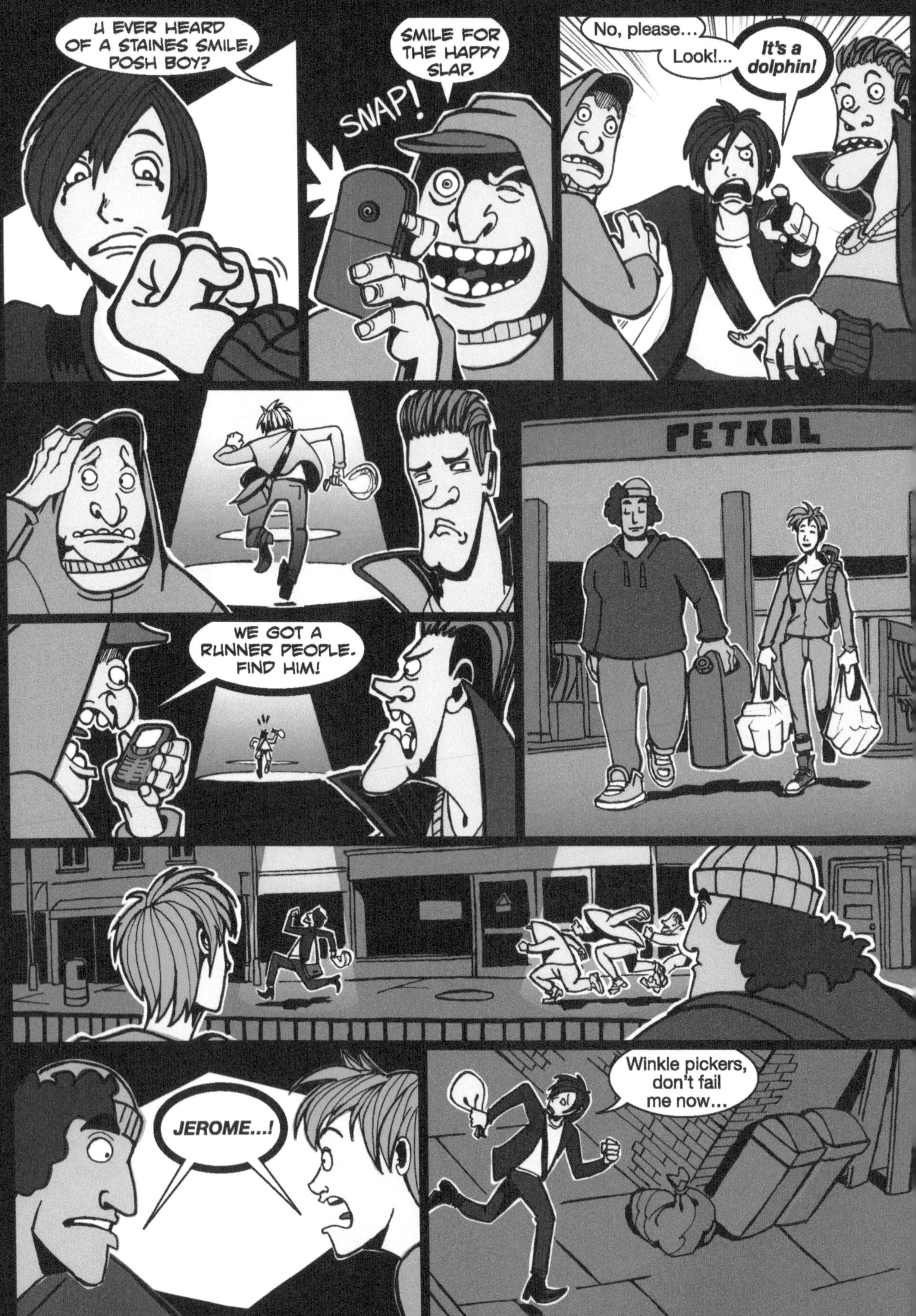

U EVER HEARD OF A STAINES SMILE, POSH BOY?
SMILE FOR THE HAPPY SLAP.
SNAP!
No, please…
Look!…
It's a dolphin!
PETROL
WE GOT A RUNNER PEOPLE. FIND HIM!
JEROME…!
Winkle pickers, don't fail me now…

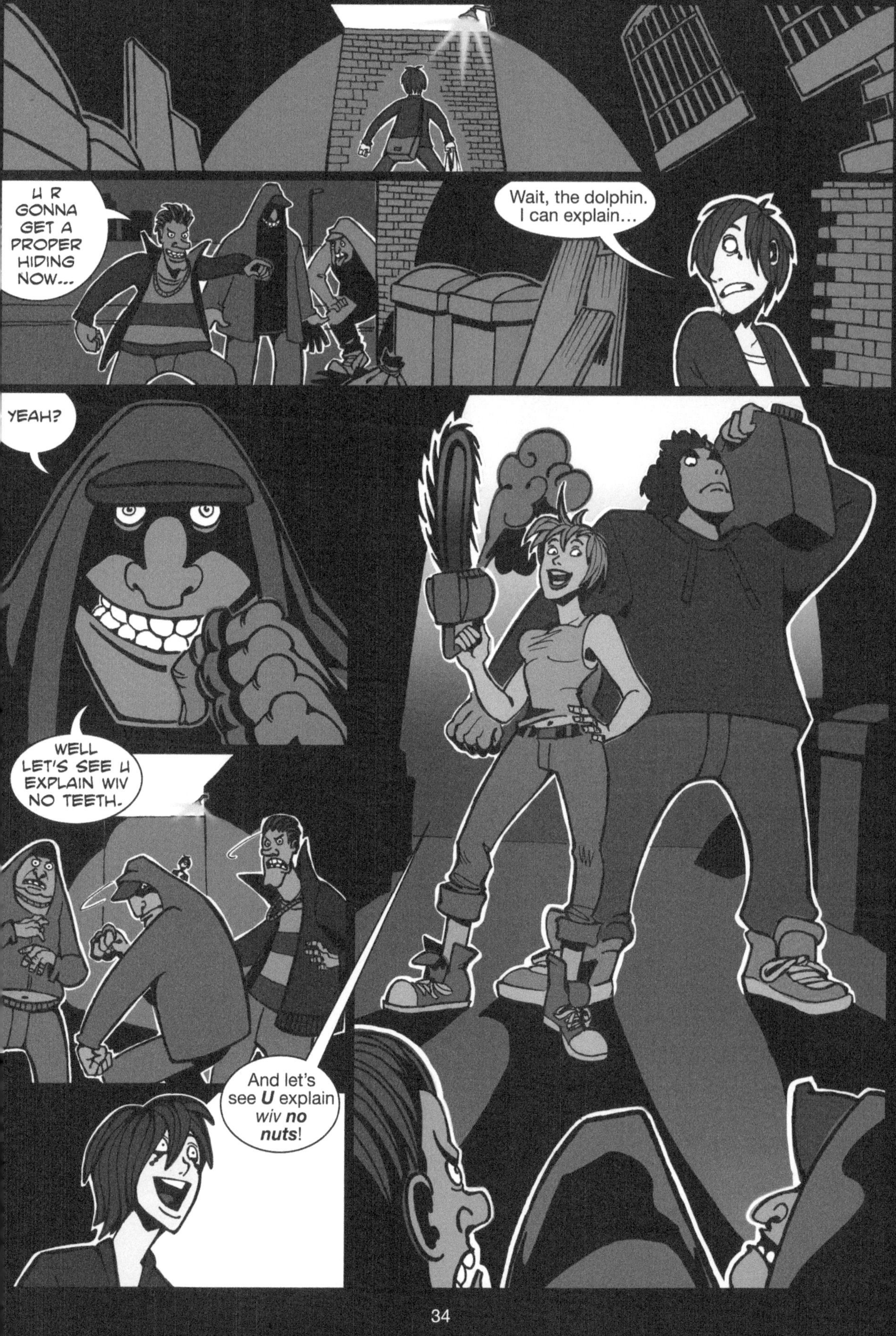
U R GONNA GET A PROPER HIDING NOW...
Wait, the dolphin. I can explain…
YEAH?
WELL LET'S SEE U EXPLAIN WIV NO TEETH.
And let's see ***U*** explain *wiv* ***no nuts***!

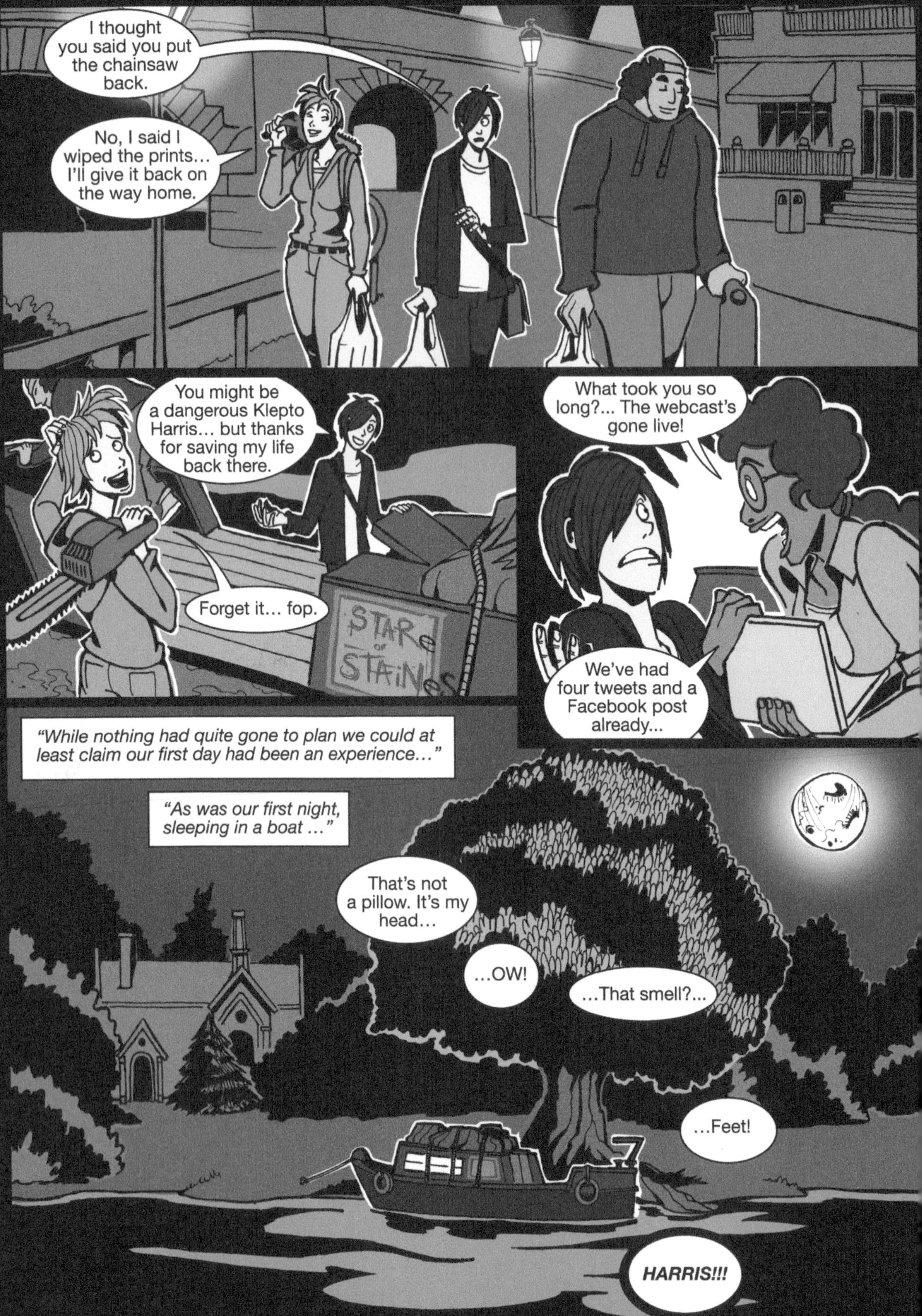
I thought you said you put the chainsaw back.
No, I said I wiped the prints… I'll give it back on the way home.
You might be a dangerous Klepto Harris… but thanks for saving my life back there.
Forget it… fop.
STARe OF STAiNeS
What took you so long?... The webcast's gone live!
We've had four tweets and a Facebook post already...
"While nothing had quite gone to plan we could at least claim our first day had been an experience…"
"As was our first night, sleeping in a boat …"
That's not a pillow. It's my head…
…OW!
…That smell?...
…Feet!
HARRIS!!!

Boyz in the HOODIES

Eyeballing

in your Dreams

Antisocial Media

Something Fishy

Shenanigans

"LEG iT"...

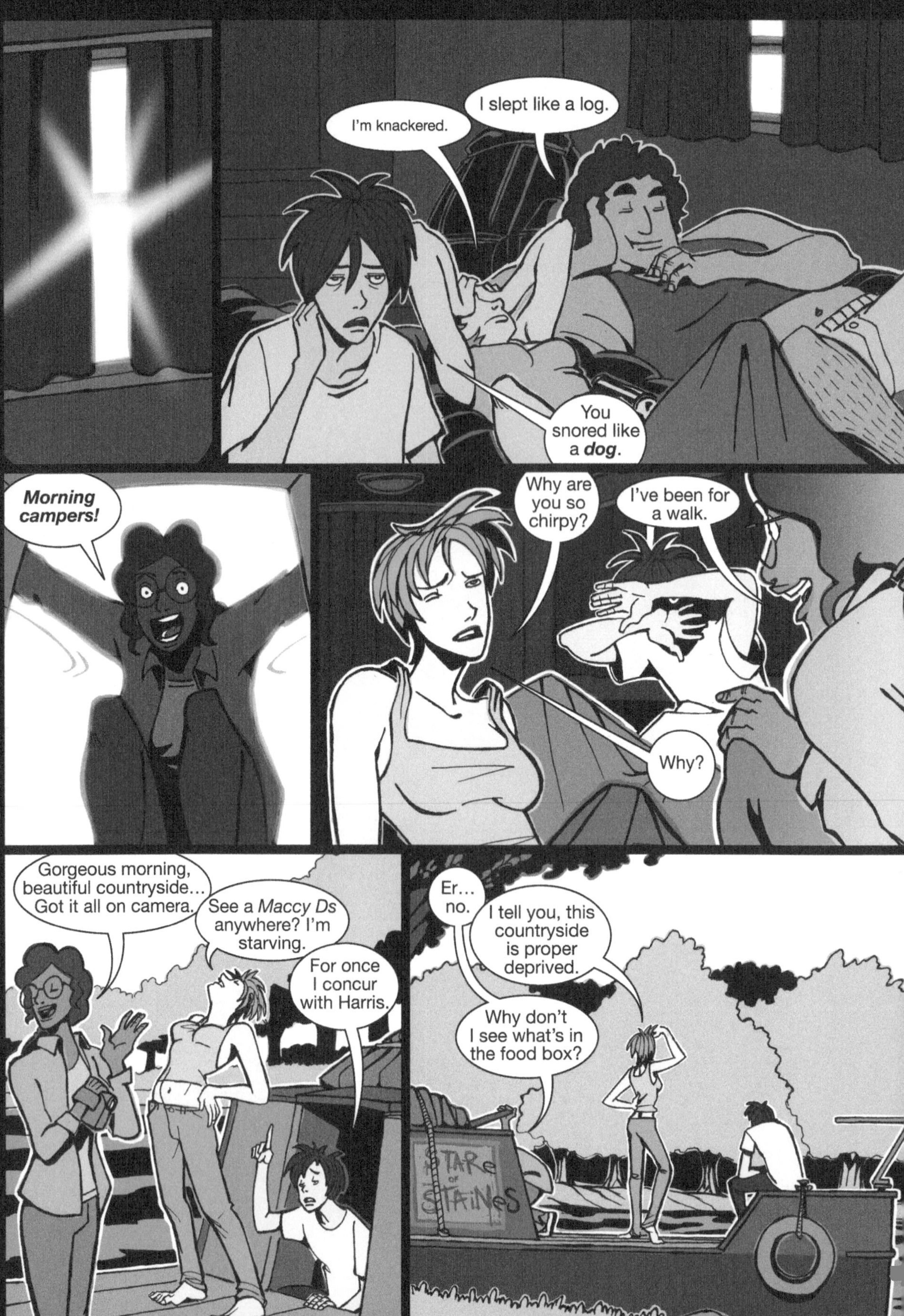
I'm knackered.
I slept like a log.
You snored like a *dog*.
Morning campers!
Why are you so chirpy?
I've been for a walk.
Why?
Gorgeous morning, beautiful countryside… Got it all on camera.
See a *Maccy Ds* anywhere? I'm starving.
For once I concur with Harris.
Er… no.
I tell you, this countryside is proper deprived.
Why don't I see what's in the food box?
STAR OF STAINES

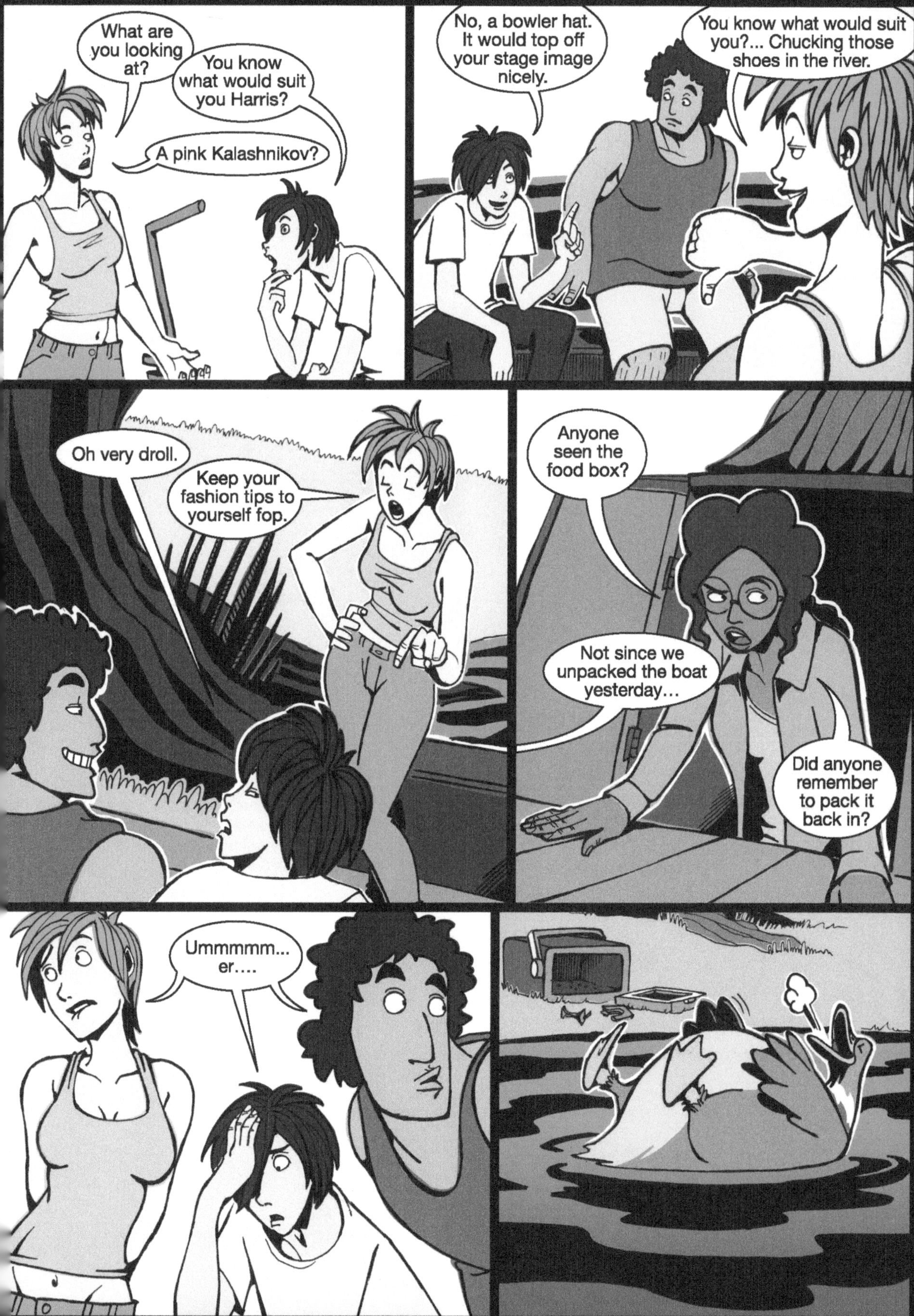

What are you looking at?
You know what would suit you Harris?
A pink Kalashnikov?
No, a bowler hat. It would top off your stage image nicely.
You know what would suit you?... Chucking those shoes in the river.
Oh very droll.
Keep your fashion tips to yourself fop.
Anyone seen the food box?
Not since we unpacked the boat yesterday…
Did anyone remember to pack it back in?
Ummmmm... er….

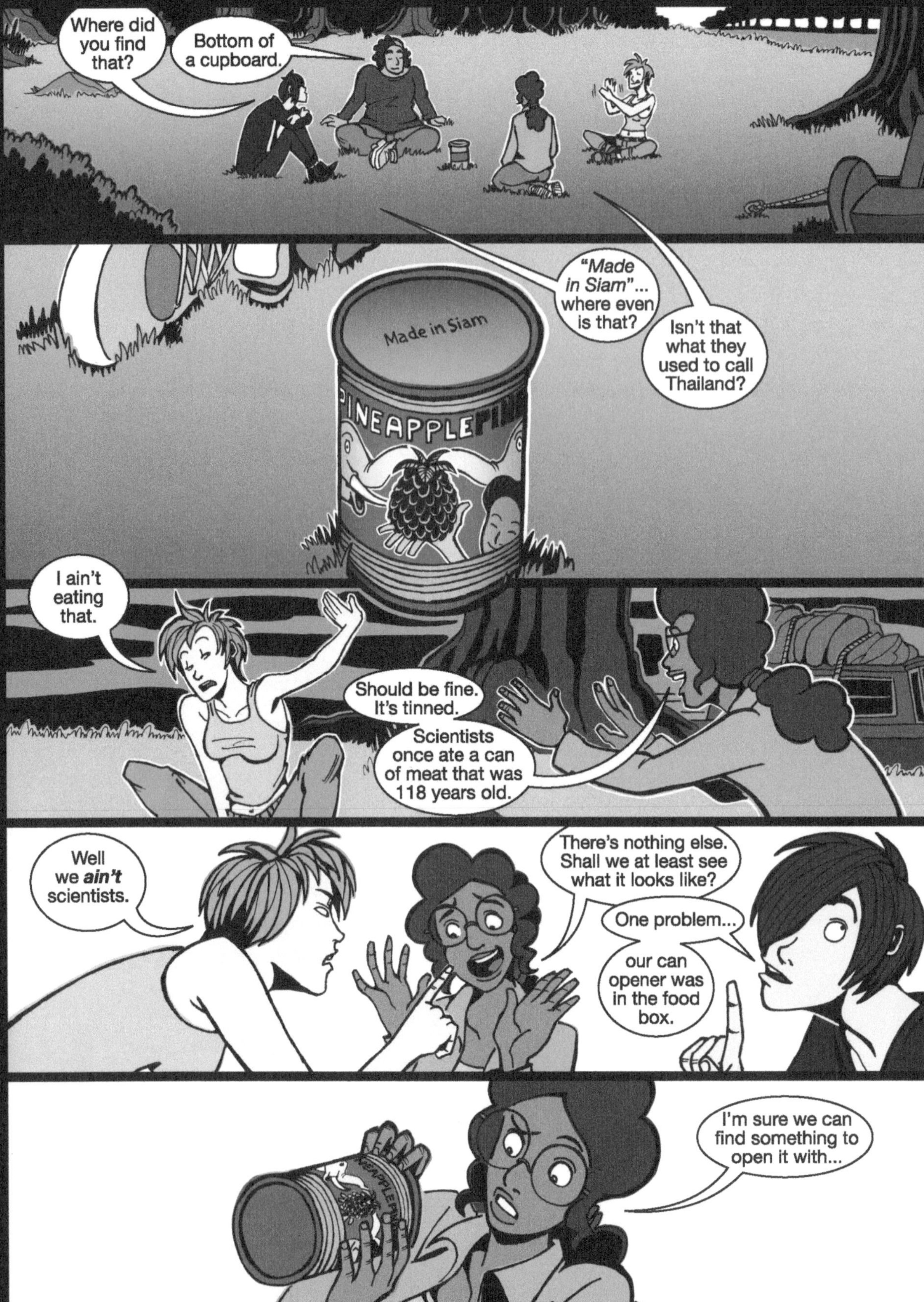
Where did you find that?
Bottom of a cupboard.
"*Made in Siam*"... where even is that?
Isn't that what they used to call Thailand?
Made in Siam
PINEAPPLE
I ain't eating that.
Should be fine. It's tinned.
Scientists once ate a can of meat that was 118 years old.
Well we ***ain't*** scientists.
There's nothing else. Shall we at least see what it looks like?
One problem...
our can opener was in the food box.
I'm sure we can find something to open it with...

AAARGHH!

NO!...

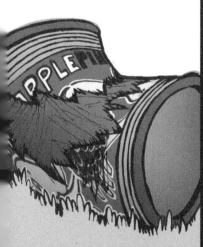

Shall we go back to Staines for supplies?

You're joking. I like my smile the way it is.

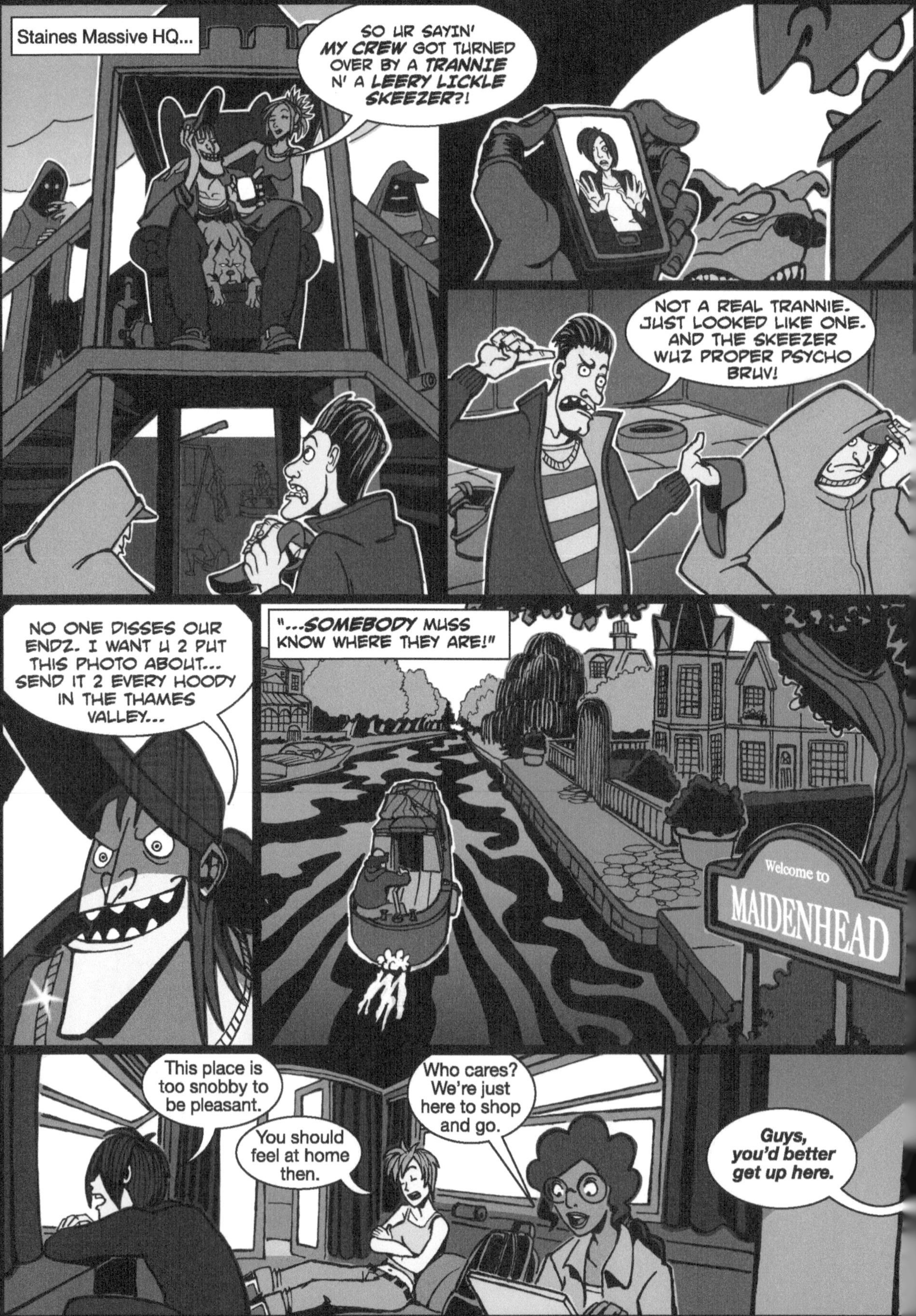
Staines Massive HQ...
SO UR SAYIN' MY CREW GOT TURNED OVER BY A TRANNIE N' A LEERY LICKLE SKEEZER?!
NOT A REAL TRANNIE. JUST LOOKED LIKE ONE. AND THE SKEEZER WUZ PROPER PSYCHO BRUV!
NO ONE DISSES OUR ENDZ. I WANT U 2 PUT THIS PHOTO ABOUT... SEND IT 2 EVERY HOODY IN THE THAMES VALLEY...
"...SOMEBODY MUSS KNOW WHERE THEY ARE!"
Welcome to
MAIDENHEAD
This place is too snobby to be pleasant.
You should feel at home then.
Who cares? We're just here to shop and go.
Guys, you'd better get up here.

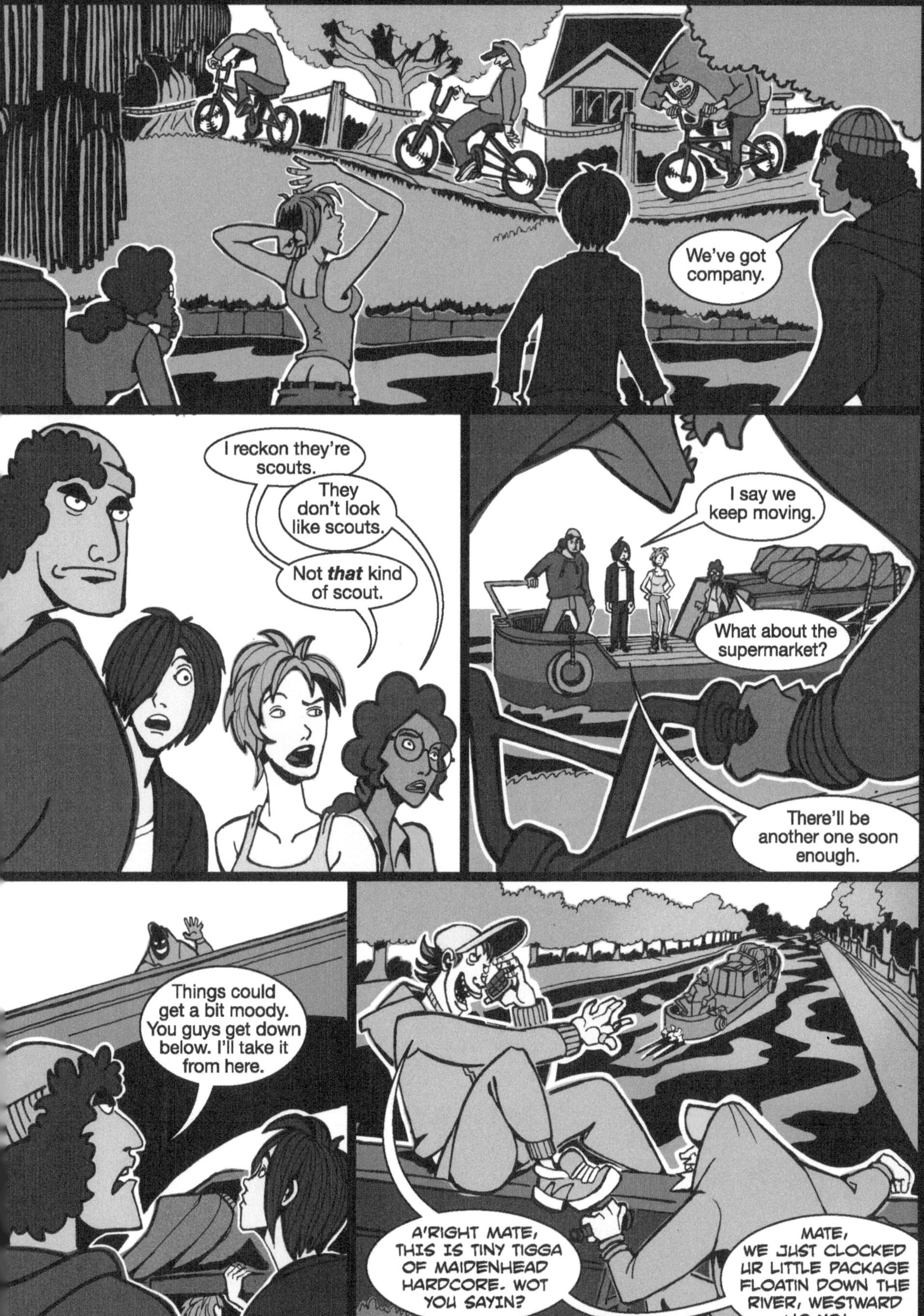
We've got company.
I reckon they're scouts.
They don't look like scouts.
Not *that* kind of scout.
I say we keep moving.
What about the supermarket?
There'll be another one soon enough.
Things could get a bit moody. You guys get down below. I'll take it from here.
A'RIGHT MATE, THIS IS TINY TIGGA OF MAIDENHEAD HARDCORE. WOT YOU SAYIN?
MATE, WE JUST CLOCKED UR LITTLE PACKAGE FLOATIN DOWN THE RIVER, WESTWARD HO YO!...

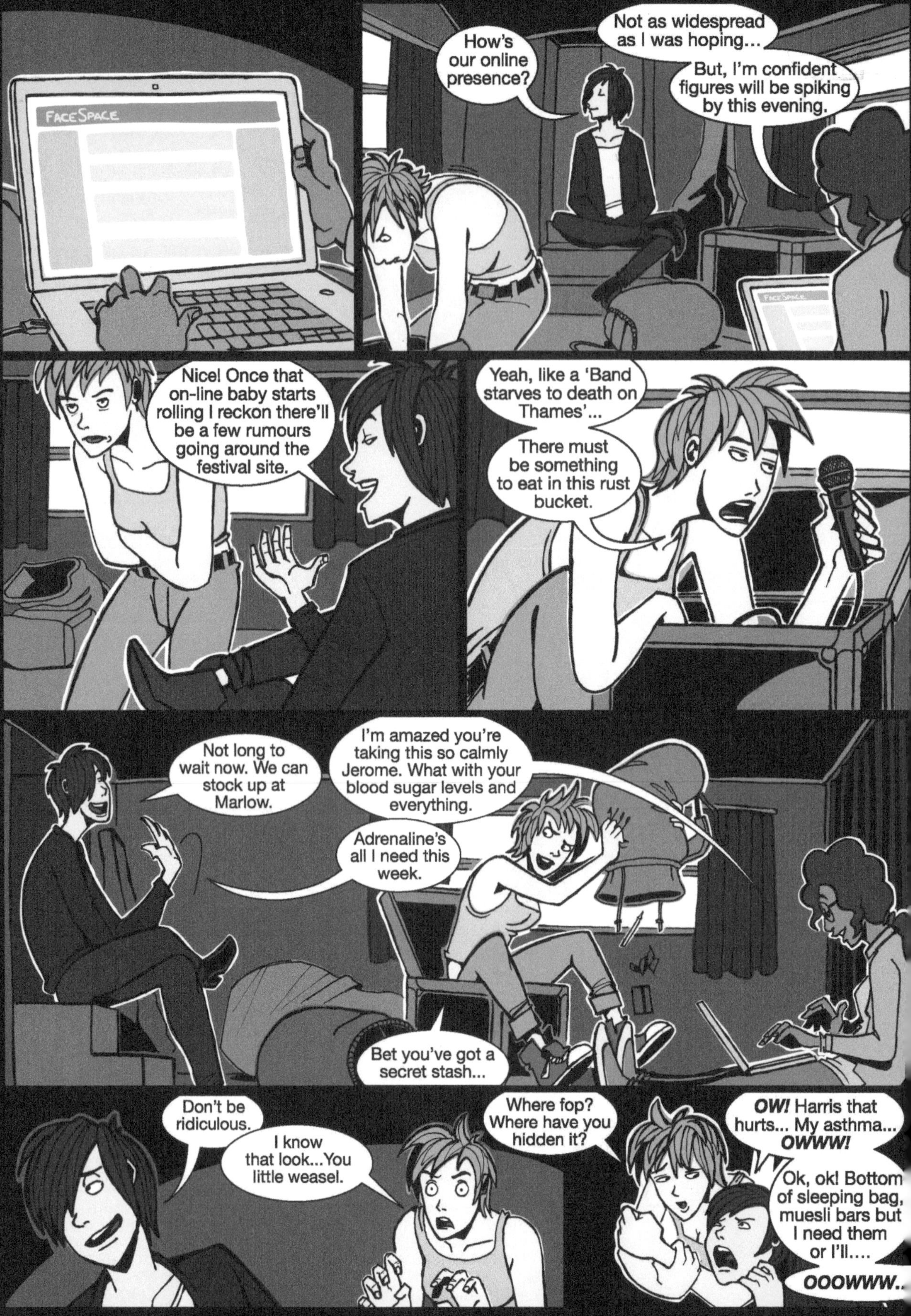
FaceSpace
How's our online presence?
Not as widespread as I was hoping…
But, I'm confident figures will be spiking by this evening.
FaceSpace
Nice! Once that on-line baby starts rolling I reckon there'll be a few rumours going around the festival site.
Yeah, like a 'Band starves to death on Thames'...
There must be something to eat in this rust bucket.
Not long to wait now. We can stock up at Marlow.
I'm amazed you're taking this so calmly Jerome. What with your blood sugar levels and everything.
Adrenaline's all I need this week.
Bet you've got a secret stash...
Don't be ridiculous.
I know that look...You little weasel.
Where fop? Where have you hidden it?
OW! Harris that hurts... My asthma... OWWW!
Ok, ok! Bottom of sleeping bag, muesli bars but I need them or I'll....
OOOWWW..

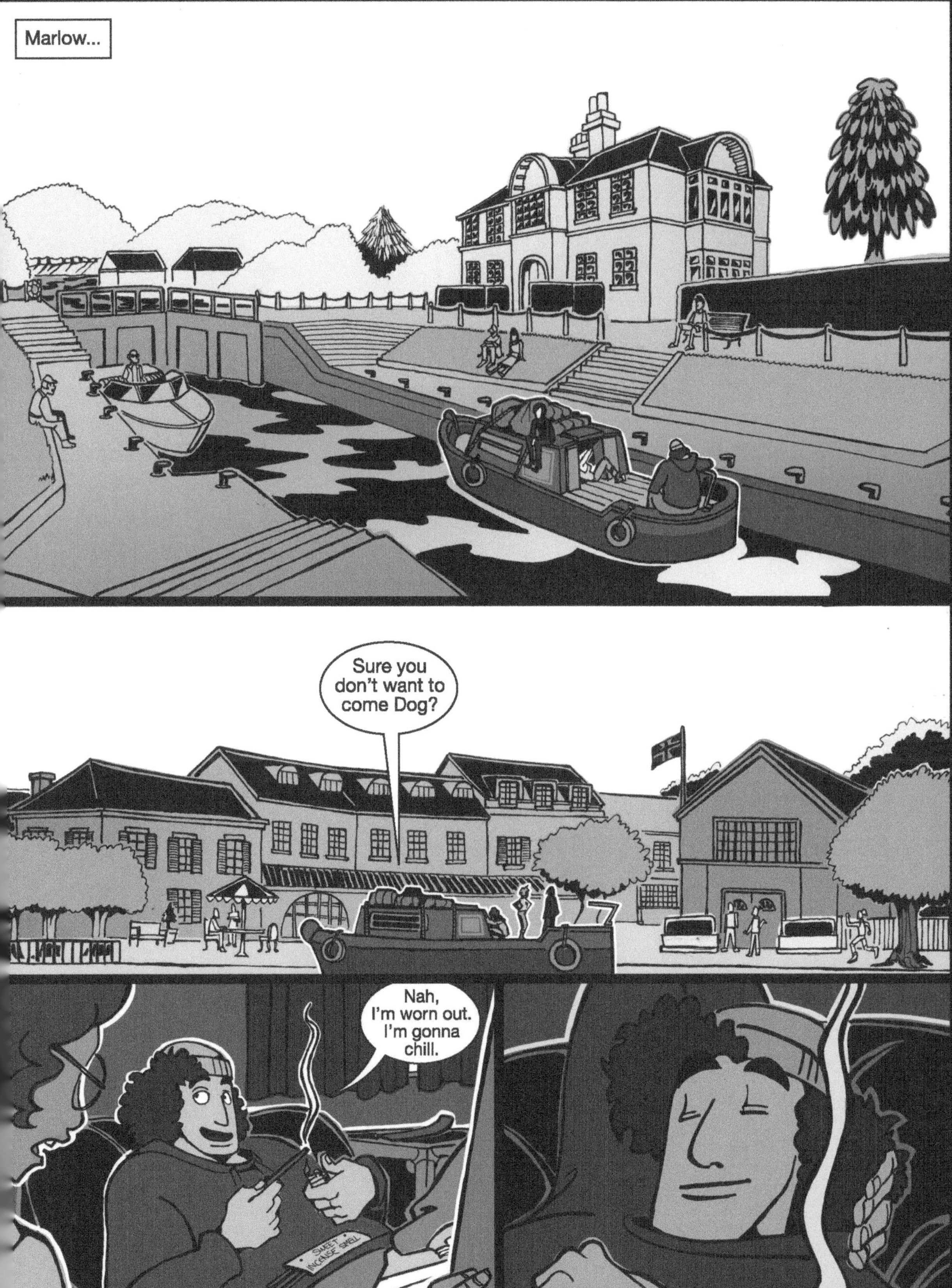
Marlow...
Sure you don't want to come Dog?
Nah, I'm worn out. I'm gonna chill.
SWEET INCENSE SMELL

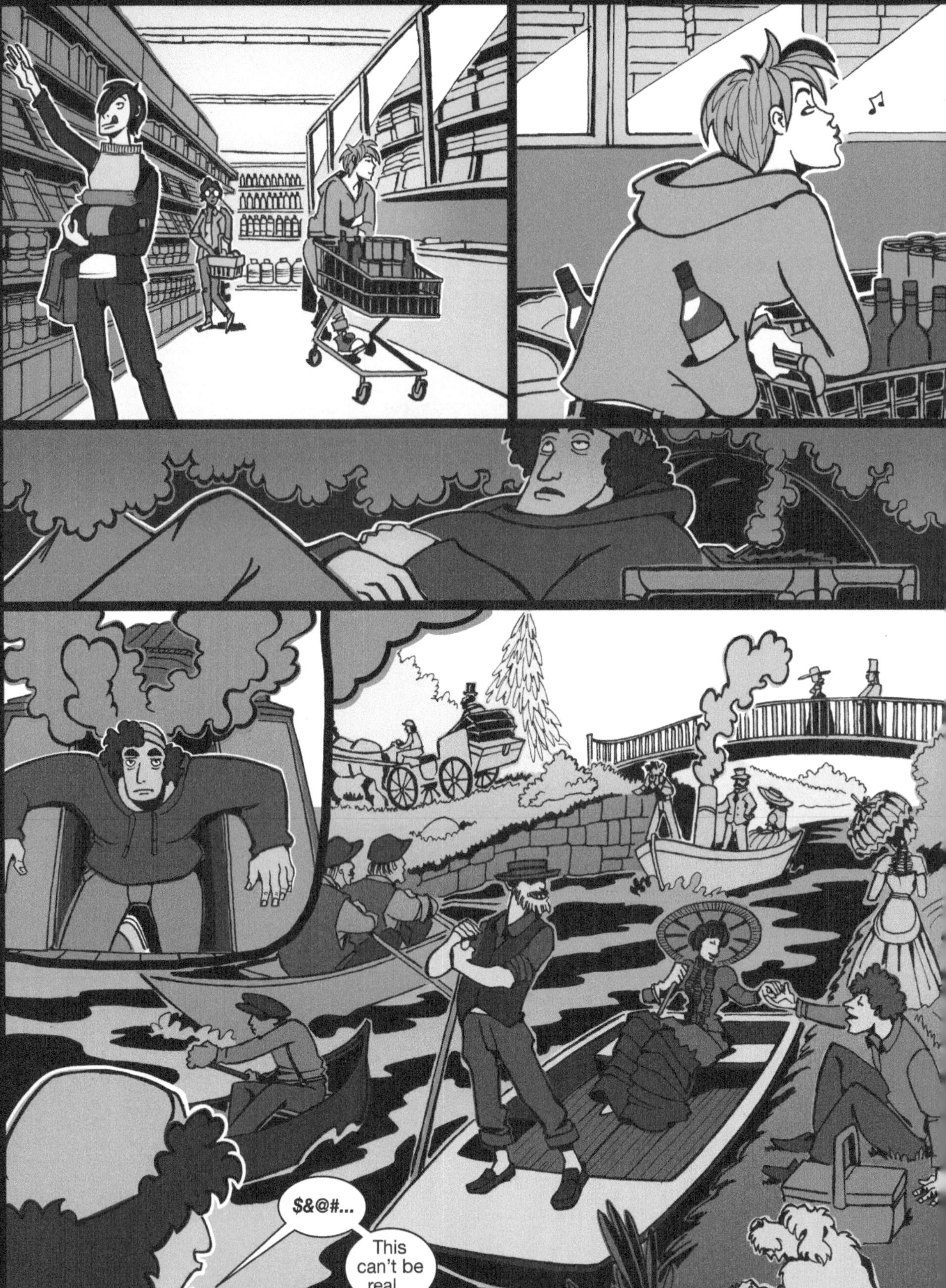
$&@#...
This can't be real...

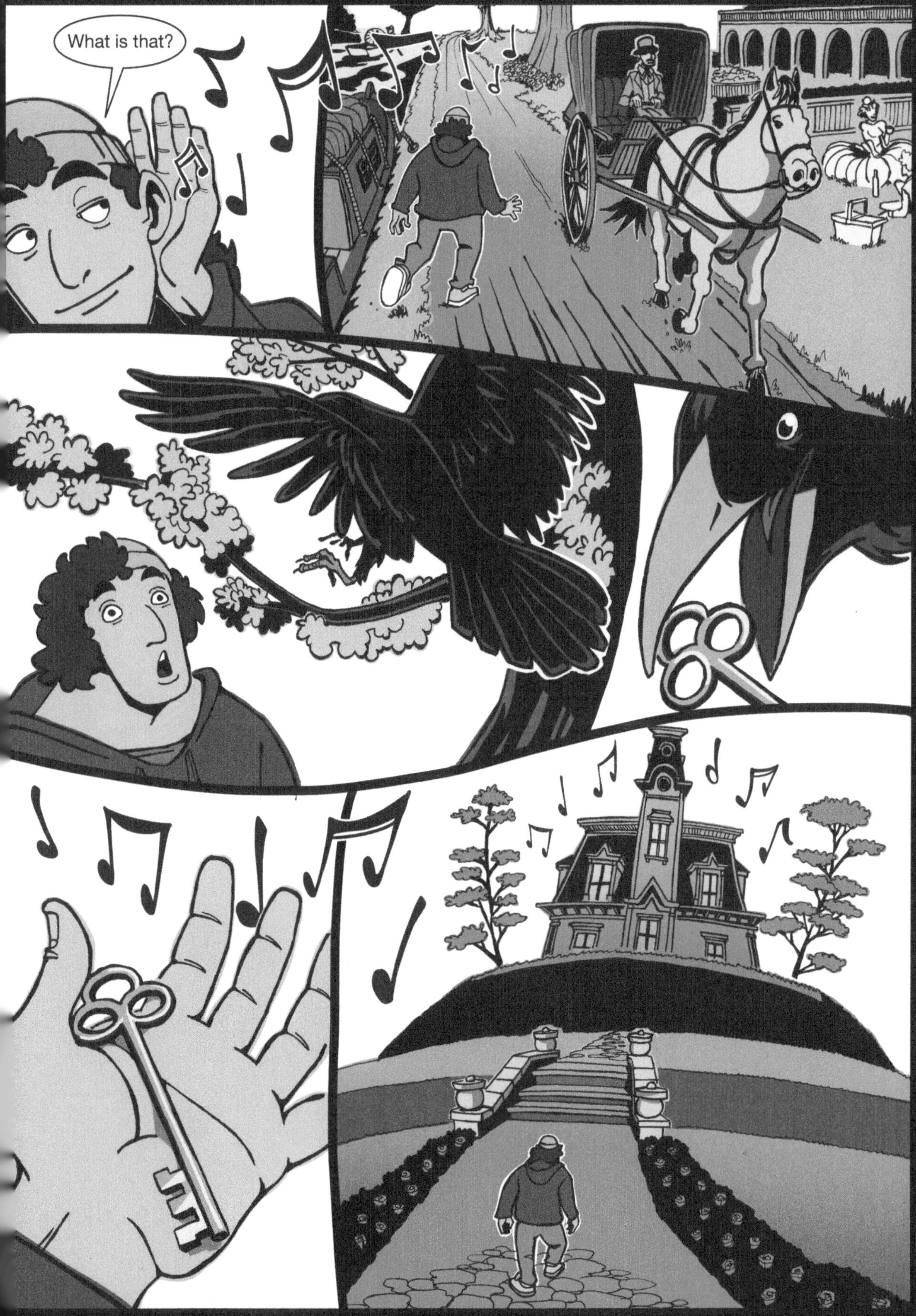
What is that?

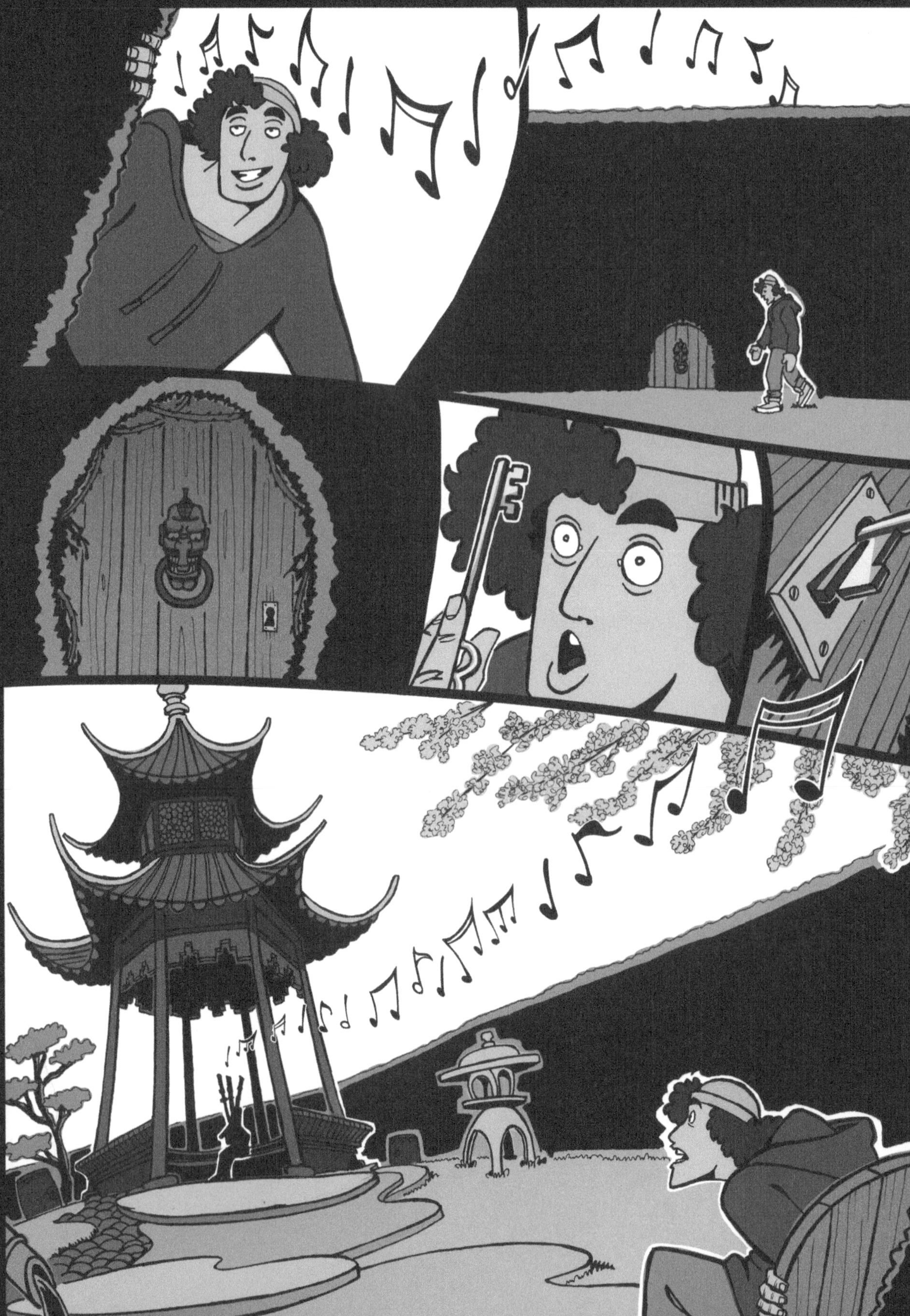

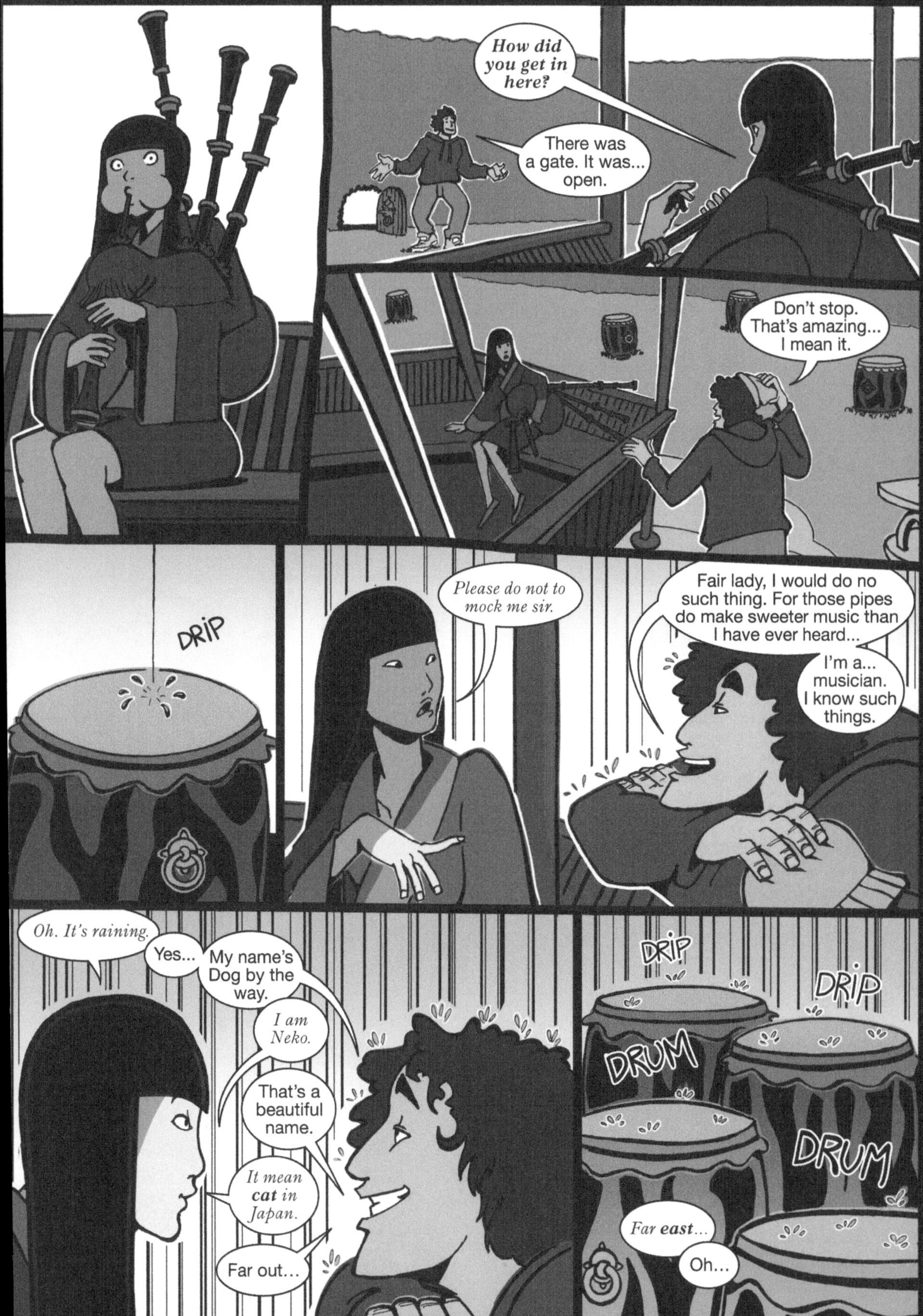
How did you get in here?
There was a gate. It was... open.
Don't stop. That's amazing... I mean it.
DRIP
Please do not to mock me sir.
Fair lady, I would do no such thing. For those pipes do make sweeter music than I have ever heard...
I'm a... musician. I know such things.
Oh. It's raining.
Yes...
My name's Dog by the way.
I am Neko.
That's a beautiful name.
It mean cat in Japan.
Far out...
DRIP
DRIP
DRUM
DRUM
Far east...
Oh...

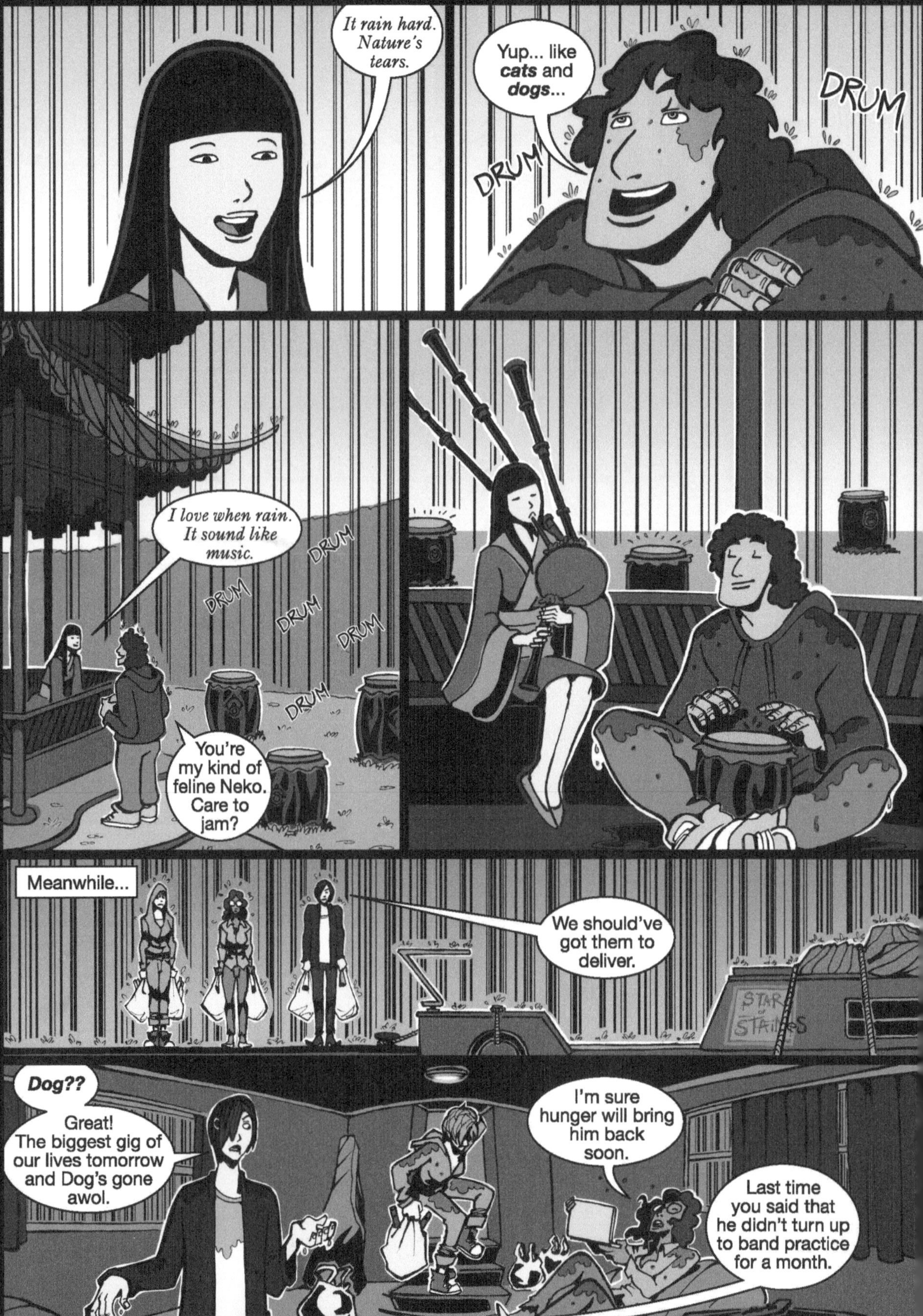
It rain hard. Nature's tears.
Yup... like ***cats*** and ***dogs***...
DRUM
DRUM
I love when rain. It sound like music.
DRUM
DRUM
DRUM
DRUM
DRUM
You're my kind of feline Neko. Care to jam?
Meanwhile...
We should've got them to deliver.
Dog??
Great! The biggest gig of our lives tomorrow and Dog's gone awol.
I'm sure hunger will bring him back soon.
Last time you said that he didn't turn up to band practice for a month.

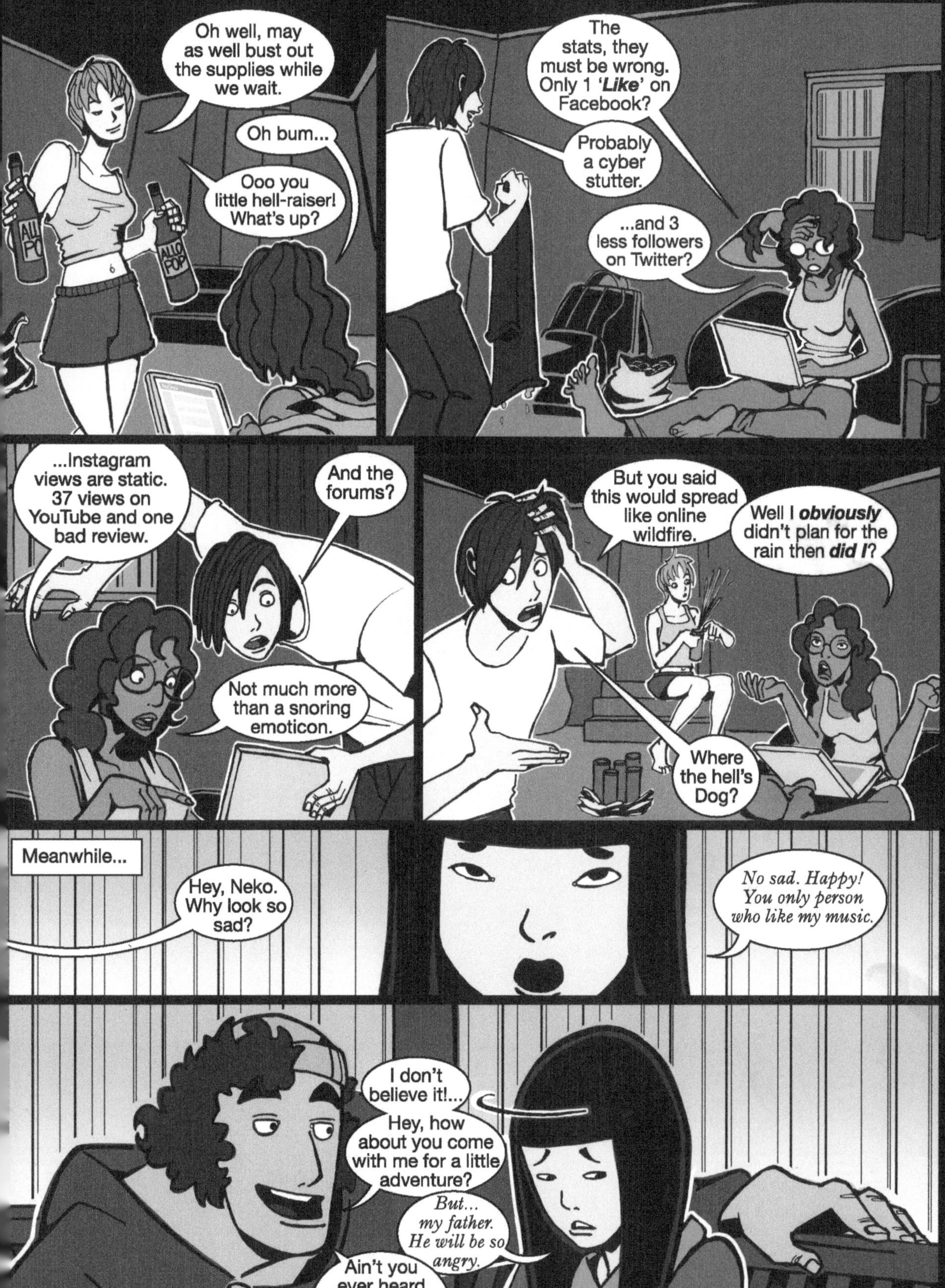
Oh well, may as well bust out the supplies while we wait.
Oh bum...
Ooo you little hell-raiser! What's up?
ALLO POP
ALLO POP
The stats, they must be wrong. Only 1 '***Like***' on Facebook?
Probably a cyber stutter.
...and 3 less followers on Twitter?
...Instagram views are static. 37 views on YouTube and one bad review.
And the forums?
Not much more than a snoring emoticon.
But you said this would spread like online wildfire.
Well I ***obviously*** didn't plan for the rain then ***did I***?
Where the hell's Dog?
Meanwhile...
Hey, Neko. Why look so sad?
No sad. Happy! You only person who like my music.
I don't believe it!...
Hey, how about you come with me for a little adventure?
But... my father. He will be so angry.
Ain't you ever heard the one about the cat with 9 lives?

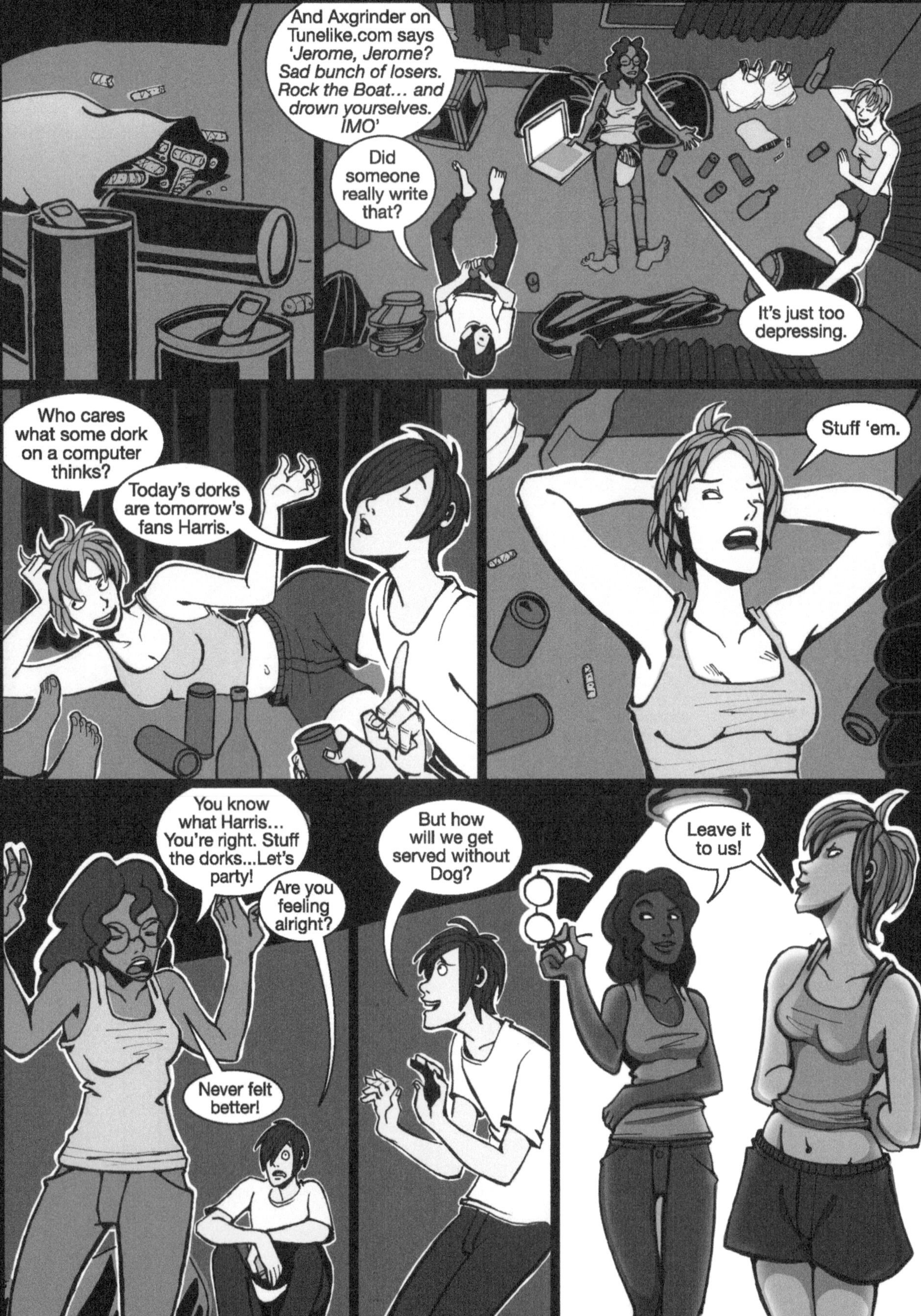
And Axgrinder on Tunelike.com says 'Jerome, Jerome? Sad bunch of losers. Rock the Boat… and drown yourselves. IMO'
Did someone really write that?
It's just too depressing.
Who cares what some dork on a computer thinks?
Today's dorks are tomorrow's fans Harris.
Stuff 'em.
You know what Harris… You're right. Stuff the dorks...Let's party!
Are you feeling alright?
Never felt better!
But how will we get served without Dog?
Leave it to us!

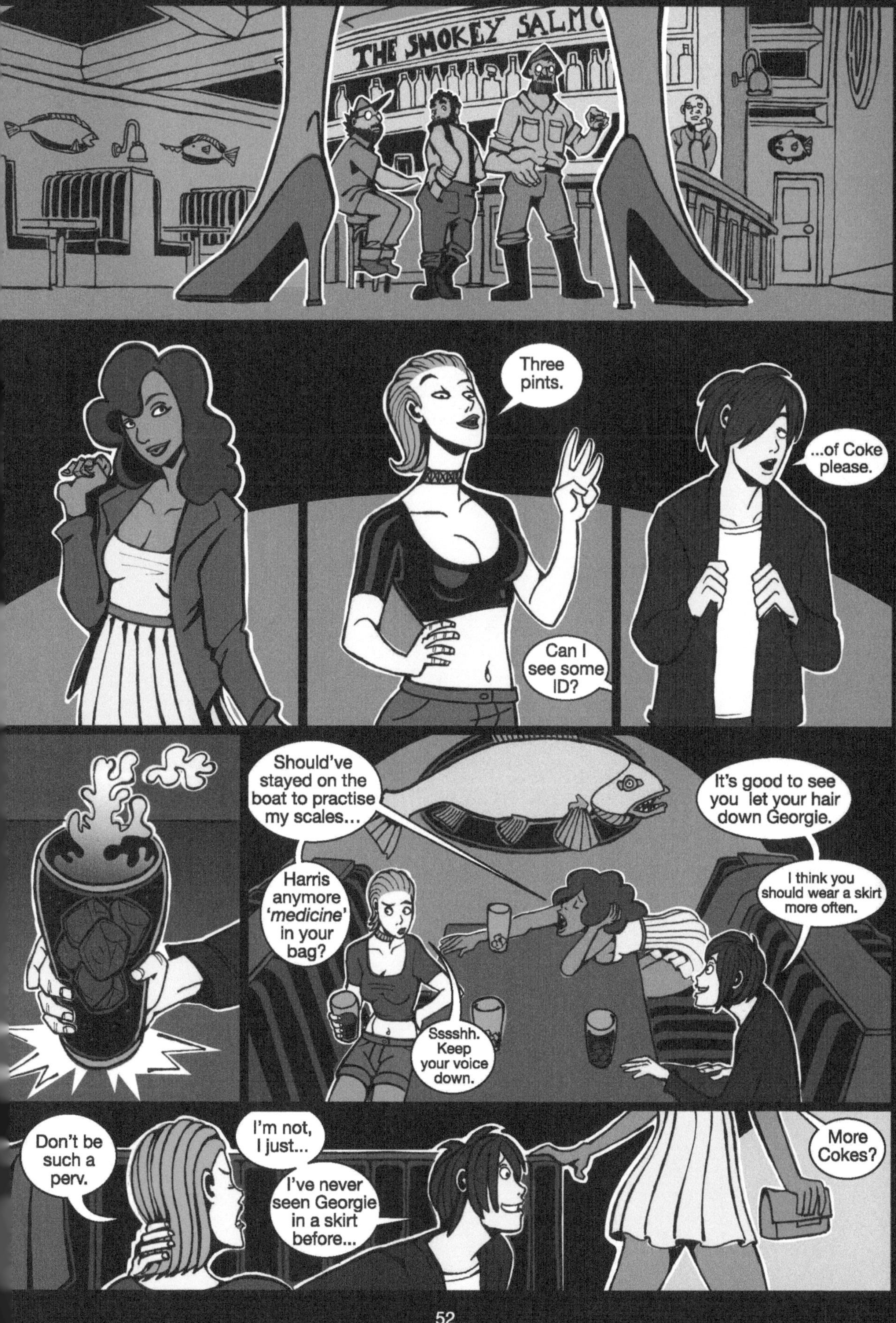
THE SMOKEY SALM
Three pints.
...of Coke please.
Can I see some ID?
Should've stayed on the boat to practise my scales...
It's good to see you let your hair down Georgie.
Harris anymore '*medicine*' in your bag?
I think you should wear a skirt more often.
Sssshh. Keep your voice down.
Don't be such a perv.
I'm not, I just...
I've never seen Georgie in a skirt before...
More Cokes?

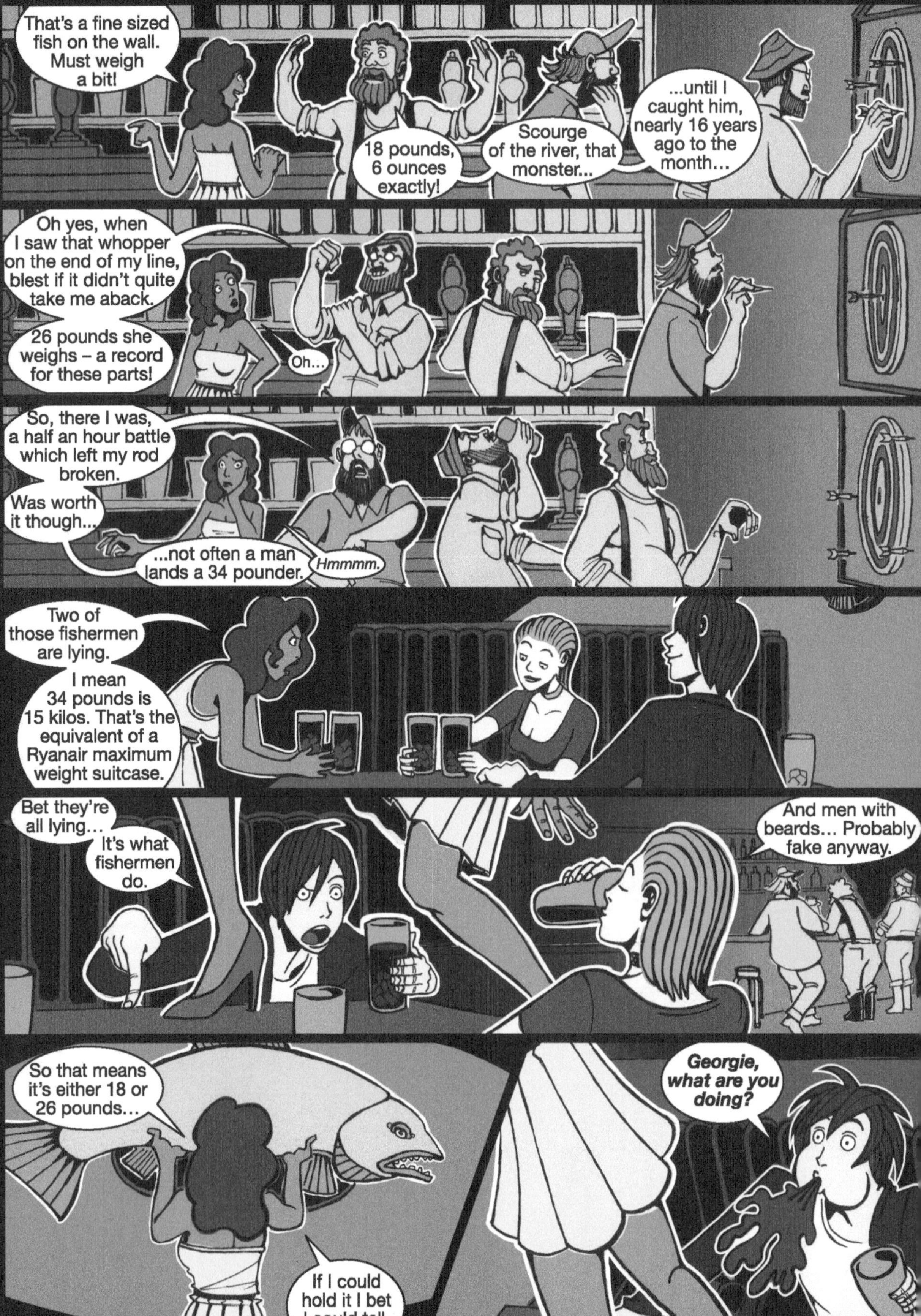
That's a fine sized fish on the wall. Must weigh a bit!
18 pounds, 6 ounces exactly!
Scourge of the river, that monster...
...until I caught him, nearly 16 years ago to the month...
Oh yes, when I saw that whopper on the end of my line, blest if it didn't quite take me aback.
26 pounds she weighs – a record for these parts!
Oh...
So, there I was, a half an hour battle which left my rod broken.
Was worth it though...
...not often a man lands a 34 pounder.
Hmmmm.
Two of those fishermen are lying.
I mean 34 pounds is 15 kilos. That's the equivalent of a Ryanair maximum weight suitcase.
Bet they're all lying...
It's what fishermen do.
And men with beards... Probably fake anyway.
So that means it's either 18 or 26 pounds...
If I could hold it I bet I could tell.
Georgie, what are you doing?

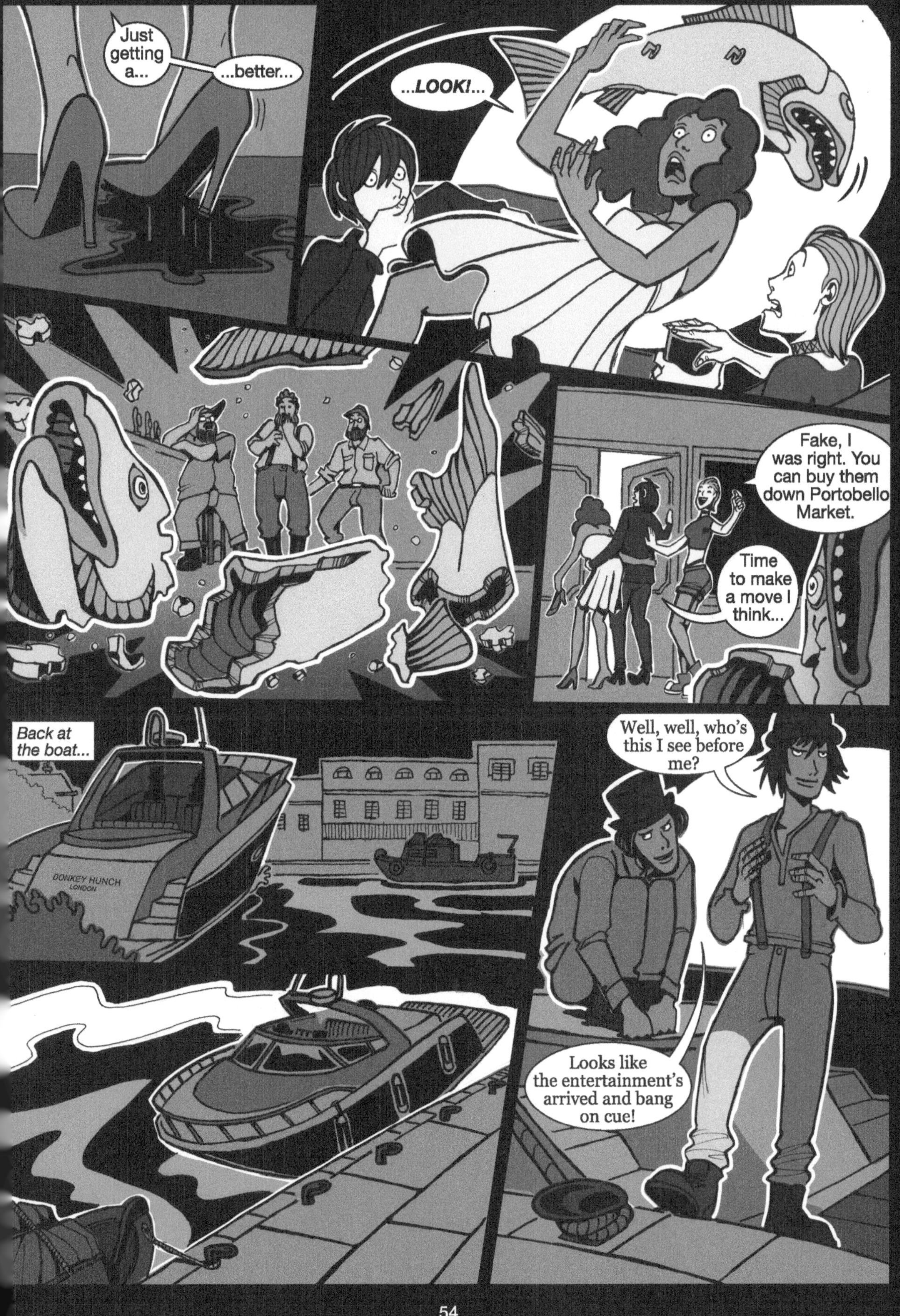

Just getting a...
...better...
...LOOK!...
Fake, I was right. You can buy them down Portobello Market.
Time to make a move I think...
Back at the boat...
DONKEY HUNCH
LONDON
Well, well, who's this I see before me?
Looks like the entertainment's arrived and bang on cue!

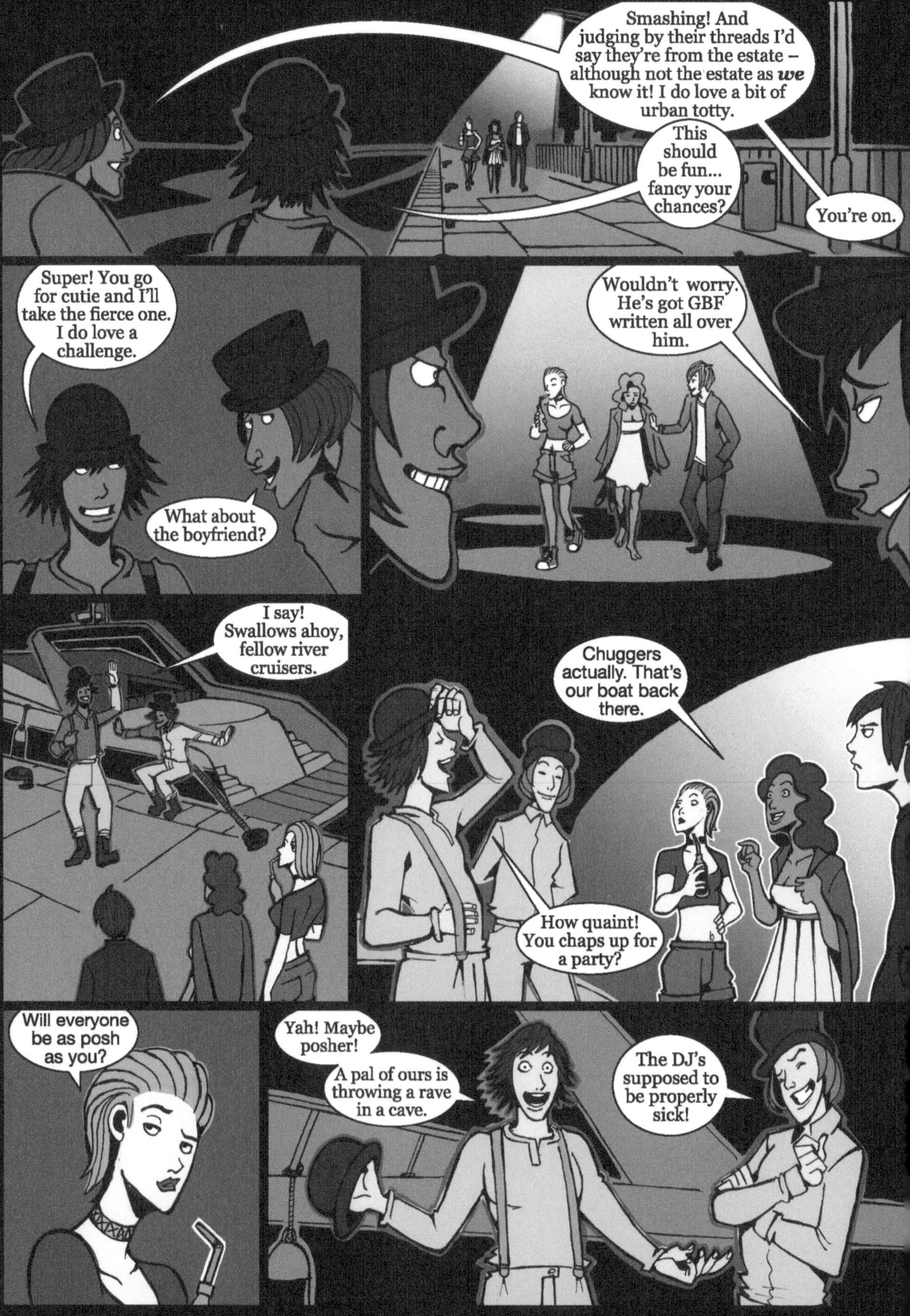
Smashing! And judging by their threads I'd say they're from the estate – although not the estate as *we* know it! I do love a bit of urban totty.
This should be fun... fancy your chances?
You're on.
Super! You go for cutie and I'll take the fierce one. I do love a challenge.
What about the boyfriend?
Wouldn't worry. He's got GBF written all over him.
I say! Swallows ahoy, fellow river cruisers.
Chuggers actually. That's our boat back there.
How quaint! You chaps up for a party?
Will everyone be as posh as you?
Yah! Maybe posher!
A pal of ours is throwing a rave in a cave.
The DJ's supposed to be properly sick!

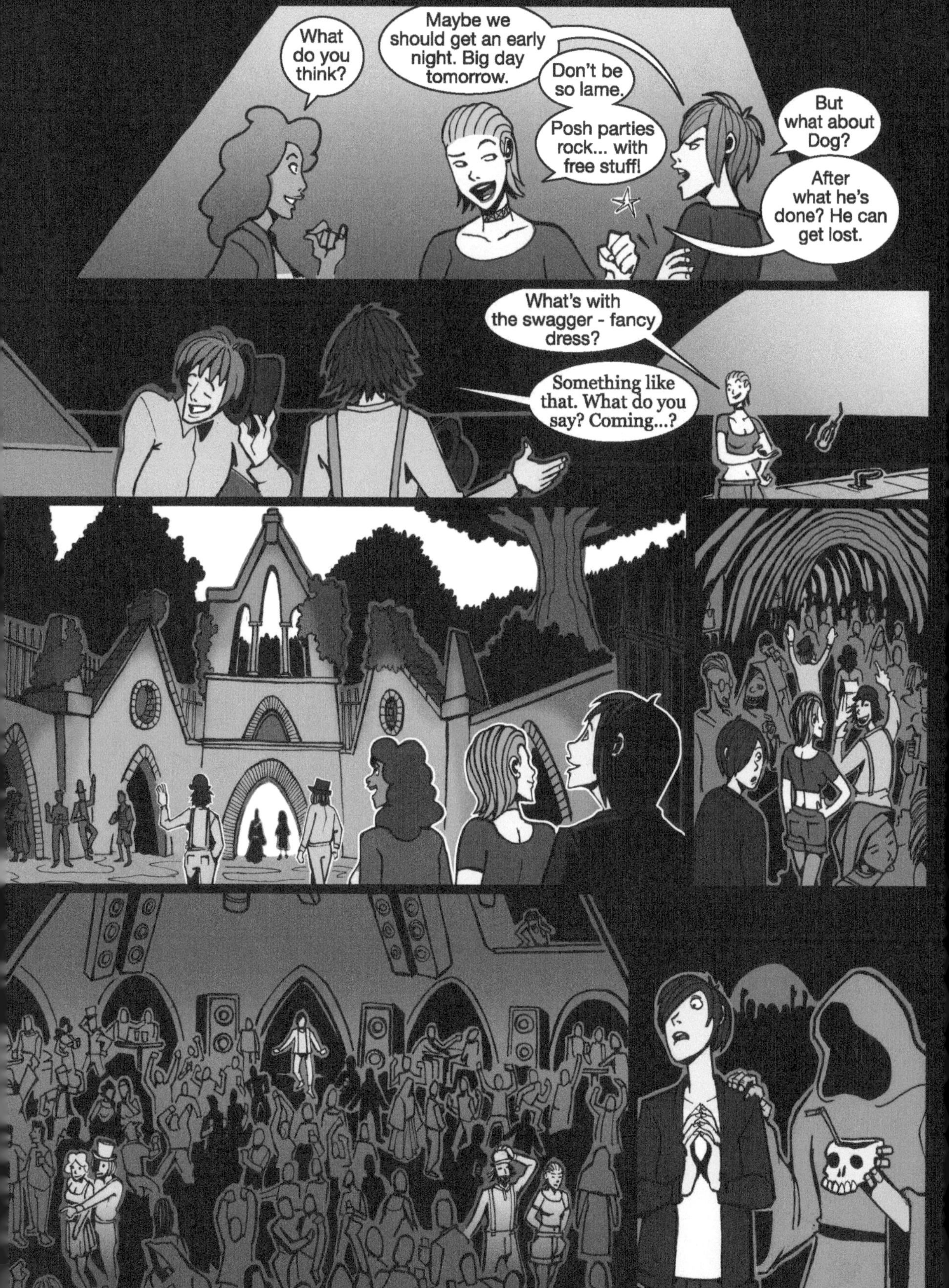

What do you think?
Maybe we should get an early night. Big day tomorrow.
Don't be so lame.
Posh parties rock... with free stuff!
But what about Dog?
After what he's done? He can get lost.
What's with the swagger - fancy dress?
Something like that. What do you say? Coming...?

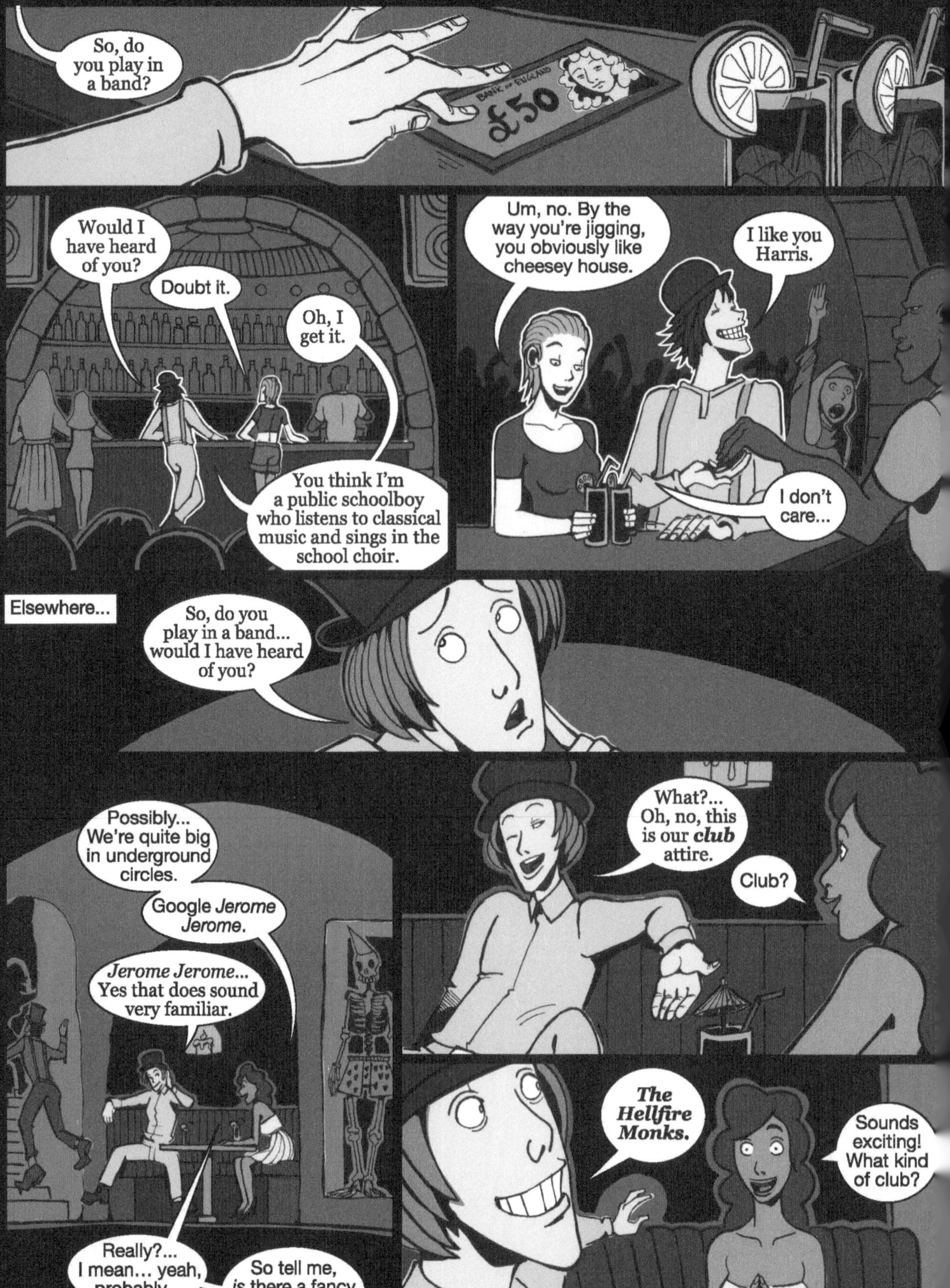
So, do you play in a band?
Would I have heard of you?
Doubt it.
Oh, I get it.
You think I'm a public schoolboy who listens to classical music and sings in the school choir.
Um, no. By the way you're jigging, you obviously like cheesey house.
I like you Harris.
I don't care...
Elsewhere...
So, do you play in a band... would I have heard of you?
Possibly... We're quite big in underground circles.
Google *Jerome Jerome*.
Jerome Jerome... Yes that does sound very familiar.
Really?... I mean... yeah, probably...
So tell me, *is* there a fancy dress theme tonight?
What?... Oh, no, this is our ***club*** attire.
Club?
The Hellfire Monks.
Sounds exciting! What kind of club?

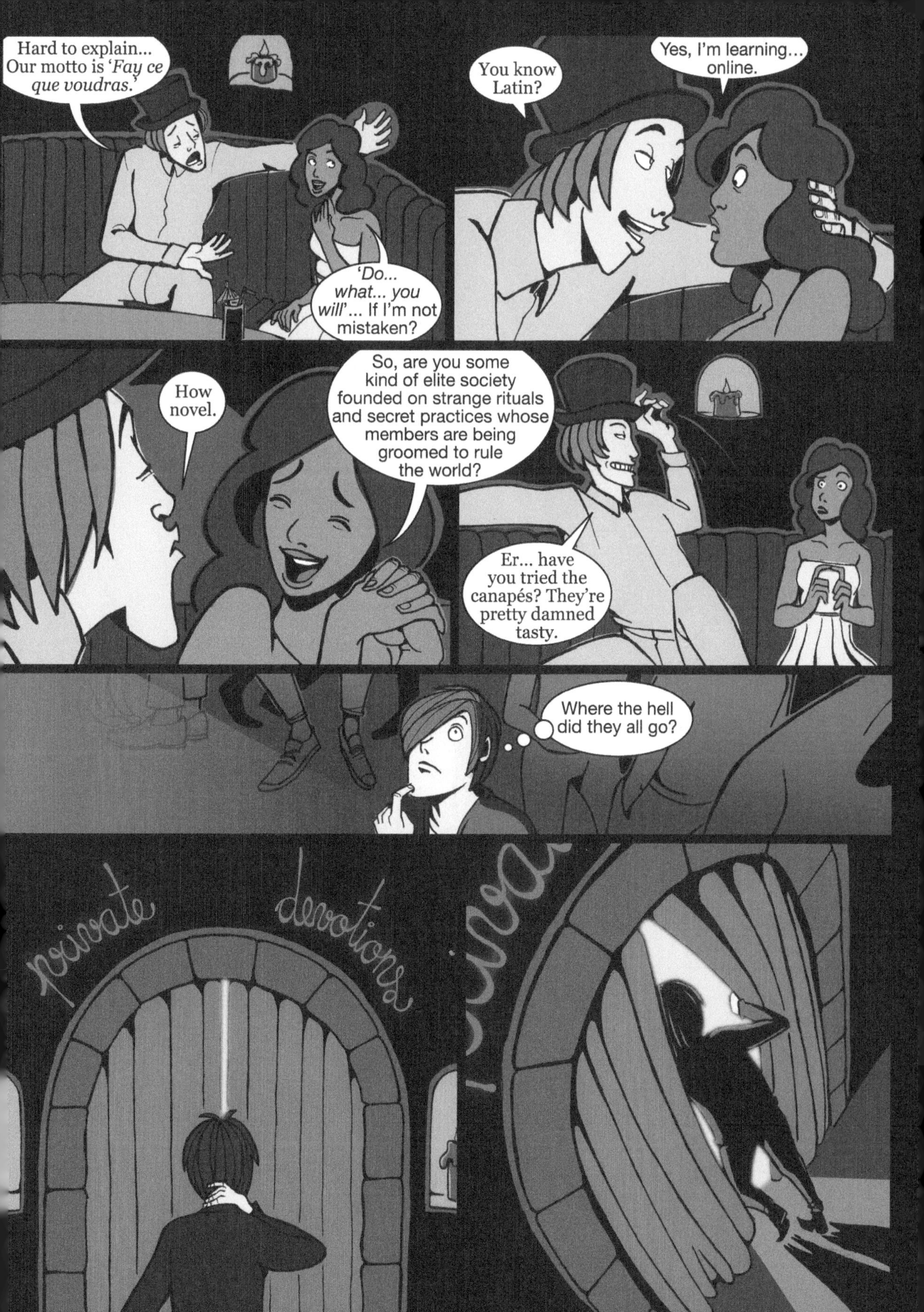
Hard to explain... Our motto is '*Fay ce que voudras*.'
'*Do... what... you will*'... If I'm not mistaken?
You know Latin?
Yes, I'm learning... online.
How novel.
So, are you some kind of elite society founded on strange rituals and secret practices whose members are being groomed to rule the world?
Er... have you tried the canapés? They're pretty damned tasty.
Where the hell did they all go?
private devotions

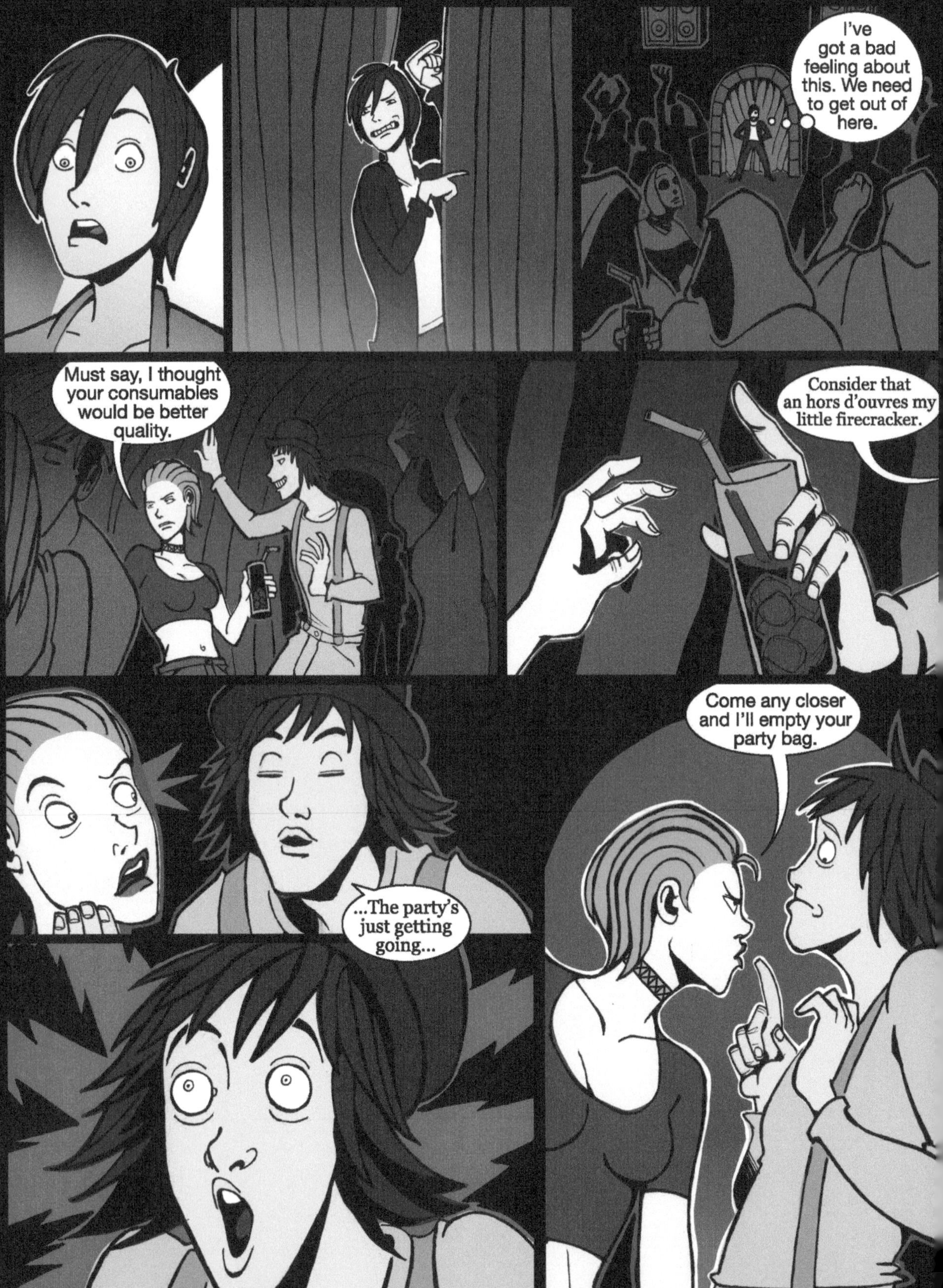
I've got a bad feeling about this. We need to get out of here.
Must say, I thought your consumables would be better quality.
Consider that an hors d'ouvres my little firecracker.
...The party's just getting going...
Come any closer and I'll empty your party bag.

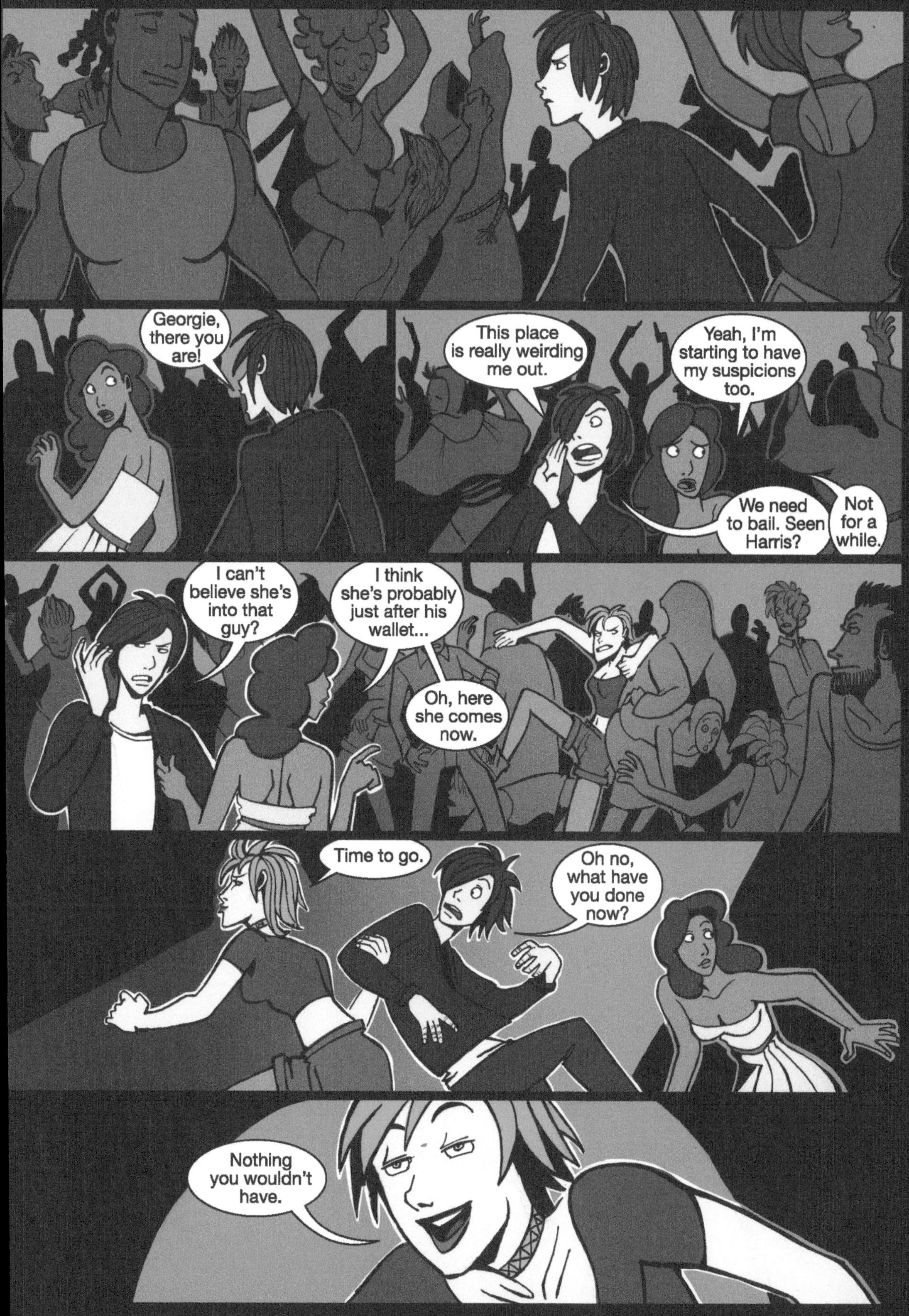
Georgie, there you are!
This place is really weirding me out.
Yeah, I'm starting to have my suspicions too.
We need to bail. Seen Harris?
Not for a while.
I can't believe she's into that guy?
I think she's probably just after his wallet...
Oh, here she comes now.
Time to go.
Oh no, what have you done now?
Nothing you wouldn't have.

Day 3

Lost dog Returns

Er... BAGPIPES?

s-NOBS revenge

anger Management issues

I predict a RioT

Why all the fuss?

RESULT !!!

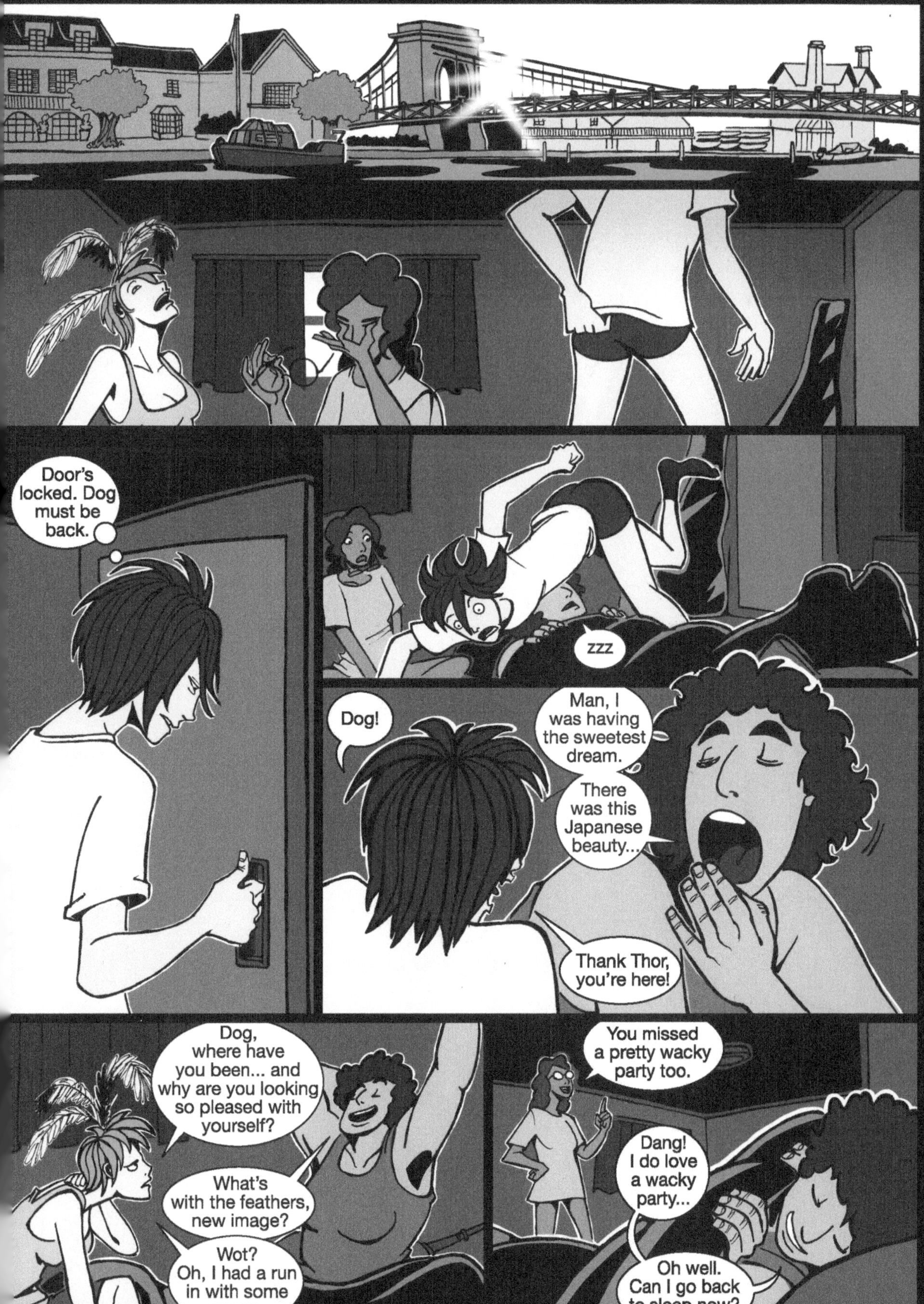
Door's locked. Dog must be back.
zzz
Dog!
Man, I was having the sweetest dream.
There was this Japanese beauty...
Thank Thor, you're here!
Dog, where have you been... and why are you looking so pleased with yourself?
What's with the feathers, new image?
Wot? Oh, I had a run in with some swans.
You missed a pretty wacky party too.
Dang! I do love a wacky party...
Oh well. Can I go back to sleep now?

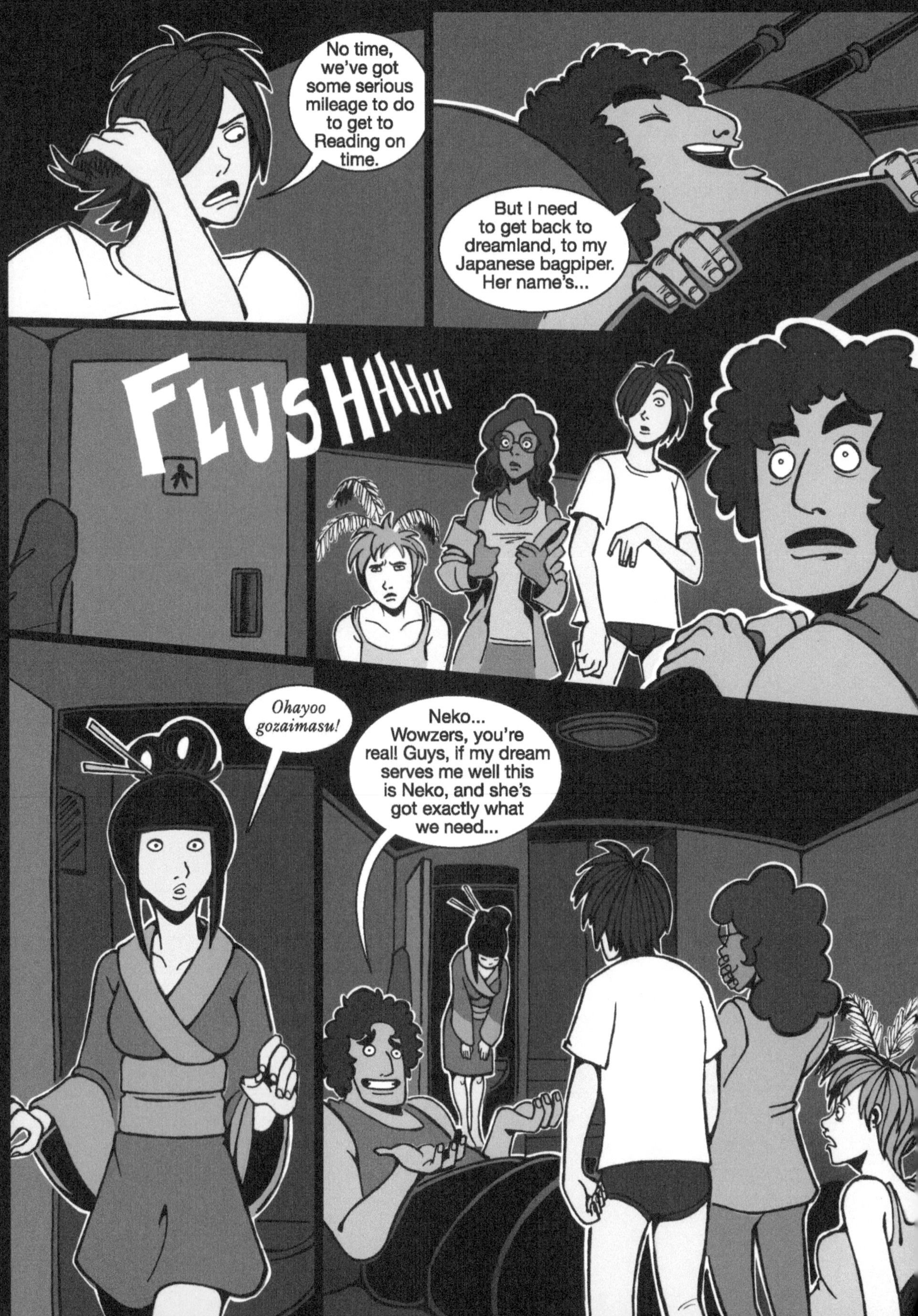
No time, we've got some serious mileage to do to get to Reading on time.
But I need to get back to dreamland, to my Japanese bagpiper. Her name's...
FLUSHHHHH
Ohayoo gozaimasu!
Neko... Wowzers, you're real! Guys, if my dream serves me well this is Neko, and she's got exactly what we need...

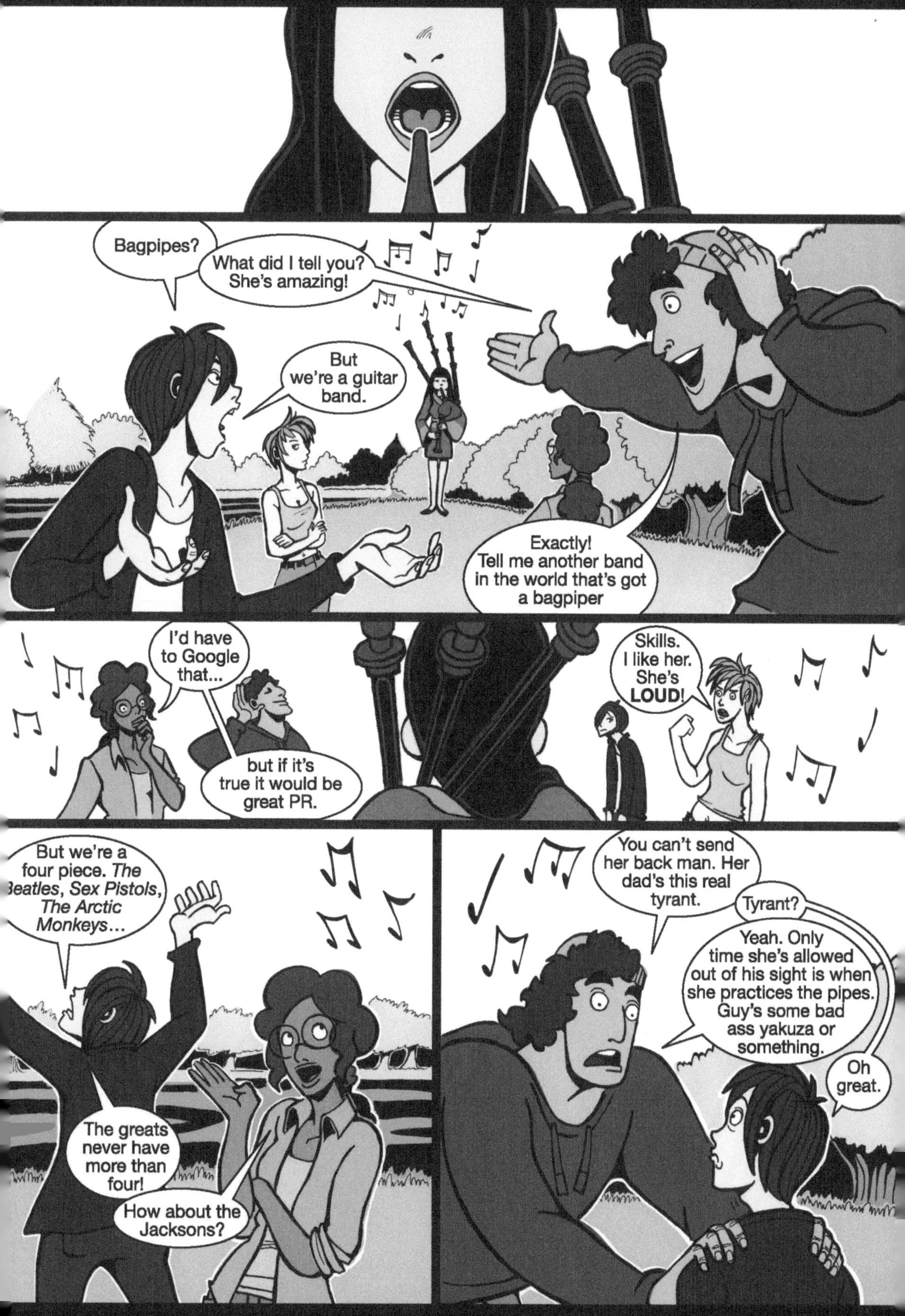
Bagpipes?
What did I tell you? She's amazing!
But we're a guitar band.
Exactly! Tell me another band in the world that's got a bagpiper
I'd have to Google that...
but if it's true it would be great PR.
Skills. I like her. She's **LOUD**!
But we're a four piece. *The Beatles*, *Sex Pistols*, *The Arctic Monkeys*...
The greats never have more than four!
How about the Jacksons?
You can't send her back man. Her dad's this real tyrant.
Tyrant?
Yeah. Only time she's allowed out of his sight is when she practices the pipes. Guy's some bad ass yakuza or something.
Oh great.

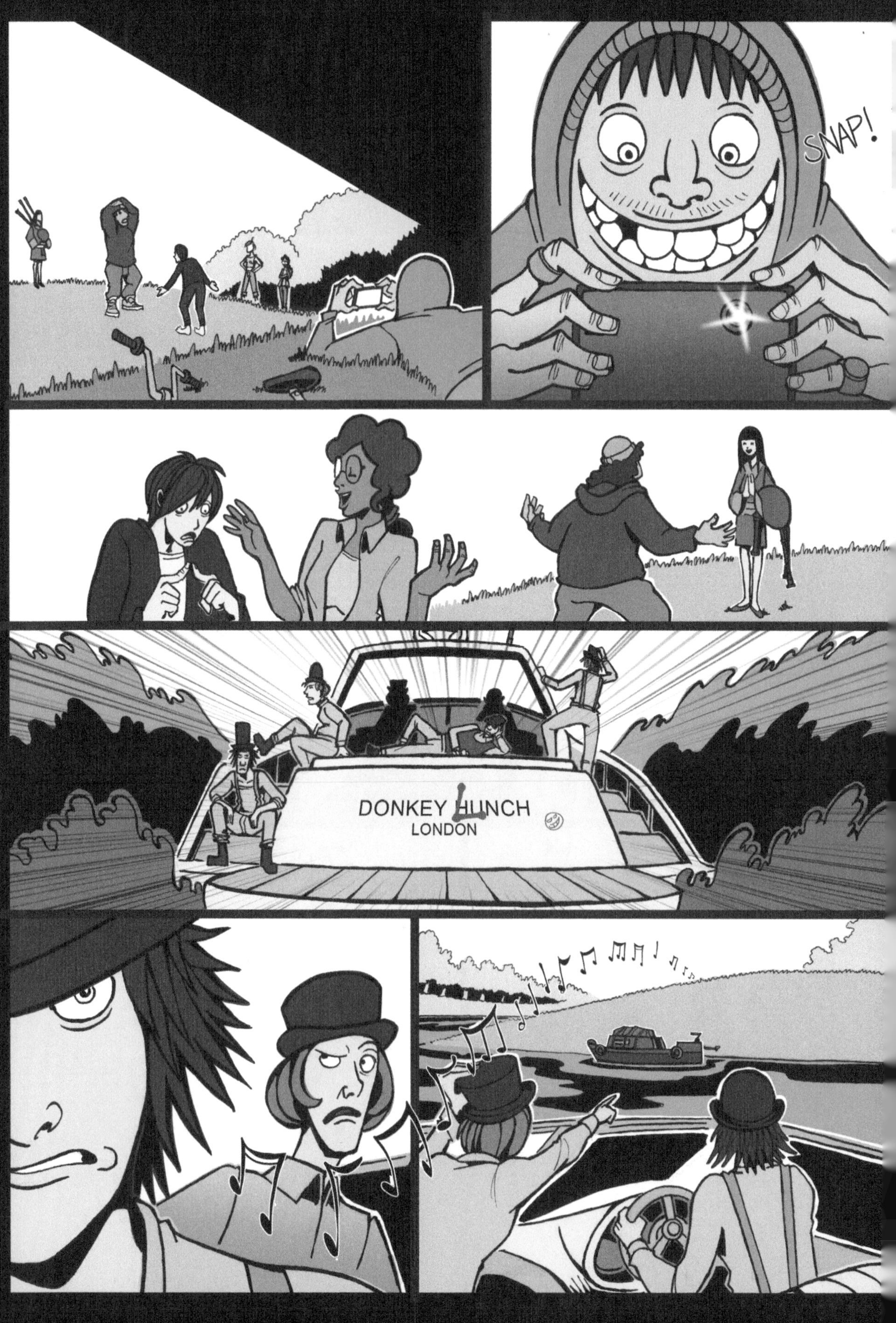
SNAP!
DONKEY HUNCH
LONDON

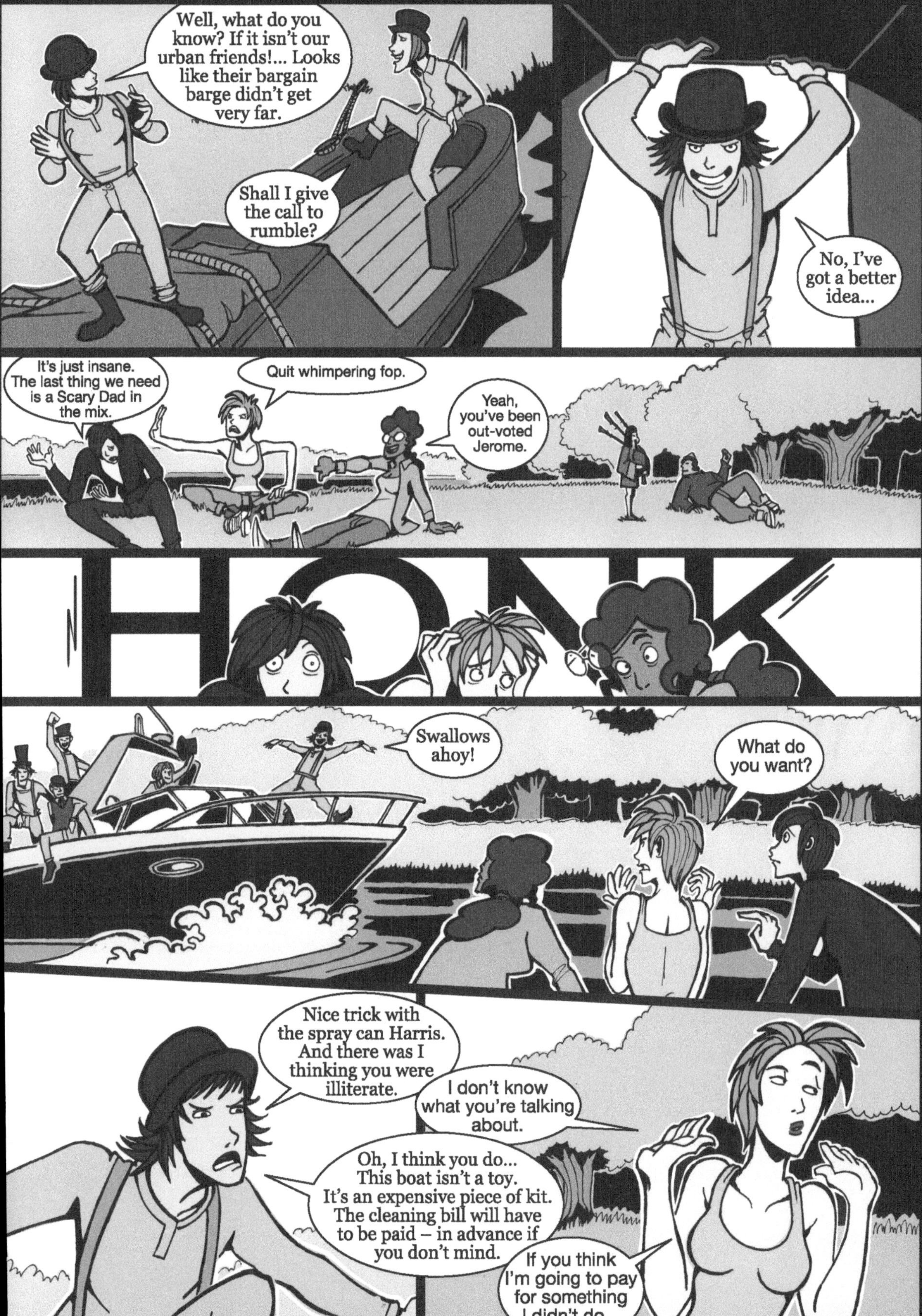

Well, what do you know? If it isn't our urban friends!... Looks like their bargain barge didn't get very far.
Shall I give the call to rumble?
No, I've got a better idea...
It's just insane. The last thing we need is a Scary Dad in the mix.
Quit whimpering fop.
Yeah, you've been out-voted Jerome.
HONK
Swallows ahoy!
What do you want?
Nice trick with the spray can Harris. And there was I thinking you were illiterate.
I don't know what you're talking about.
Oh, I think you do... This boat isn't a toy. It's an expensive piece of kit. The cleaning bill will have to be paid – in advance if you don't mind.
If you think I'm going to pay for something I didn't do...

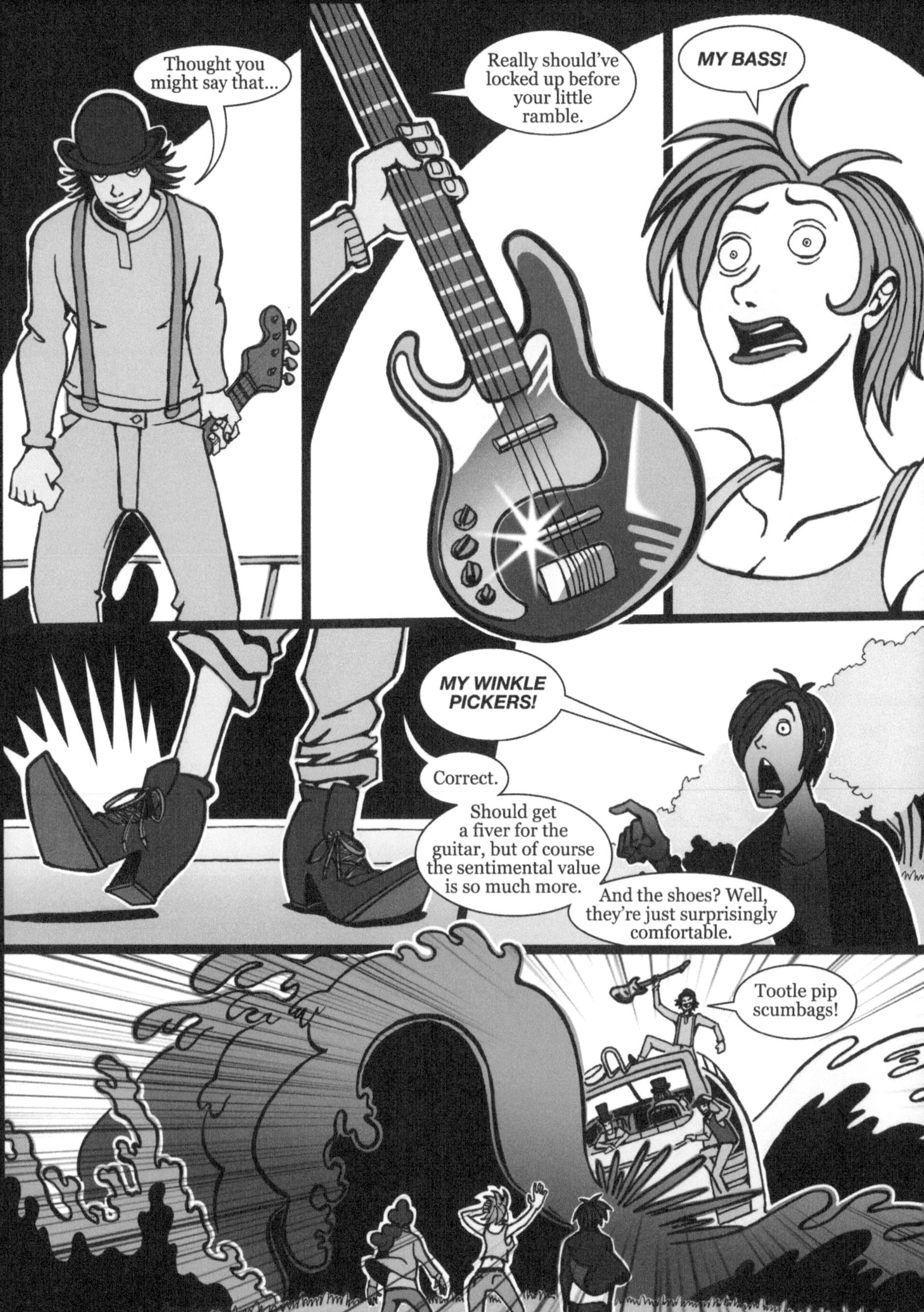

Thought you might say that...
Really should've locked up before your little ramble.
MY BASS!
MY WINKLE PICKERS!
Correct.
Should get a fiver for the guitar, but of course the sentimental value is so much more.
And the shoes? Well, they're just surprisingly comfortable.
Tootle pip scumbags!

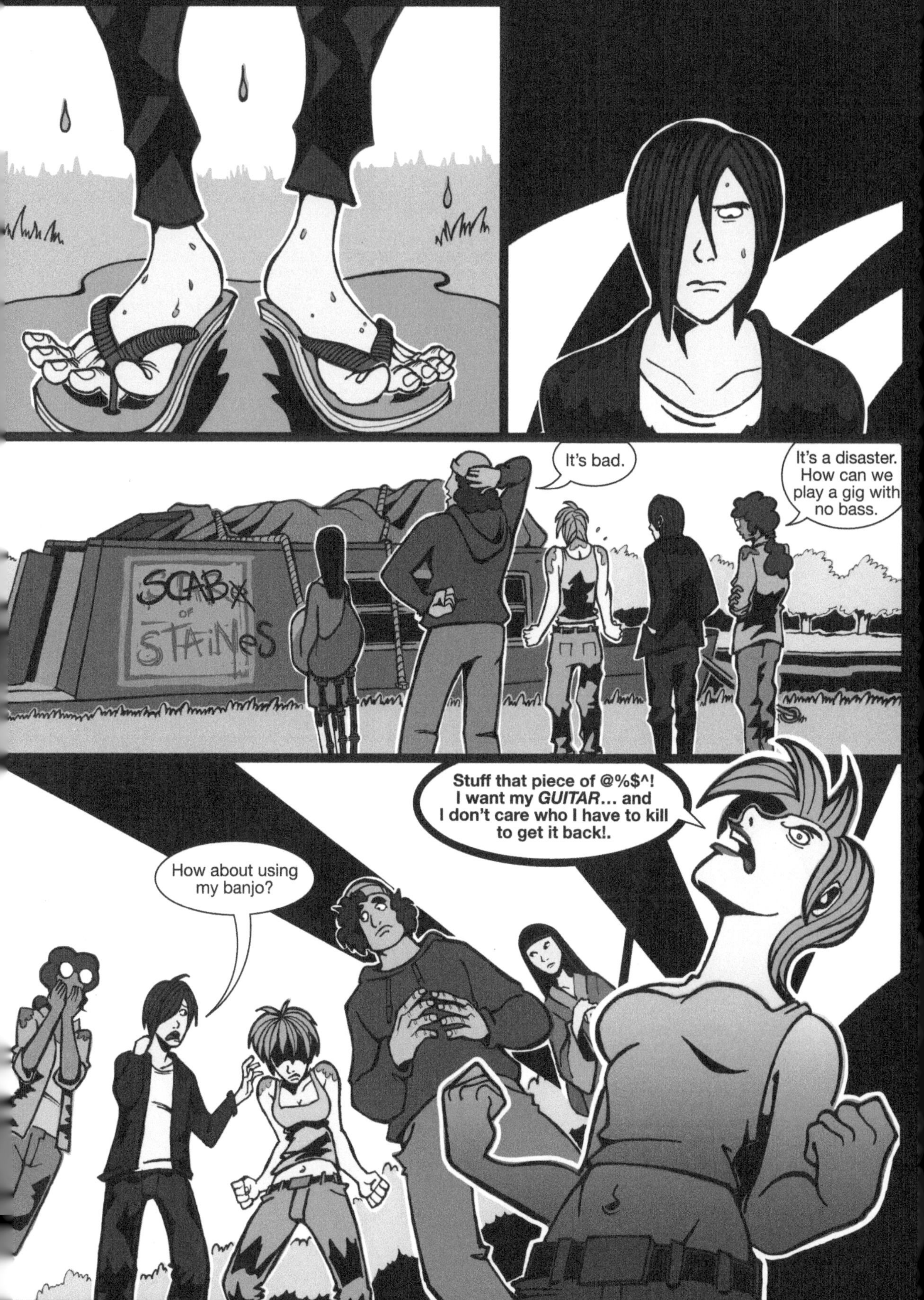
It's bad.
It's a disaster. How can we play a gig with no bass.
SCAB of STAINeS
Stuff that piece of @%$^! I want my *GUITAR*… and I don't care who I have to kill to get it back!.
How about using my banjo?

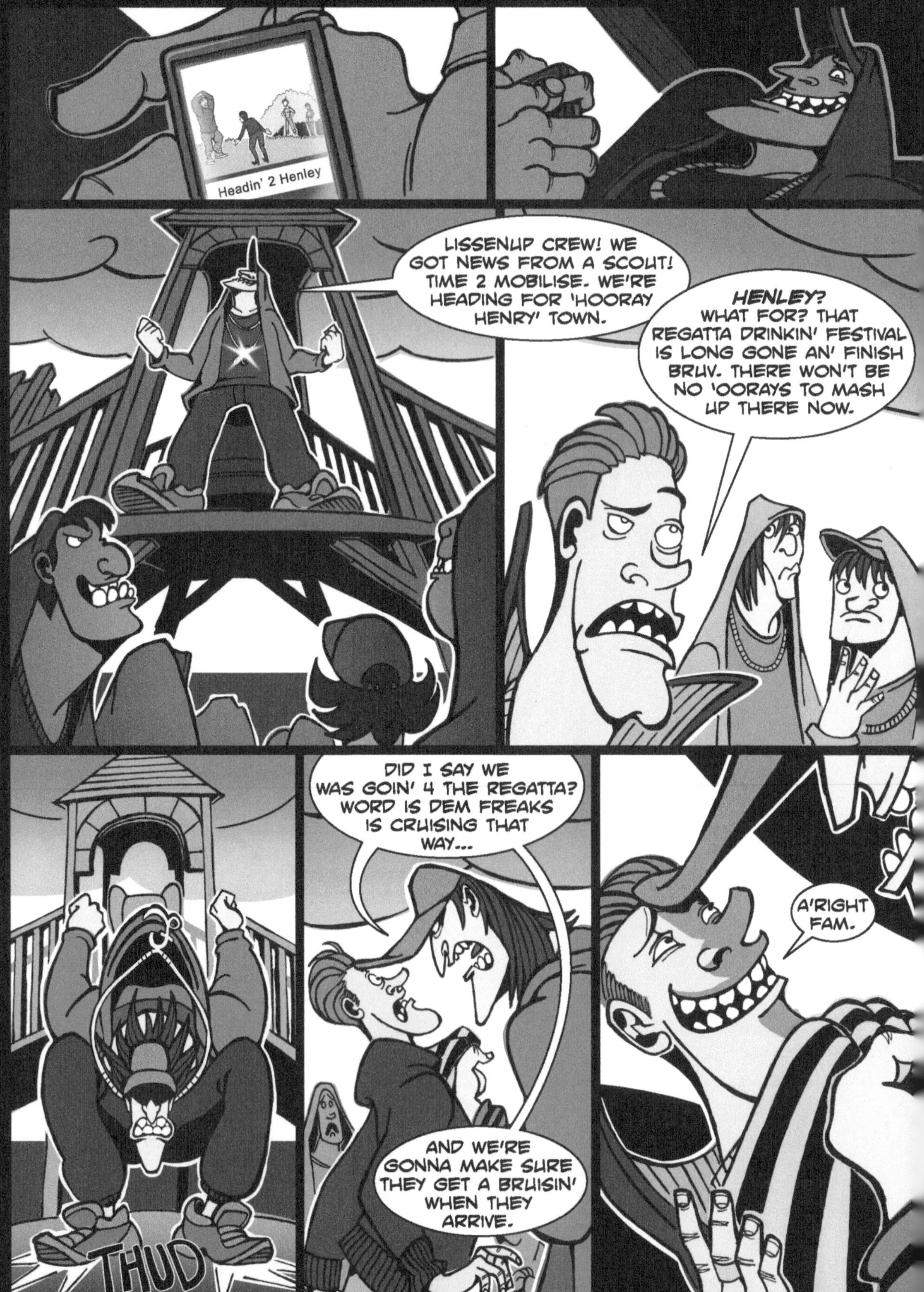
Headin' 2 Henley
LISSENUP CREW! WE GOT NEWS FROM A SCOUT! TIME 2 MOBILISE. WE'RE HEADING FOR 'HOORAY HENRY' TOWN.
HENLEY? WHAT FOR? THAT REGATTA DRINKIN' FESTIVAL IS LONG GONE AN' FINISH BRUV. THERE WON'T BE NO 'OORAYS TO MASH UP THERE NOW.
THUD
DID I SAY WE WAS GOIN' 4 THE REGATTA? WORD IS DEM FREAKS IS CRUISING THAT WAY...
AND WE'RE GONNA MAKE SURE THEY GET A BRUISIN' WHEN THEY ARRIVE.
A'RIGHT FAM.

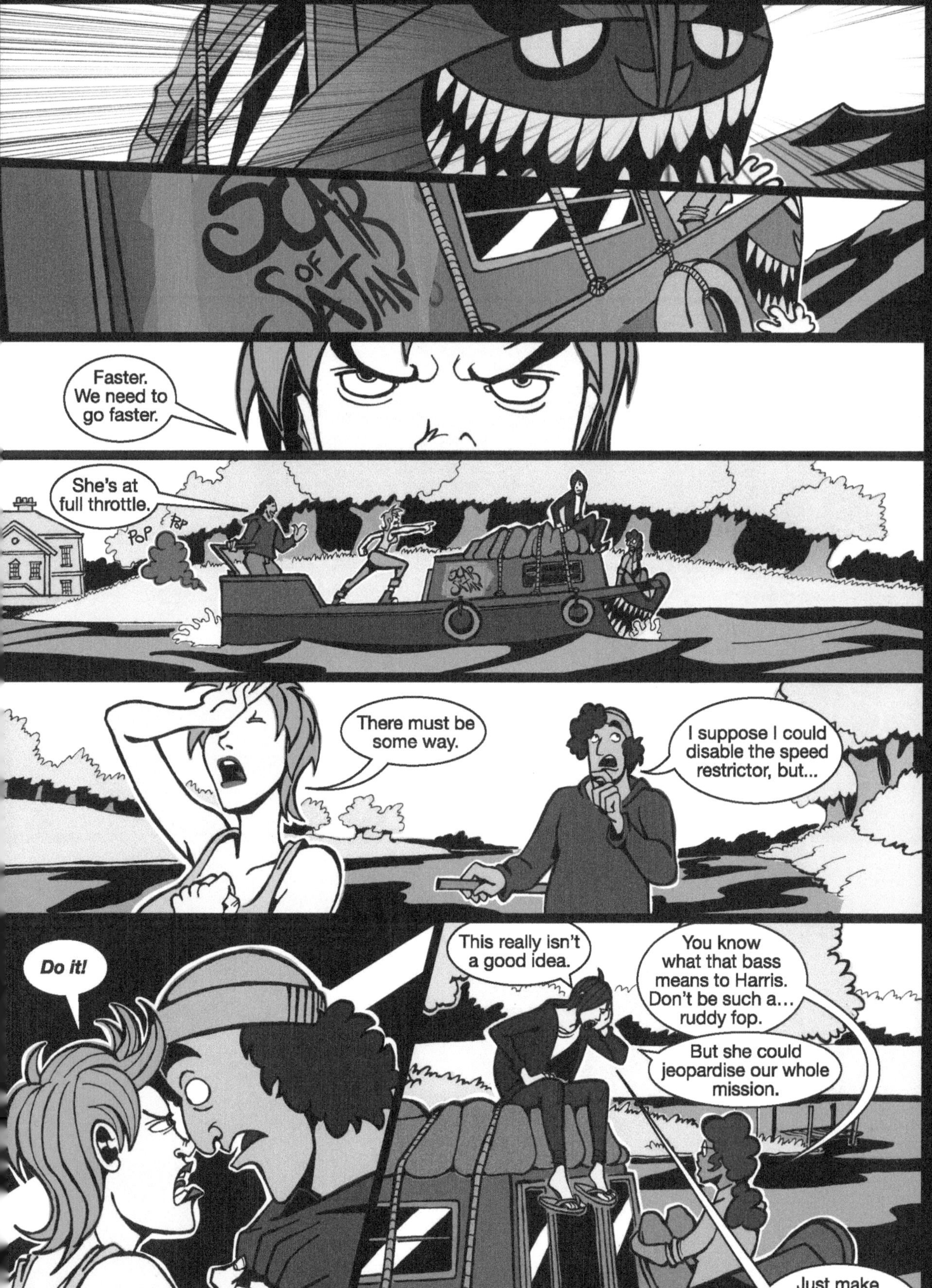
SOAP OF SATAN
Faster. We need to go faster.
She's at full throttle.
POP POP
There must be some way.
I suppose I could disable the speed restrictor, but...
Do it!
This really isn't a good idea.
You know what that bass means to Harris. Don't be such a... ruddy fop.
But she could jeopardise our whole mission.
Just make sure you hide that chainsaw...

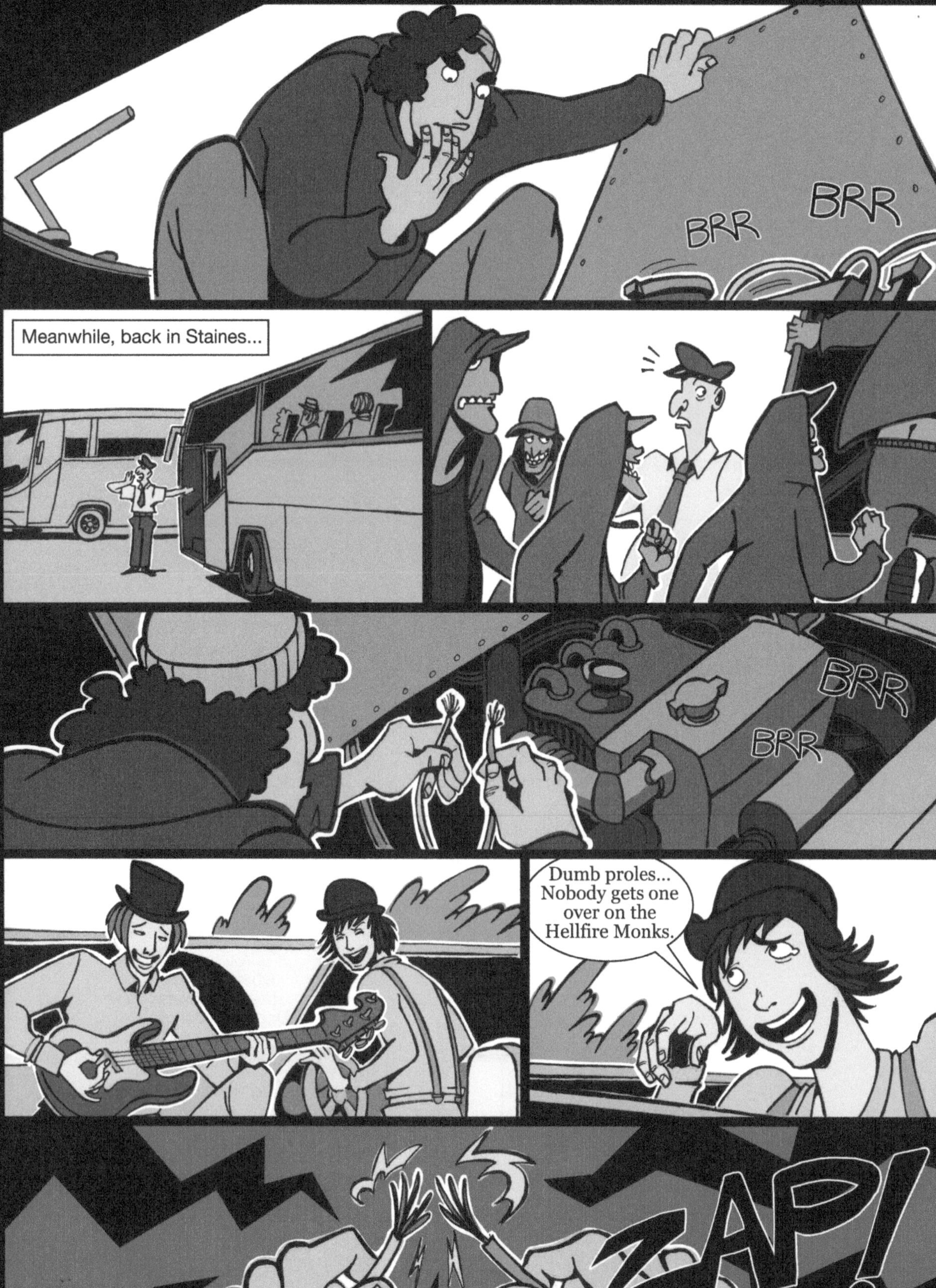
BRR
BRR
Meanwhile, back in Staines...
BRR
BRR
Dumb proles... Nobody gets one over on the Hellfire Monks.
ZAP!

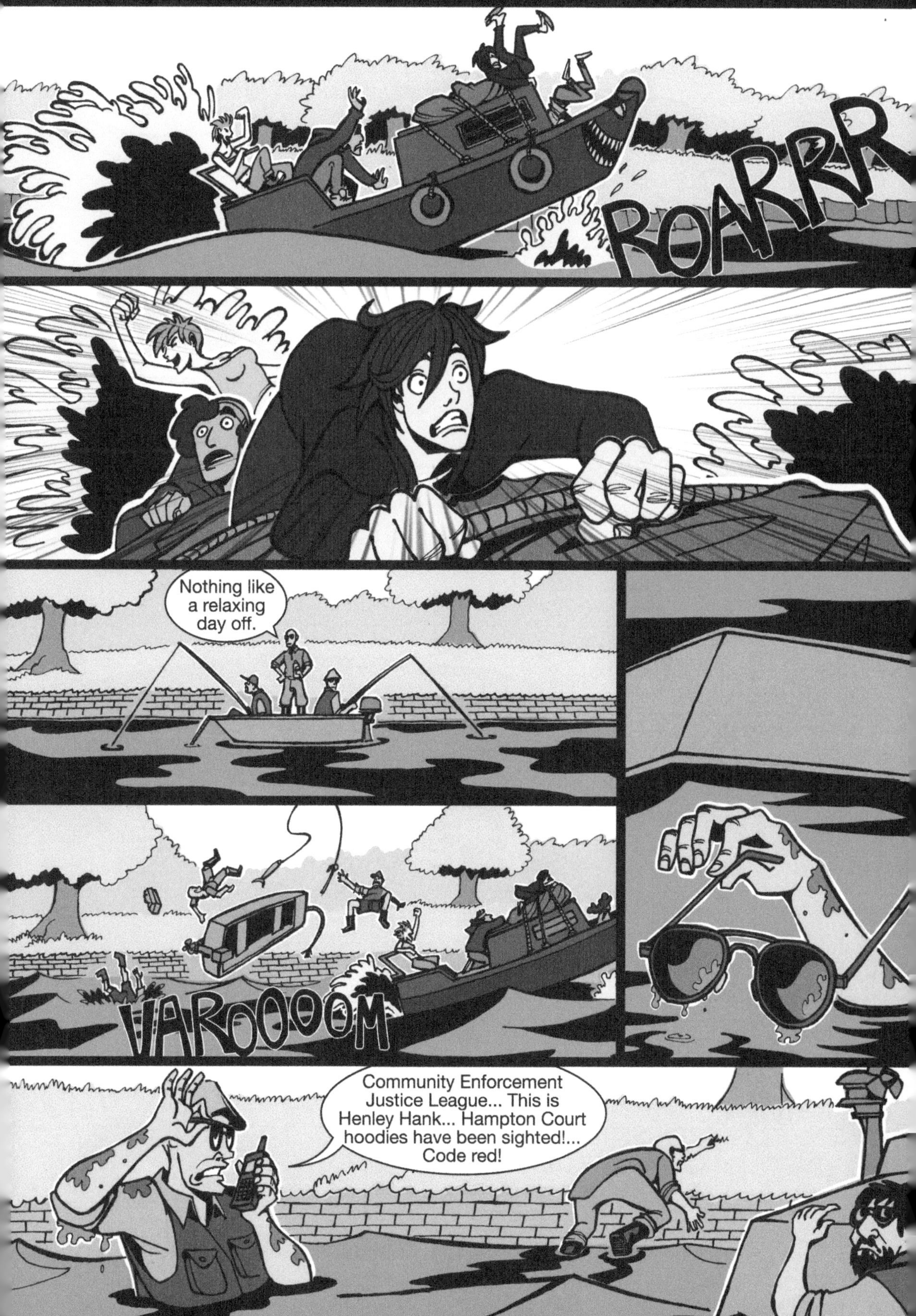
ROARRR
Nothing like a relaxing day off.
VAROOOOM
Community Enforcement Justice League... This is Henley Hank... Hampton Court hoodies have been sighted!... Code red!

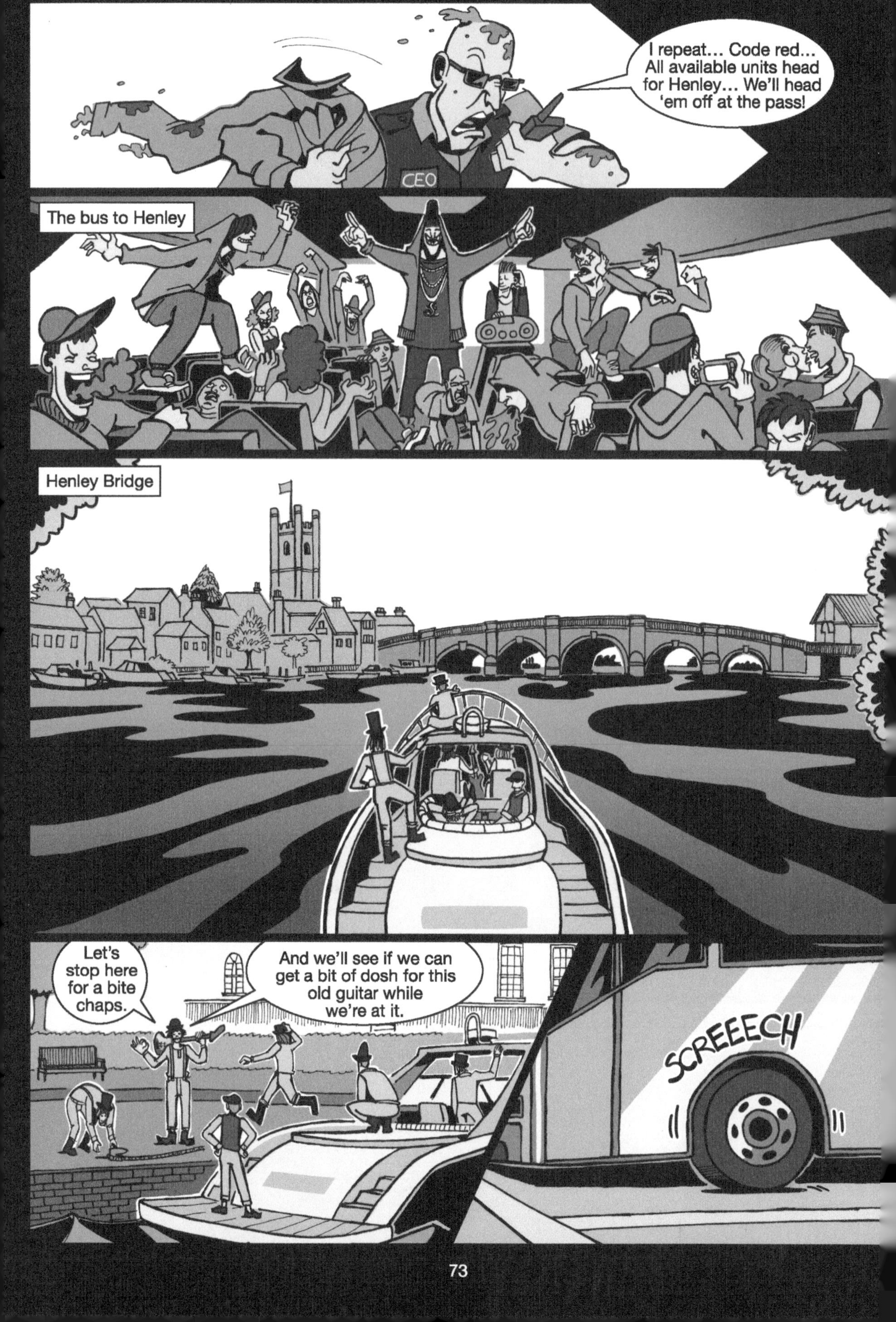
I repeat... Code red... All available units head for Henley... We'll head 'em off at the pass!
CEO
The bus to Henley
Henley Bridge
Let's stop here for a bite chaps.
And we'll see if we can get a bit of dosh for this old guitar while we're at it.
SCREEECH

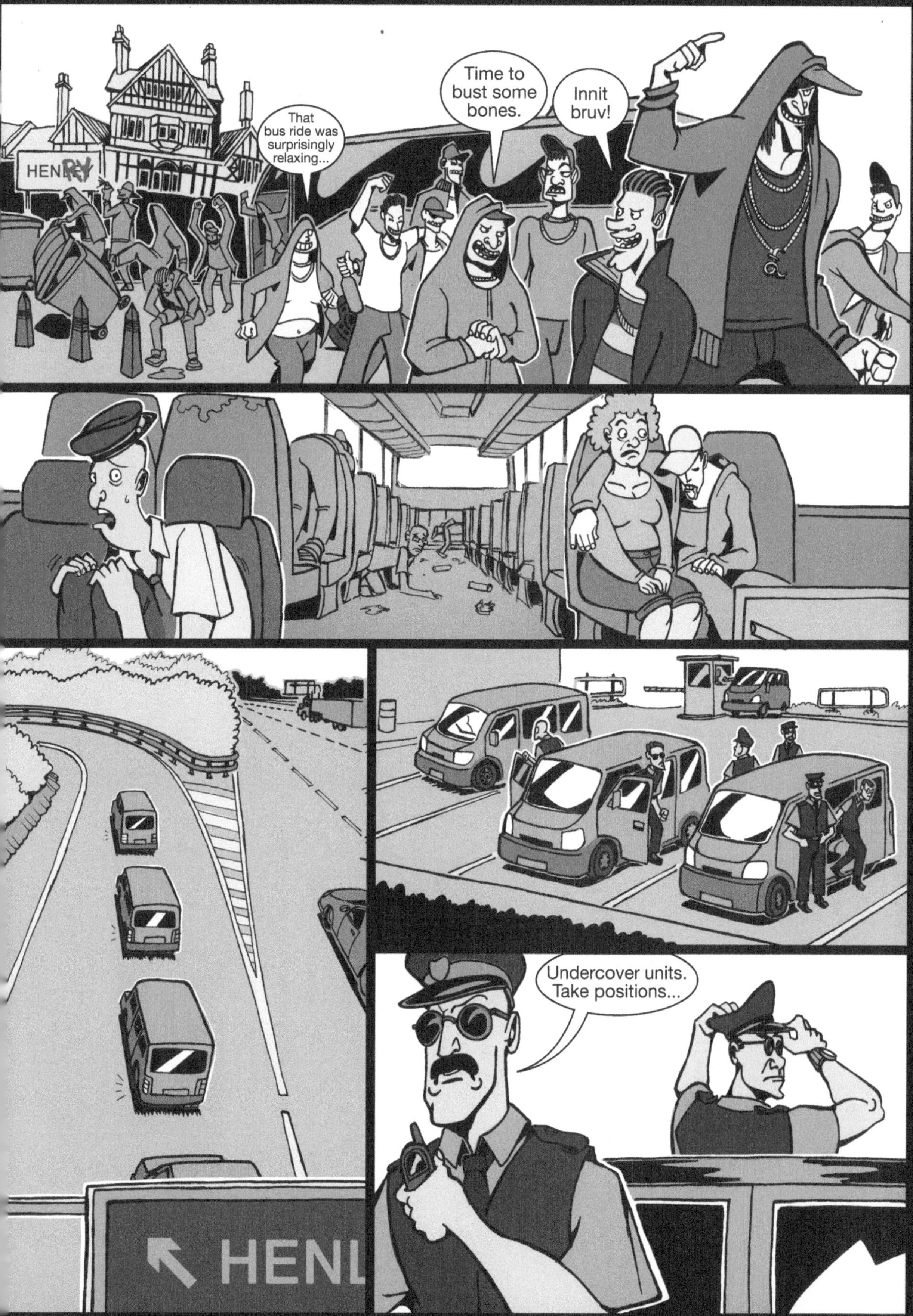
HENRY
That bus ride was surprisingly relaxing...
Time to bust some bones.
Innit bruv!
Undercover units. Take positions...
HENL

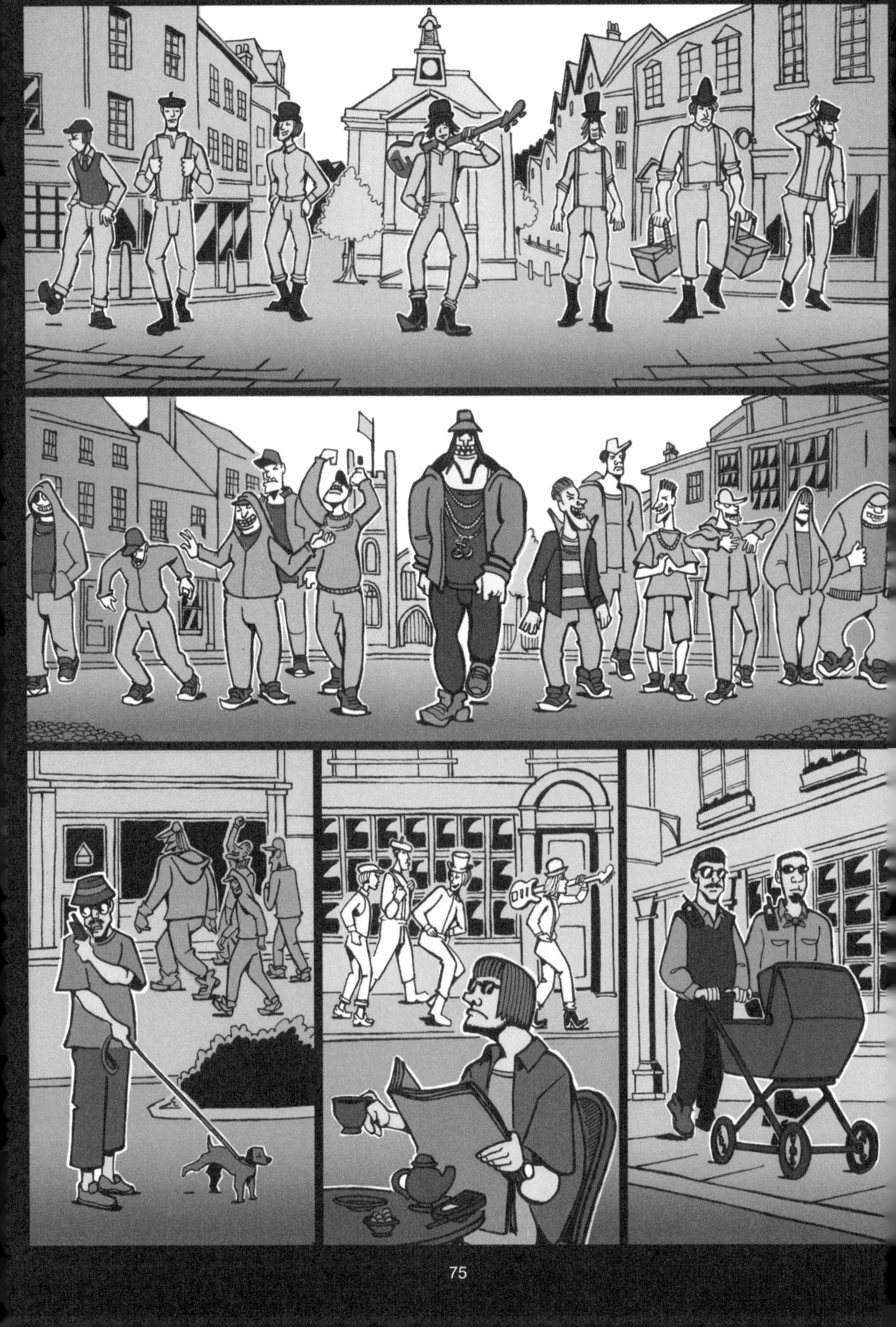

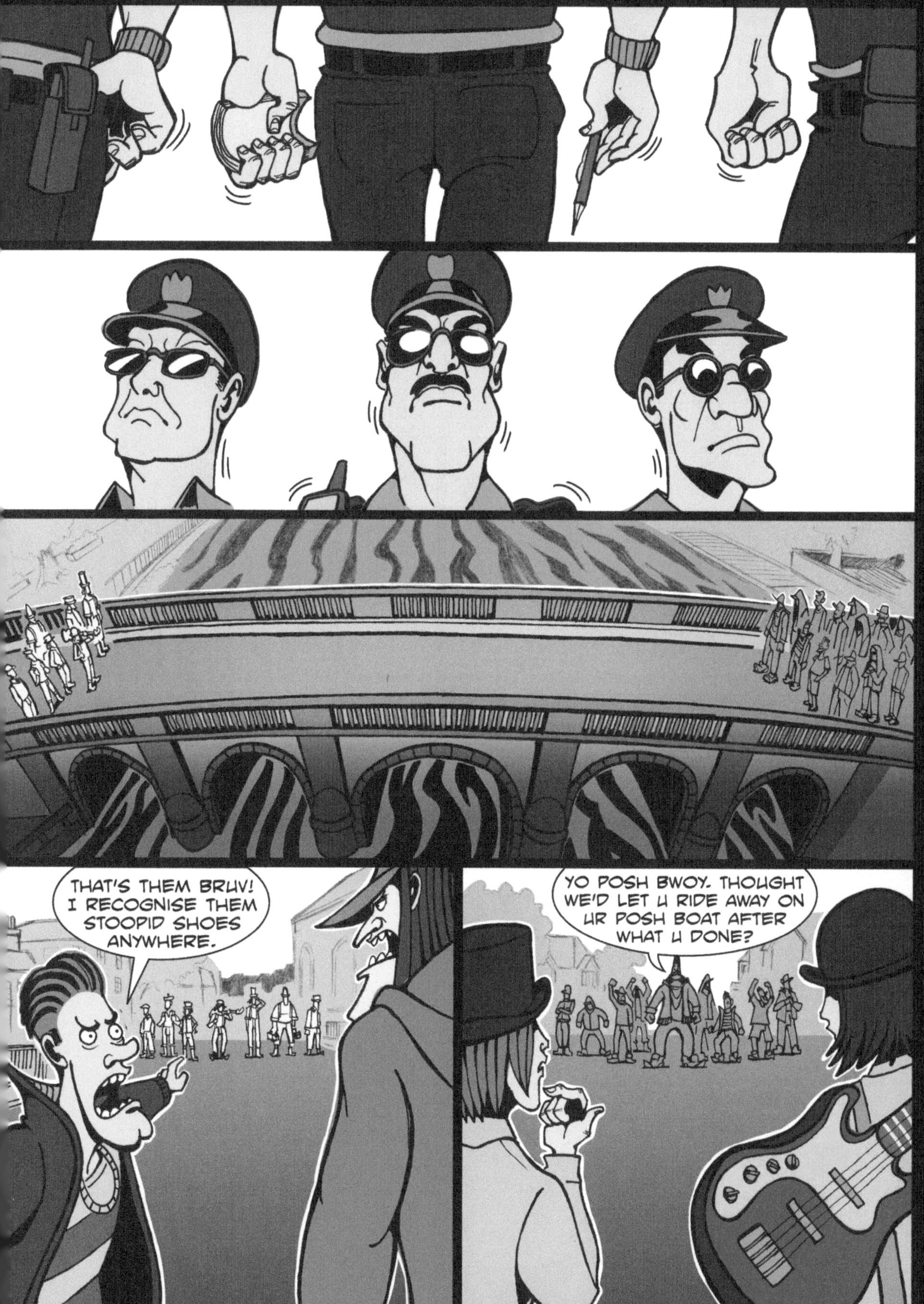
THAT'S THEM BRUV! I RECOGNISE THEM STOOPID SHOES ANYWHERE.
YO POSH BWOY. THOUGHT WE'D LET U RIDE AWAY ON UR POSH BOAT AFTER WHAT U DONE?

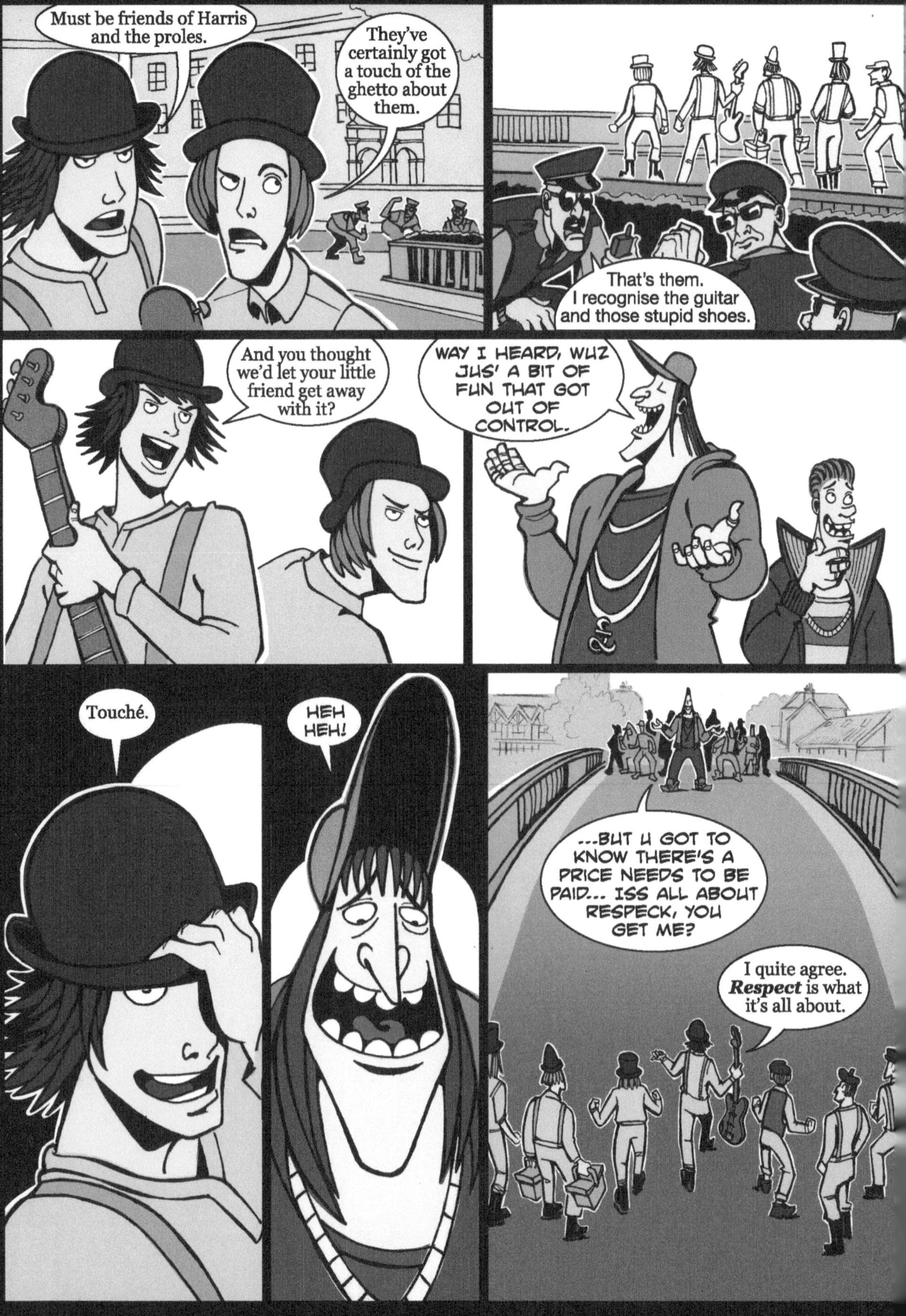
Must be friends of Harris and the proles.
They've certainly got a touch of the ghetto about them.
That's them. I recognise the guitar and those stupid shoes.
And you thought we'd let your little friend get away with it?
WAY I HEARD, WUZ JUS' A BIT OF FUN THAT GOT OUT OF CONTROL.
Touché.
HEH HEH!
...BUT U GOT TO KNOW THERE'S A PRICE NEEDS TO BE PAID... ISS ALL ABOUT RESPECK, YOU GET ME?
I quite agree. ***Respect*** is what it's all about.

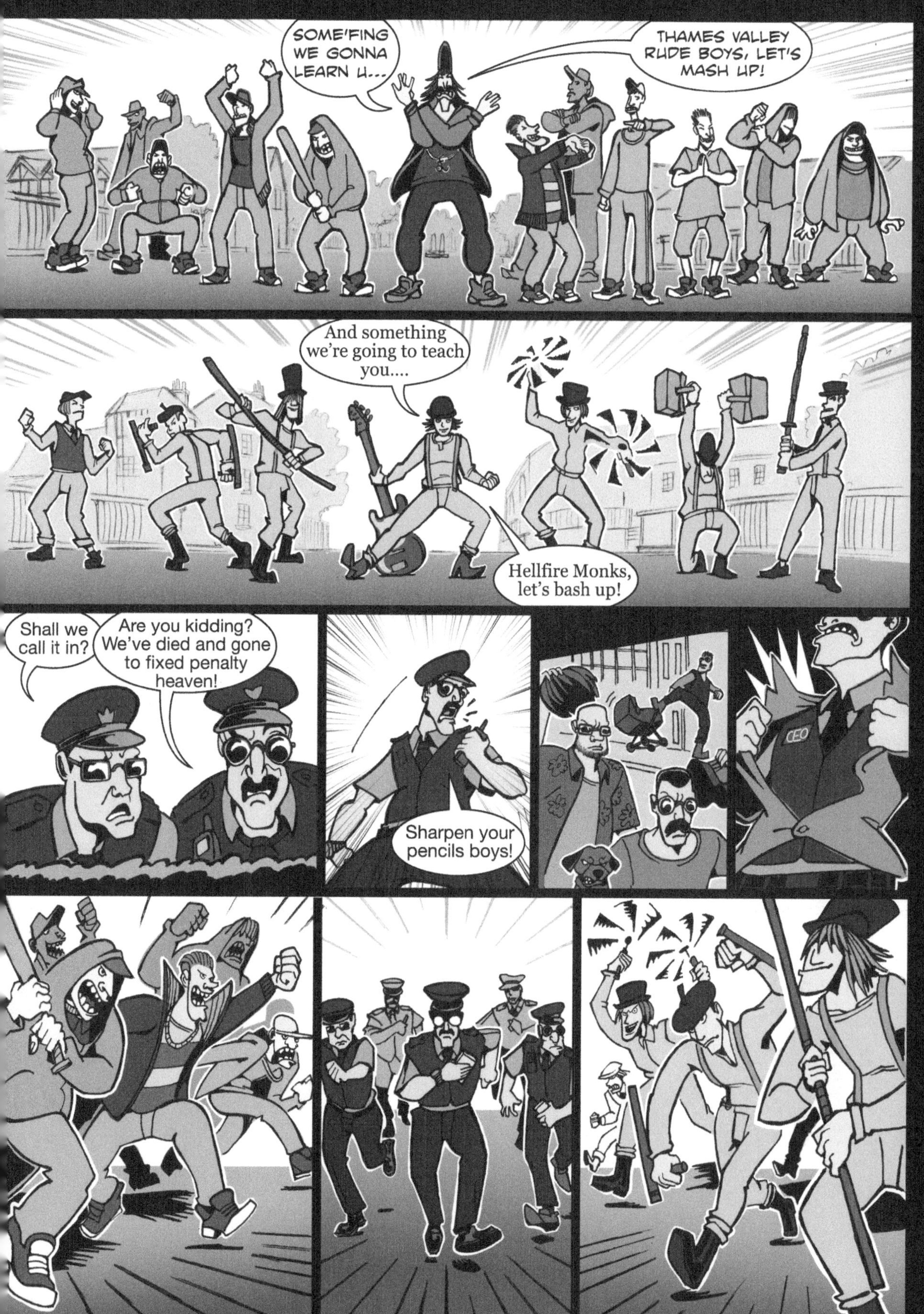
SOME'FING WE GONNA LEARN U...
THAMES VALLEY RUDE BOYS, LET'S MASH UP!
And something we're going to teach you....
Hellfire Monks, let's bash up!
Shall we call it in?
Are you kidding? We've died and gone to fixed penalty heaven!
Sharpen your pencils boys!
CEO

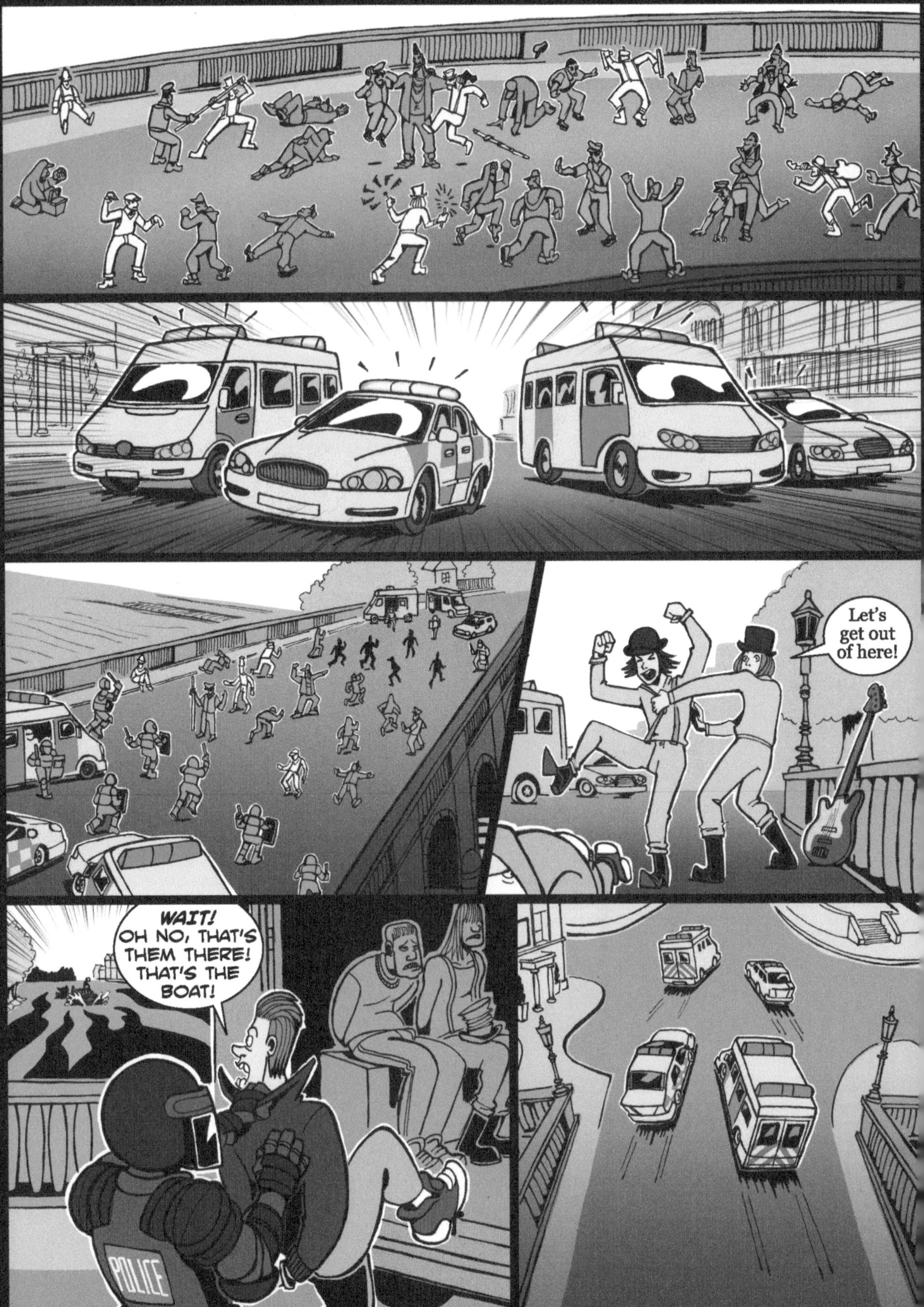
Let's get out of here!
WAIT! OH NO, THAT'S THEM THERE! THAT'S THE BOAT!
POLICE

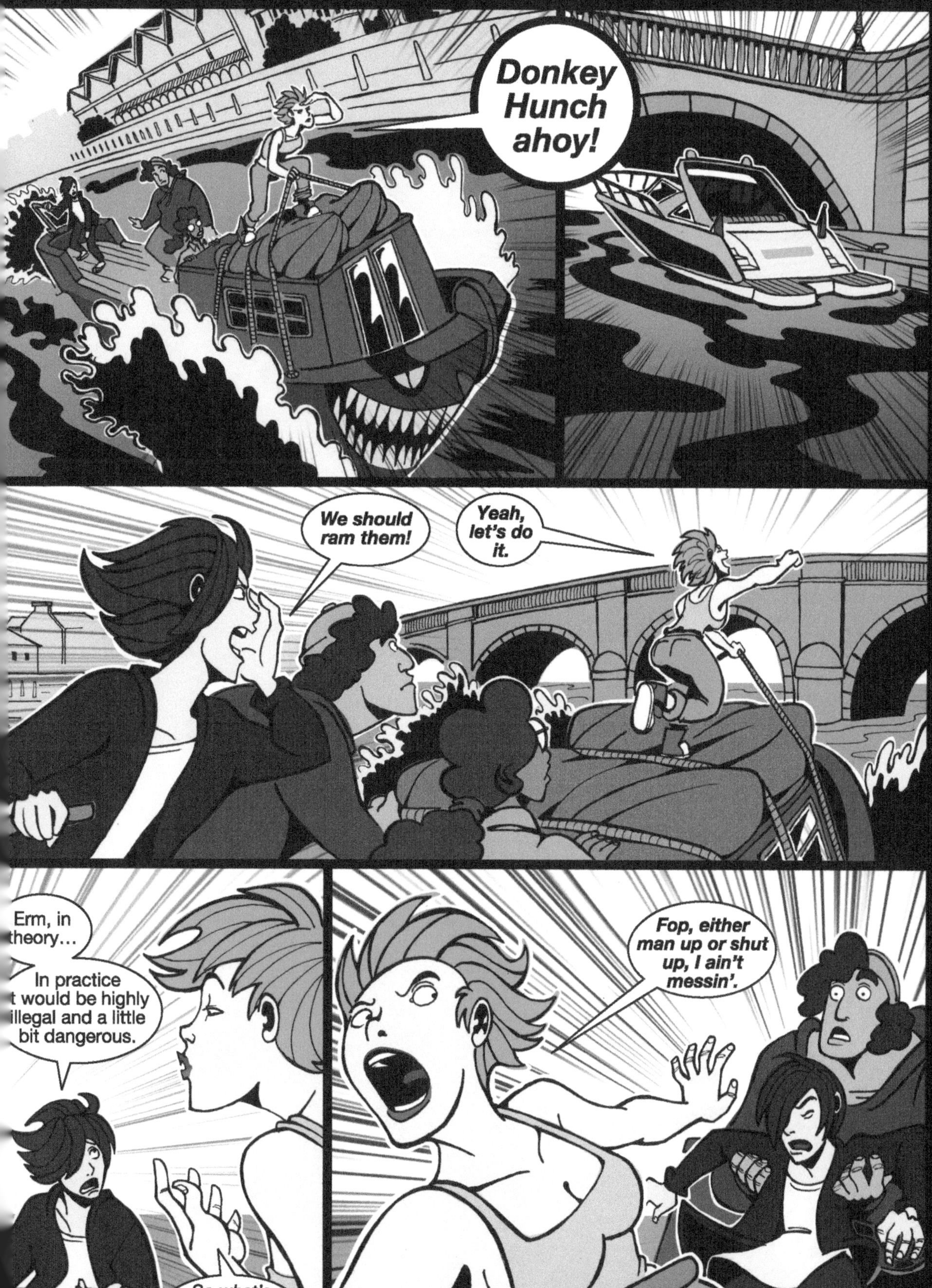
Donkey Hunch ahoy!
We should ram them!
Yeah, let's do it.
Erm, in theory…
In practice it would be highly illegal and a little bit dangerous.
So what's the point sayin' it?
Fop, either man up or shut up, I ain't messin'.

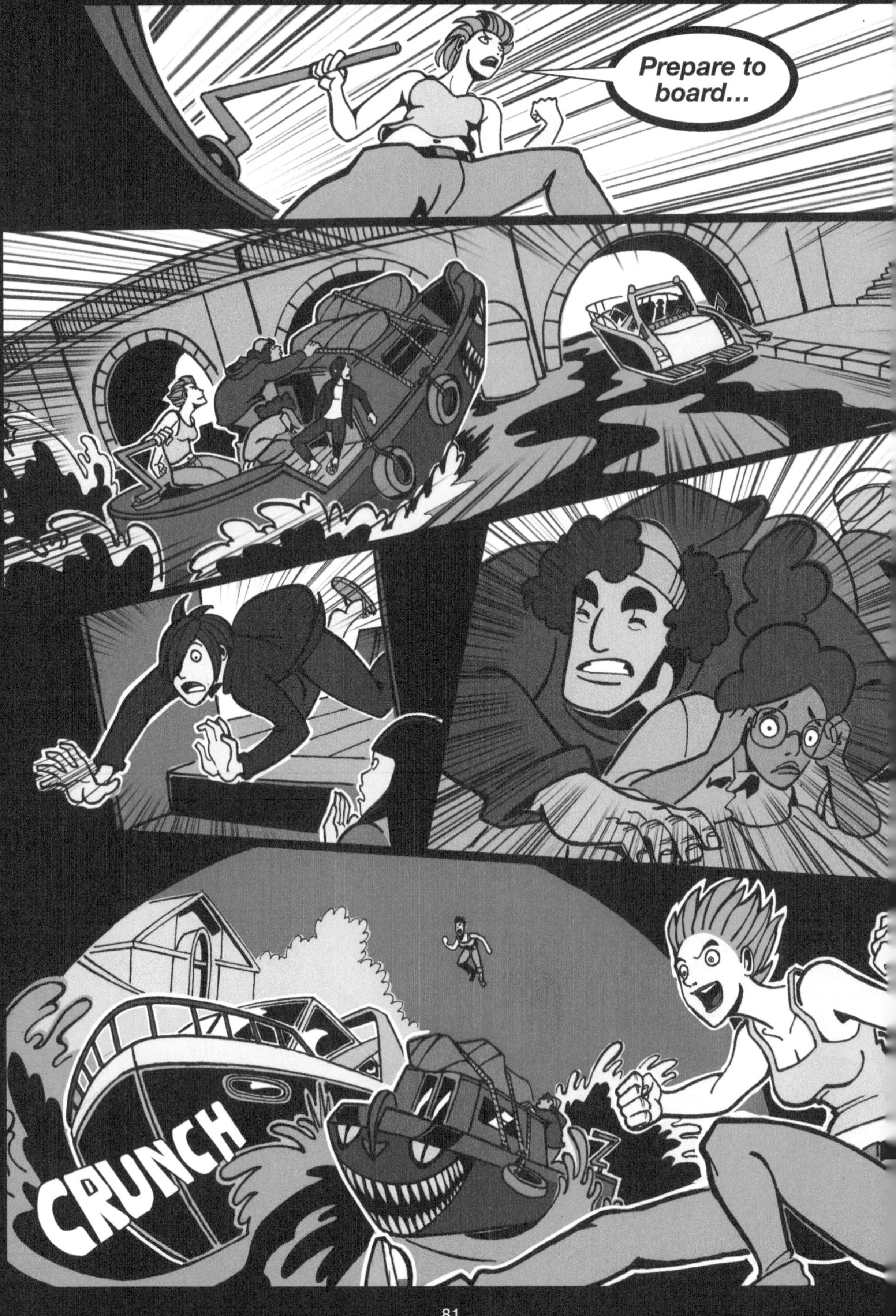
Prepare to board...
CRUNCH

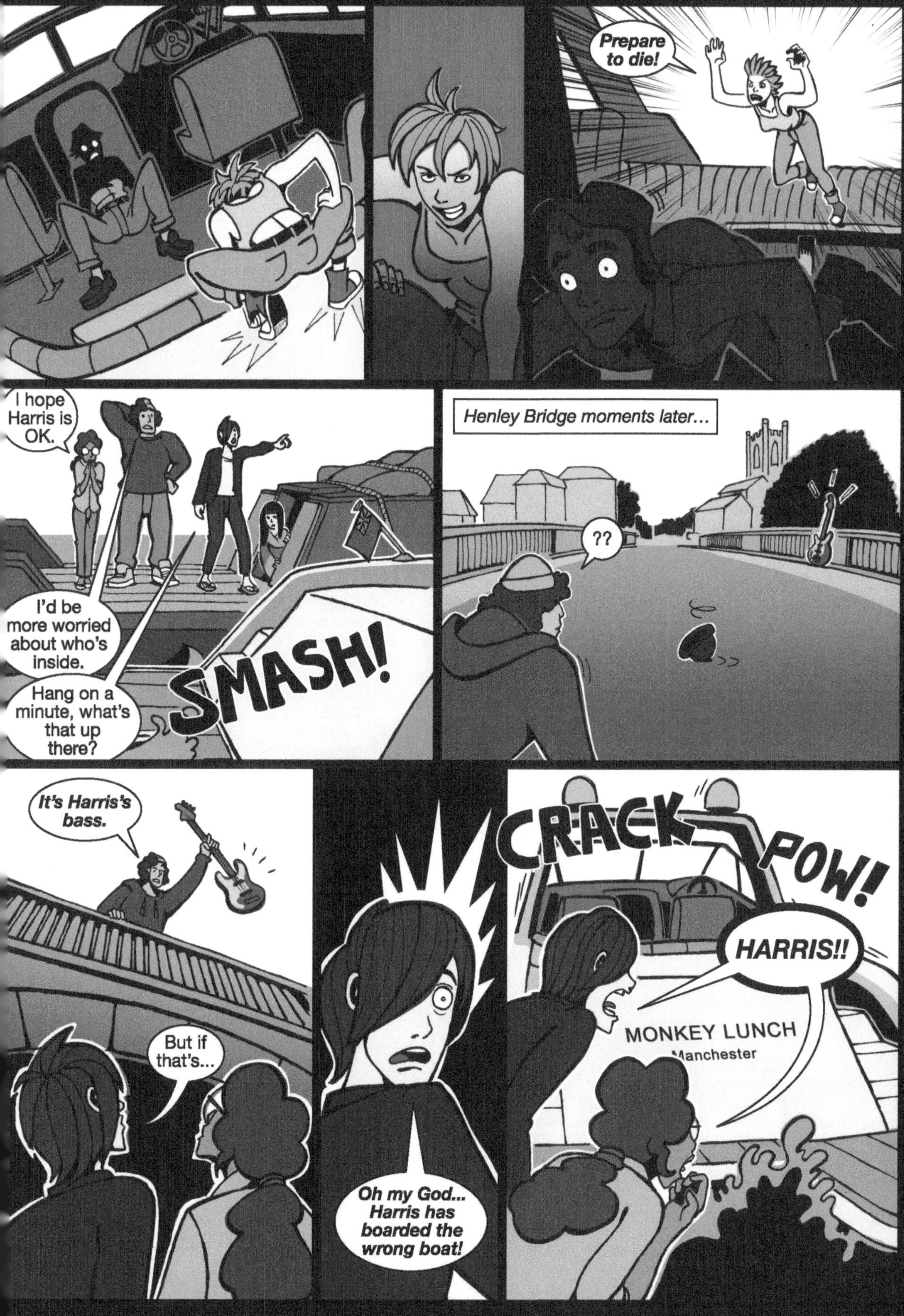
Prepare to die!
I hope Harris is OK.
I'd be more worried about who's inside.
Hang on a minute, what's that up there?
SMASH!
Henley Bridge moments later…
??
It's Harris's bass.
But if that's…
Oh my God... Harris has boarded the wrong boat!
CRACK
POW!
HARRIS!!
MONKEY LUNCH
Manchester

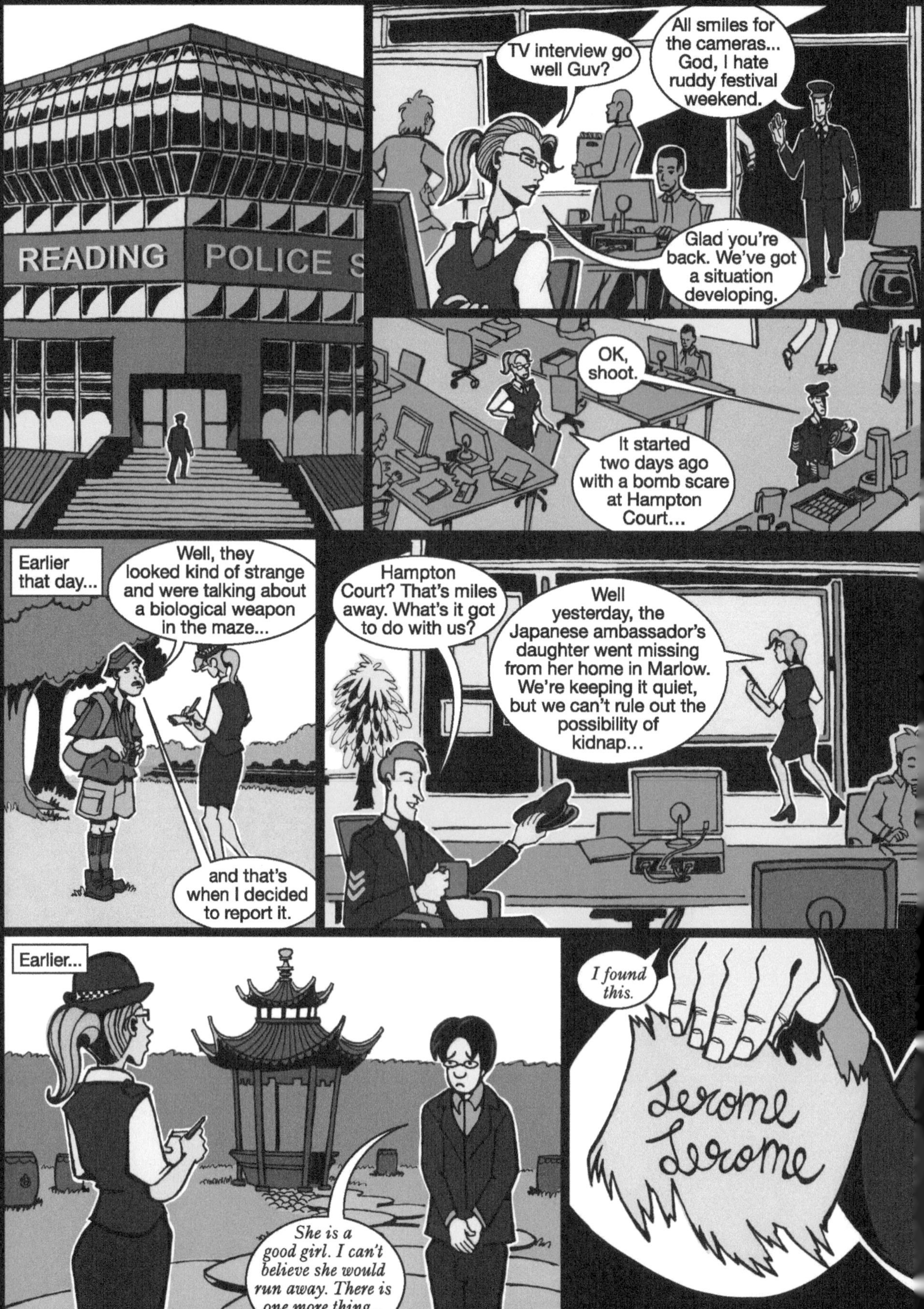
READING POLICE S
TV interview go well Guv?
All smiles for the cameras... God, I hate ruddy festival weekend.
Glad you're back. We've got a situation developing.
OK, shoot.
It started two days ago with a bomb scare at Hampton Court…
Earlier that day...
Well, they looked kind of strange and were talking about a biological weapon in the maze...
and that's when I decided to report it.
Hampton Court? That's miles away. What's it got to do with us?
Well yesterday, the Japanese ambassador's daughter went missing from her home in Marlow. We're keeping it quiet, but we can't rule out the possibility of kidnap…
Earlier...
She is a good girl. I can't believe she would run away. There is one more thing...
I found this.
Jerome Jerome

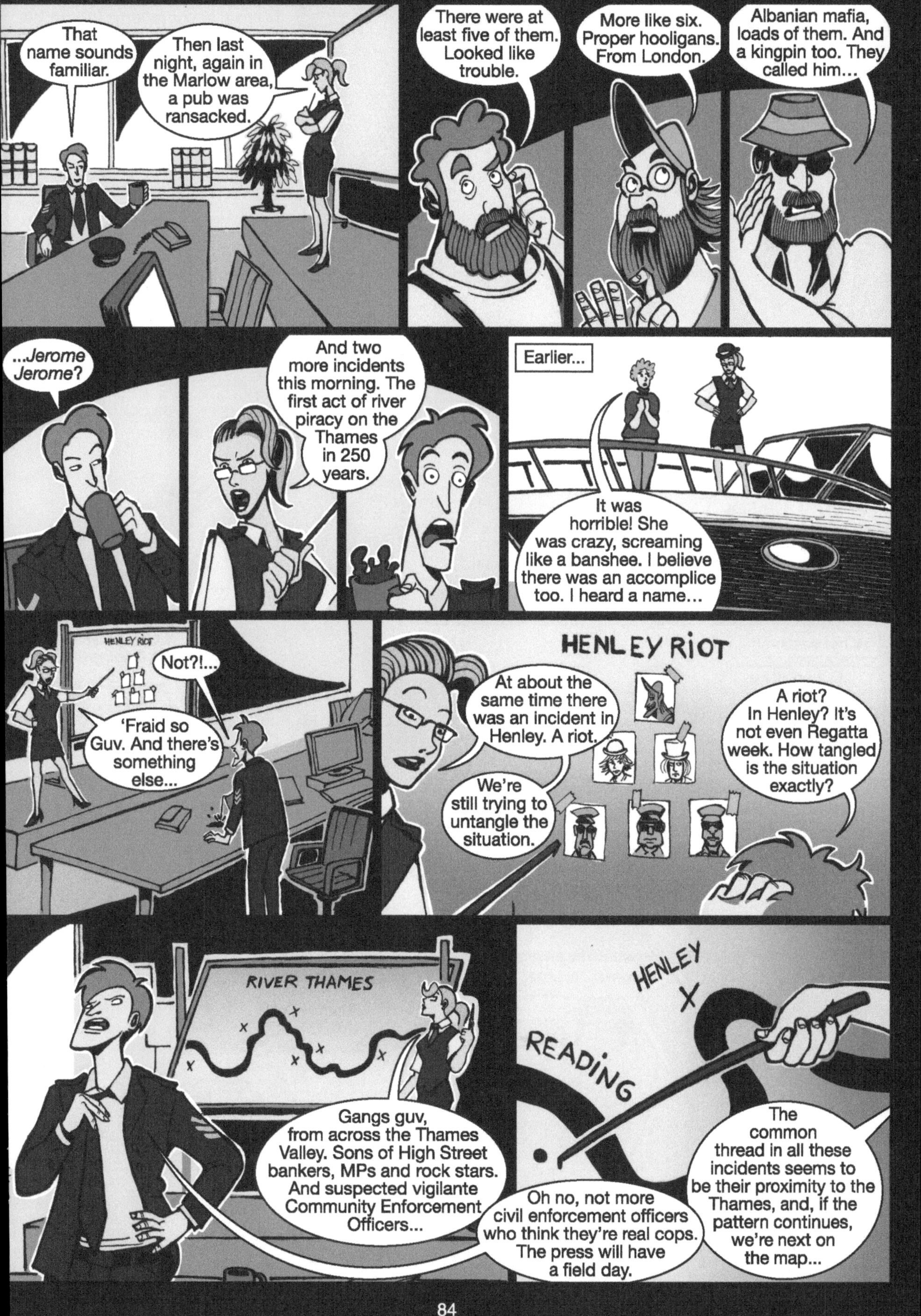
That name sounds familiar.
Then last night, again in the Marlow area, a pub was ransacked.
There were at least five of them. Looked like trouble.
More like six. Proper hooligans. From London.
Albanian mafia, loads of them. And a kingpin too. They called him...
...Jerome Jerome?
And two more incidents this morning. The first act of river piracy on the Thames in 250 years.
Earlier...
It was horrible! She was crazy, screaming like a banshee. I believe there was an accomplice too. I heard a name...
HENLEY RIOT
Not?!...
'Fraid so Guv. And there's something else...
HENLEY RIOT
At about the same time there was an incident in Henley. A riot.
We're still trying to untangle the situation.
A riot? In Henley? It's not even Regatta week. How tangled is the situation exactly?
RIVER THAMES
Gangs guv, from across the Thames Valley. Sons of High Street bankers, MPs and rock stars. And suspected vigilante Community Enforcement Officers...
Oh no, not more civil enforcement officers who think they're real cops. The press will have a field day.
HENLEY
READING
The common thread in all these incidents seems to be their proximity to the Thames, and, if the pattern continues, we're next on the map...

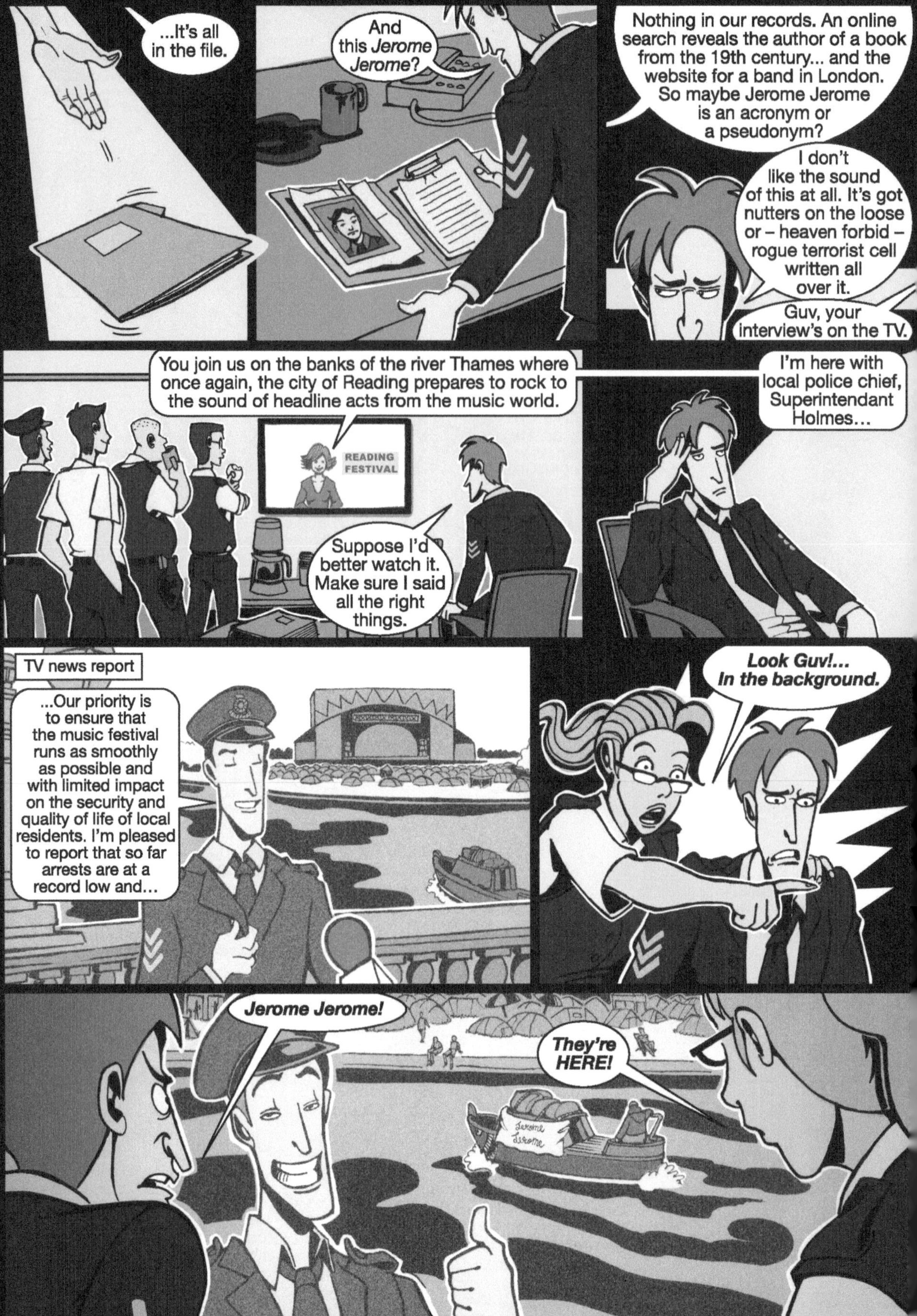

...It's all in the file.
And this *Jerome Jerome*?
Nothing in our records. An online search reveals the author of a book from the 19th century... and the website for a band in London. So maybe Jerome Jerome is an acronym or a pseudonym?
I don't like the sound of this at all. It's got nutters on the loose or – heaven forbid – rogue terrorist cell written all over it.
Guv, your interview's on the TV.
You join us on the banks of the river Thames where once again, the city of Reading prepares to rock to the sound of headline acts from the music world.
READING FESTIVAL
Suppose I'd better watch it. Make sure I said all the right things.
I'm here with local police chief, Superintendant Holmes...
TV news report
...Our priority is to ensure that the music festival runs as smoothly as possible and with limited impact on the security and quality of life of local residents. I'm pleased to report that so far arrests are at a record low and...
Look Guv!... In the background.
Jerome Jerome!
They're HERE!

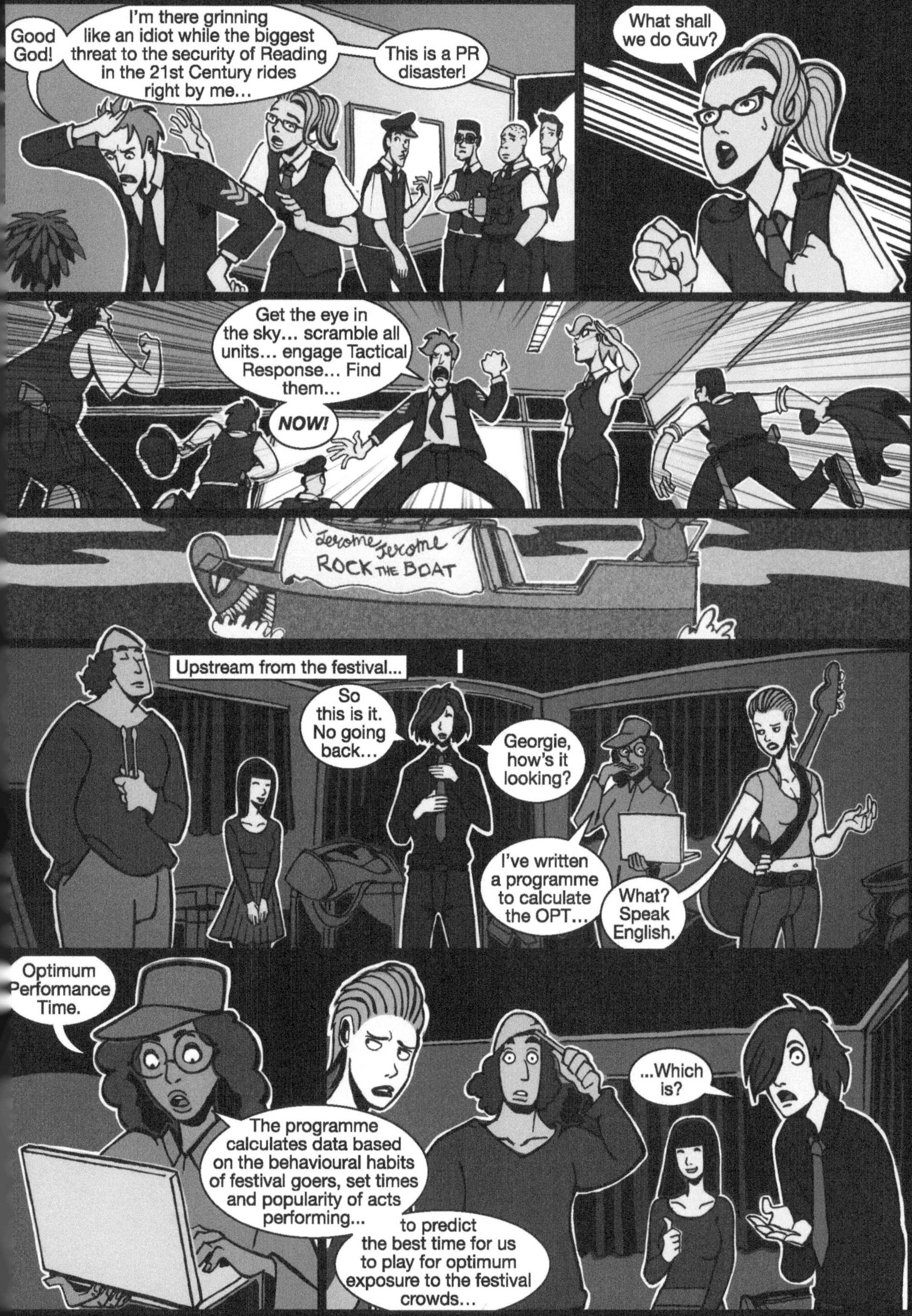
Good God!
I'm there grinning like an idiot while the biggest threat to the security of Reading in the 21st Century rides right by me...
This is a PR disaster!
What shall we do Guv?
Get the eye in the sky... scramble all units... engage Tactical Response... Find them...
NOW!
Jerome Jerome
ROCK THE BOAT
Upstream from the festival...
So this is it. No going back...
Georgie, how's it looking?
I've written a programme to calculate the OPT...
What? Speak English.
Optimum Performance Time.
The programme calculates data based on the behavioural habits of festival goers, set times and popularity of acts performing...
to predict the best time for us to play for optimum exposure to the festival crowds...
...Which is?

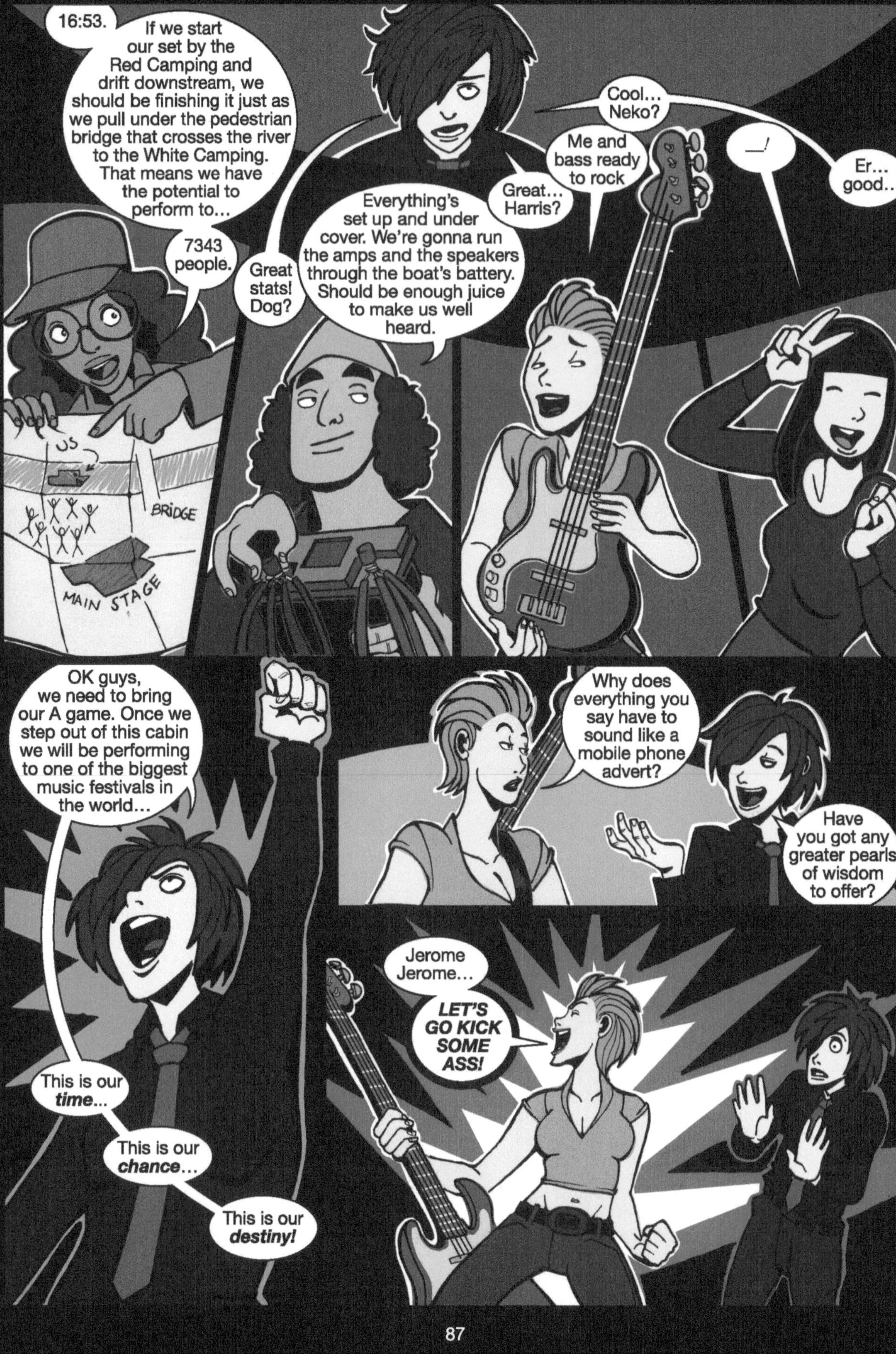
16:53.
If we start our set by the Red Camping and drift downstream, we should be finishing it just as we pull under the pedestrian bridge that crosses the river to the White Camping. That means we have the potential to perform to…
7343 people.
Great stats! Dog?
Everything's set up and under cover. We're gonna run the amps and the speakers through the boat's battery. Should be enough juice to make us well heard.
Great… Harris?
Me and bass ready to rock
Cool… Neko?
^_^!
Er… good…
US
BRIDGE
MAIN STAGE
OK guys, we need to bring our A game. Once we step out of this cabin we will be performing to one of the biggest music festivals in the world…
This is our *time*...
This is our *chance*...
This is our *destiny!*
Why does everything you say have to sound like a mobile phone advert?
Have you got any greater pearls of wisdom to offer?
Jerome Jerome…
LET'S GO KICK SOME ASS!

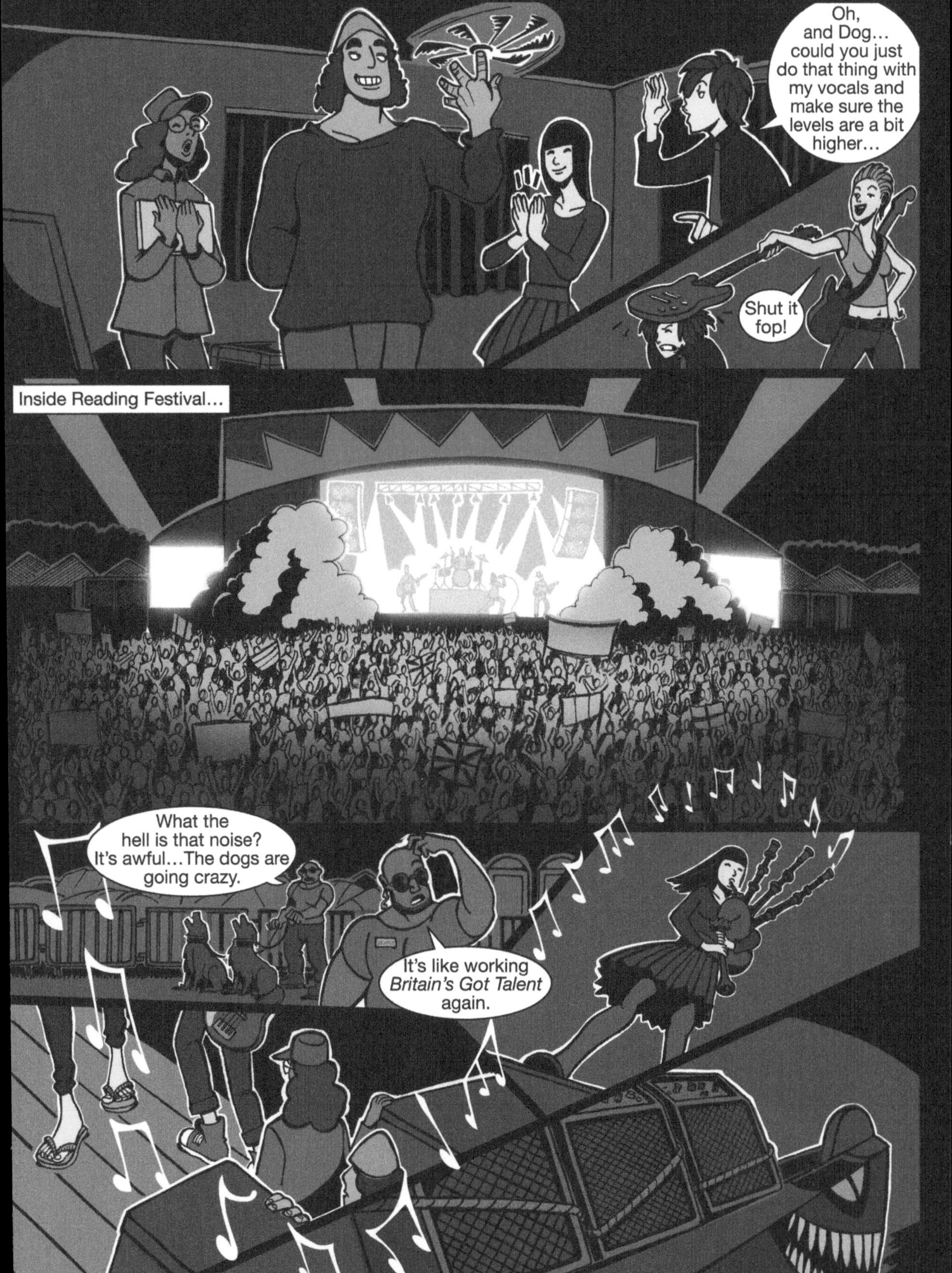

Oh, and Dog… could you just do that thing with my vocals and make sure the levels are a bit higher…
Shut it fop!
Inside Reading Festival…
What the hell is that noise? It's awful…The dogs are going crazy.
It's like working *Britain's Got Talent* again.

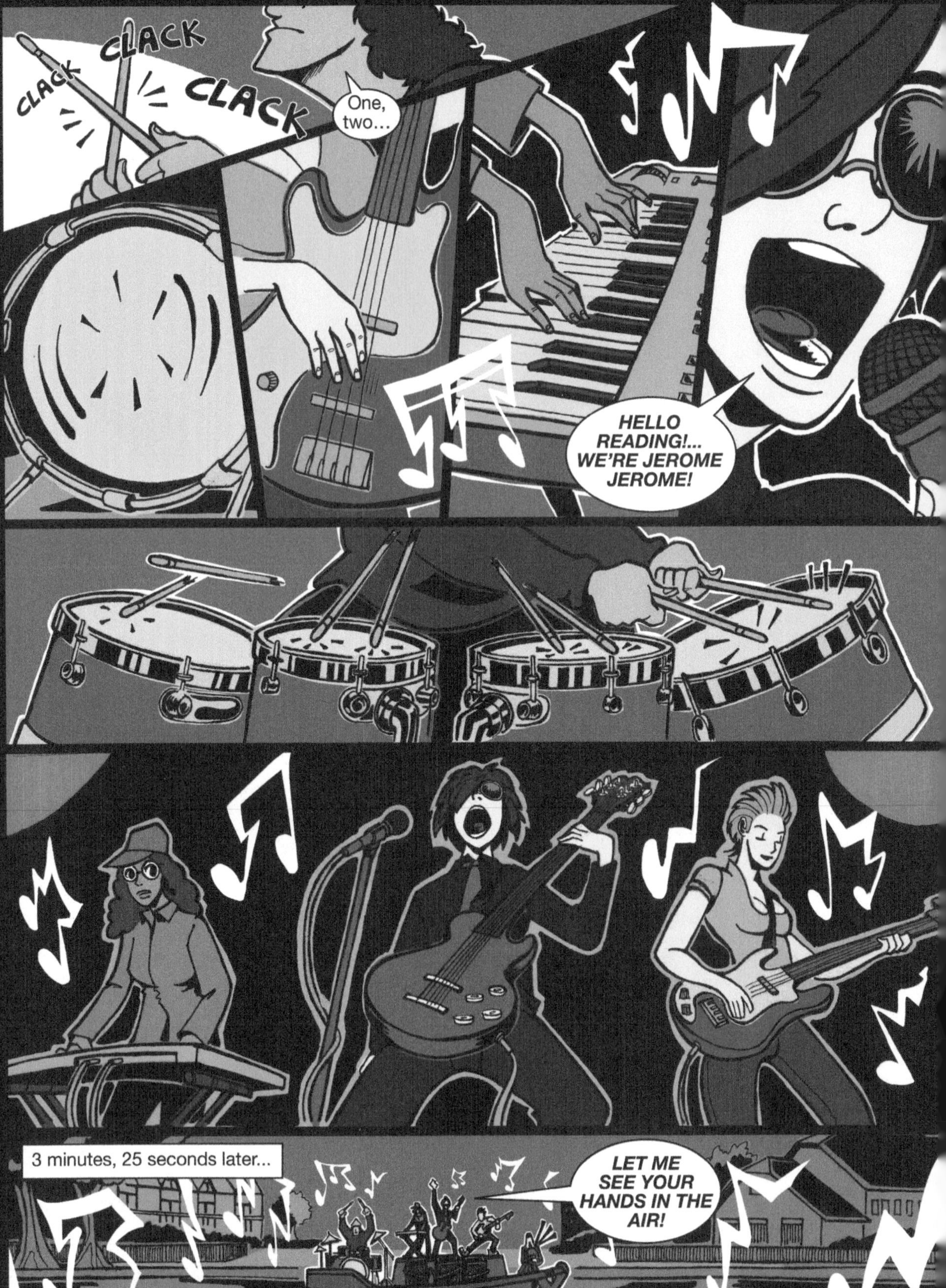
CLACK
CLACK
CLACK
CLACK
One, two...
HELLO READING!... WE'RE JEROME JEROME!
3 minutes, 25 seconds later...
LET ME SEE YOUR HANDS IN THE AIR!

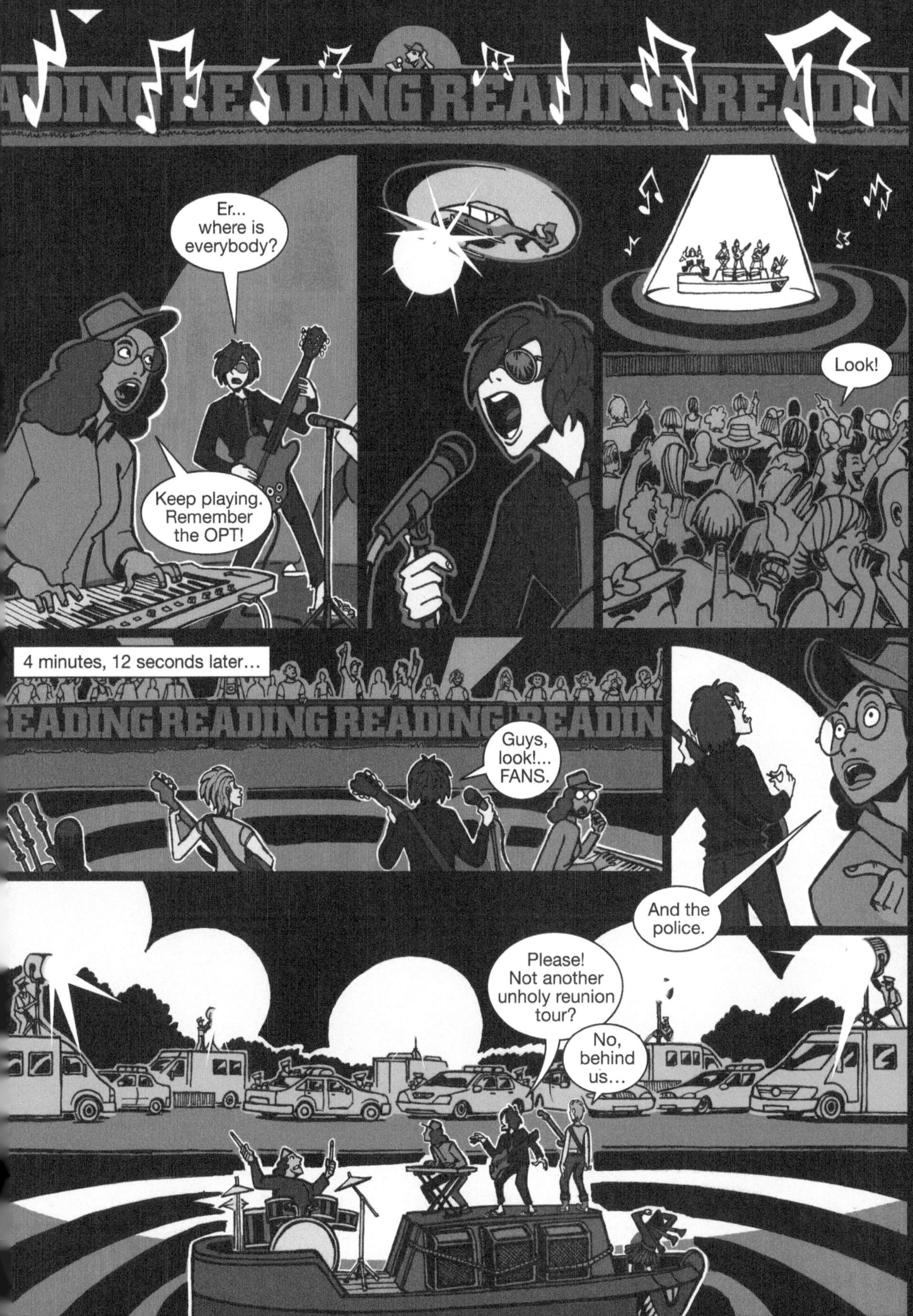
READING READING READING READIN
Er... where is everybody?
Keep playing. Remember the OPT!
Look!
4 minutes, 12 seconds later…
READING READING READING READIN
Guys, look!... FANS.
And the police.
Please! Not another unholy reunion tour?
No, behind us…

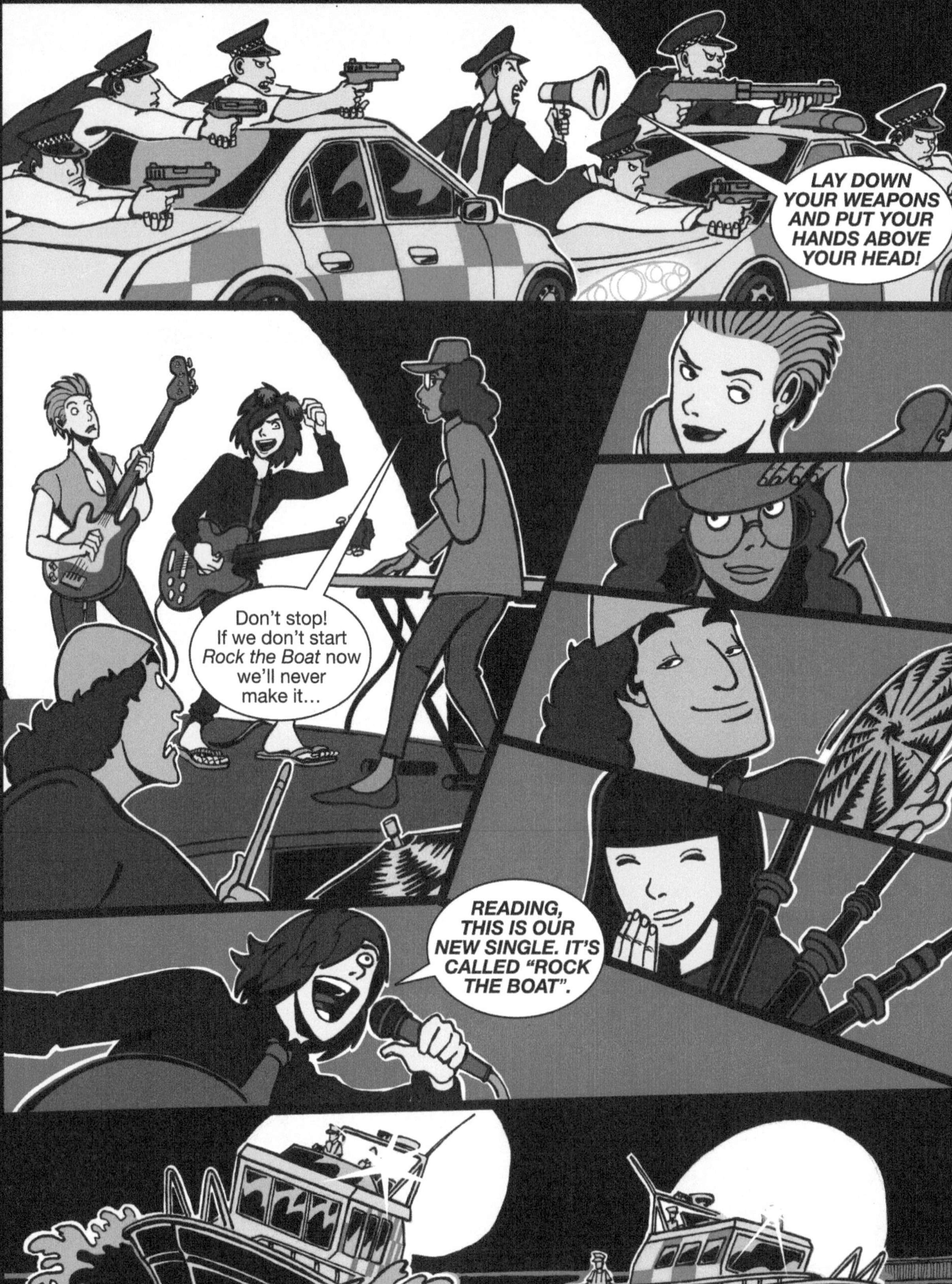
LAY DOWN YOUR WEAPONS AND PUT YOUR HANDS ABOVE YOUR HEAD!
Don't stop! If we don't start *Rock the Boat* now we'll never make it...
READING, THIS IS OUR NEW SINGLE. IT'S CALLED "ROCK THE BOAT".

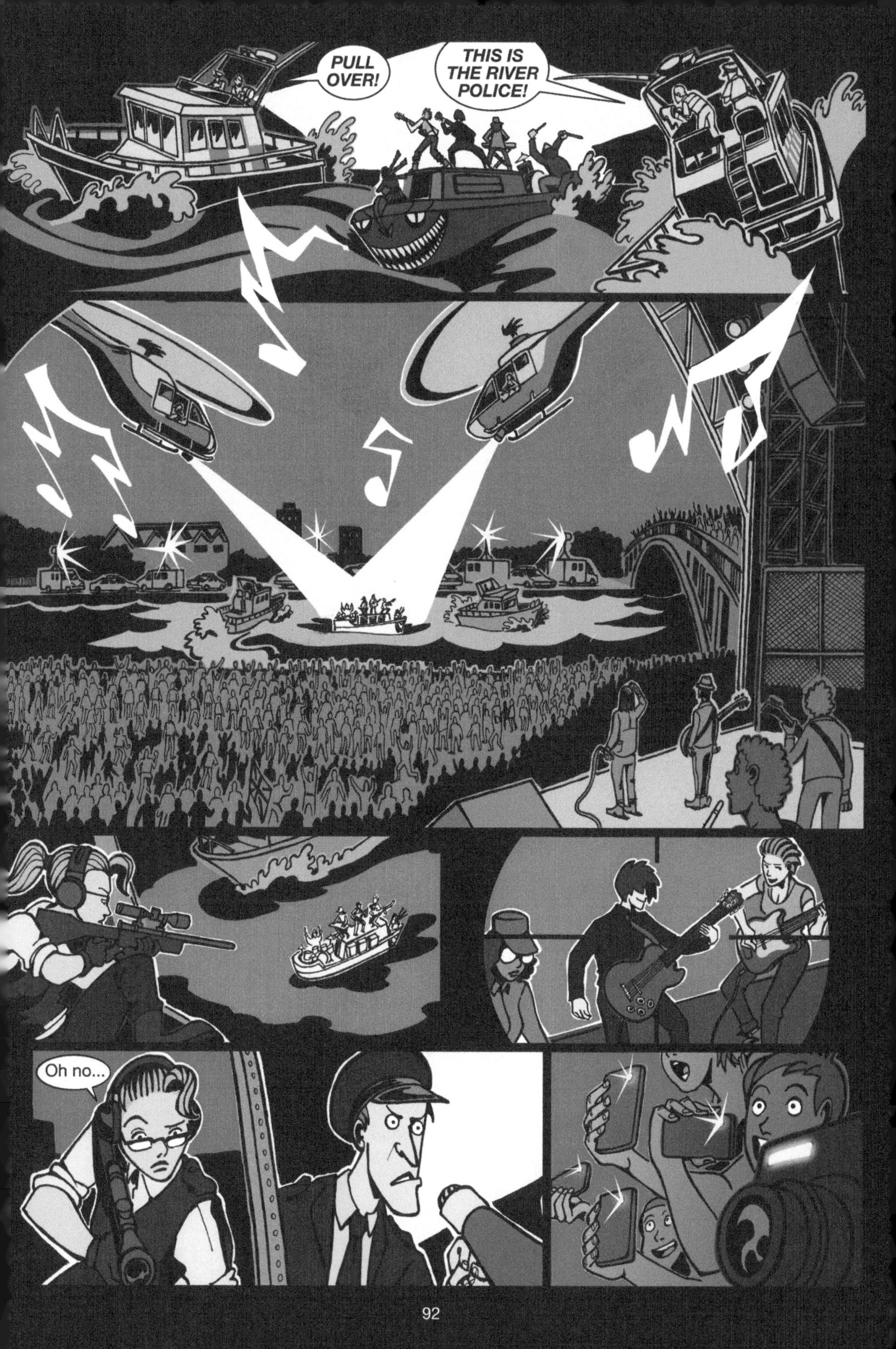
PULL OVER!
THIS IS THE RIVER POLICE!
Oh no...

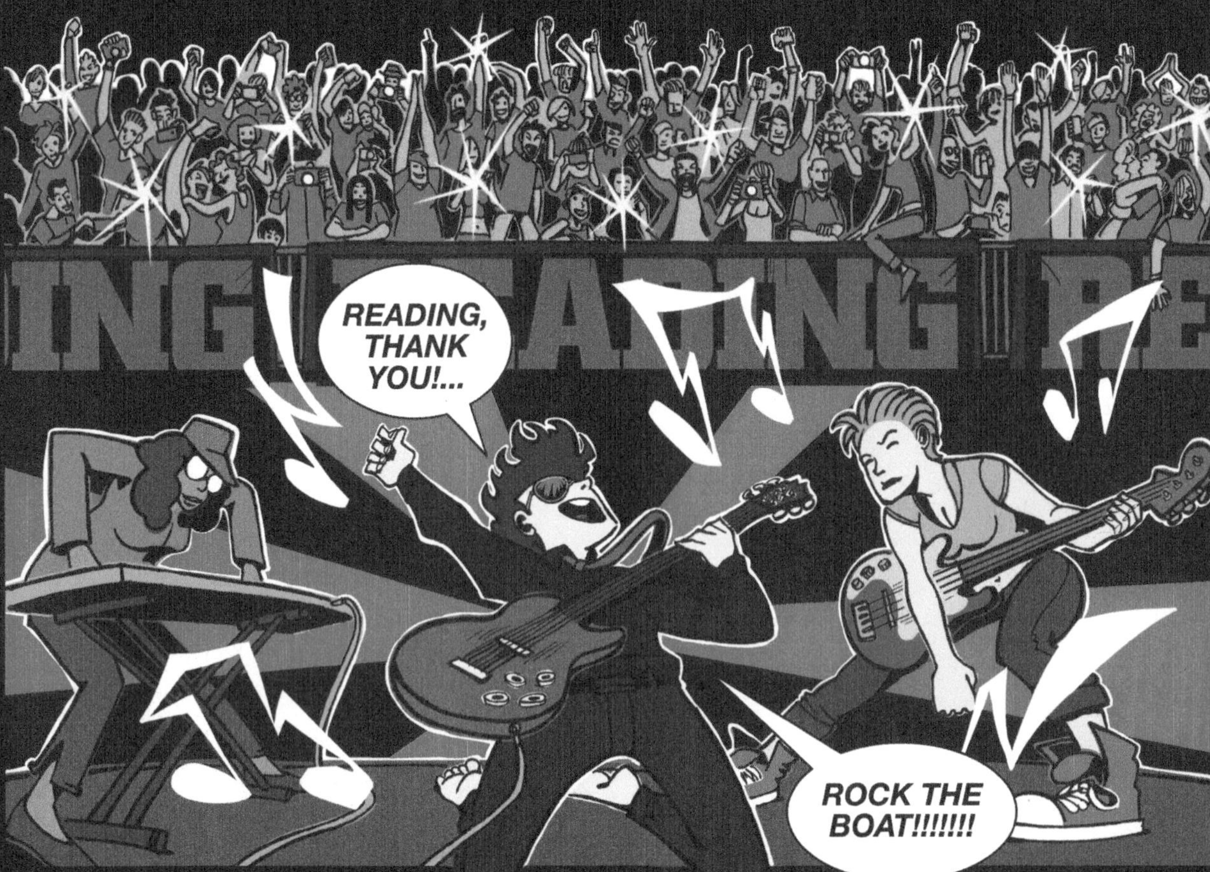
READING, THANK YOU!...
ROCK THE BOAT!!!!!!!

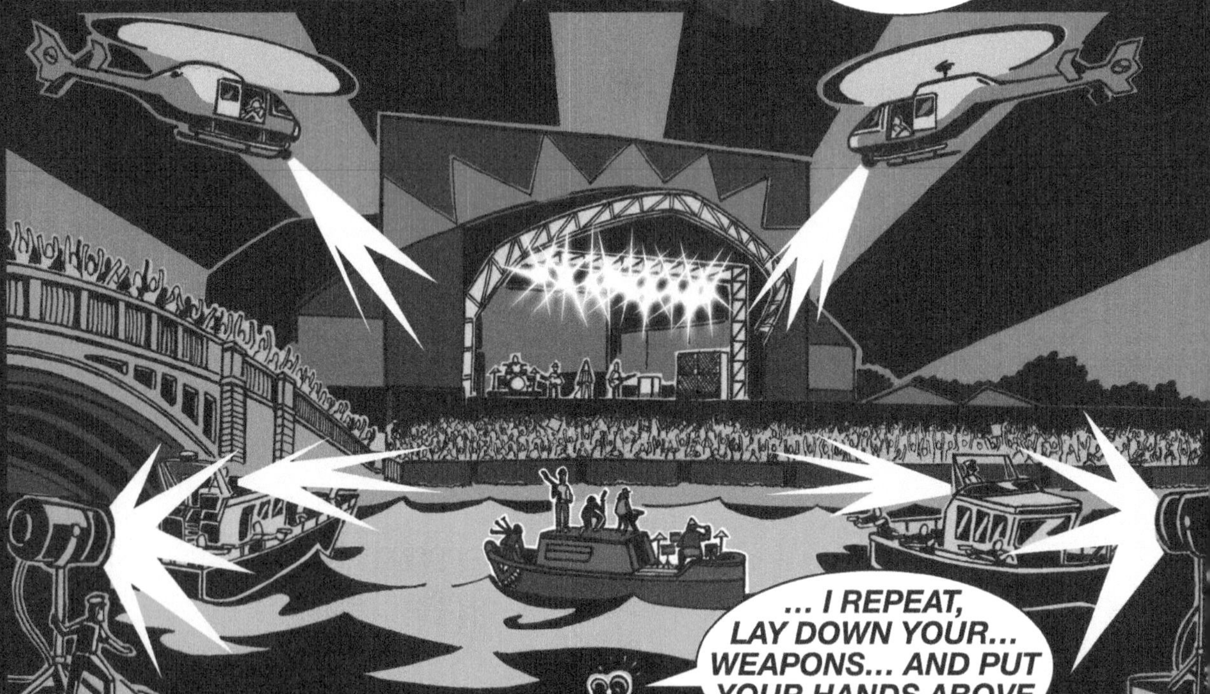
... I REPEAT, LAY DOWN YOUR... WEAPONS... AND PUT YOUR HANDS ABOVE YOUR HEAD.

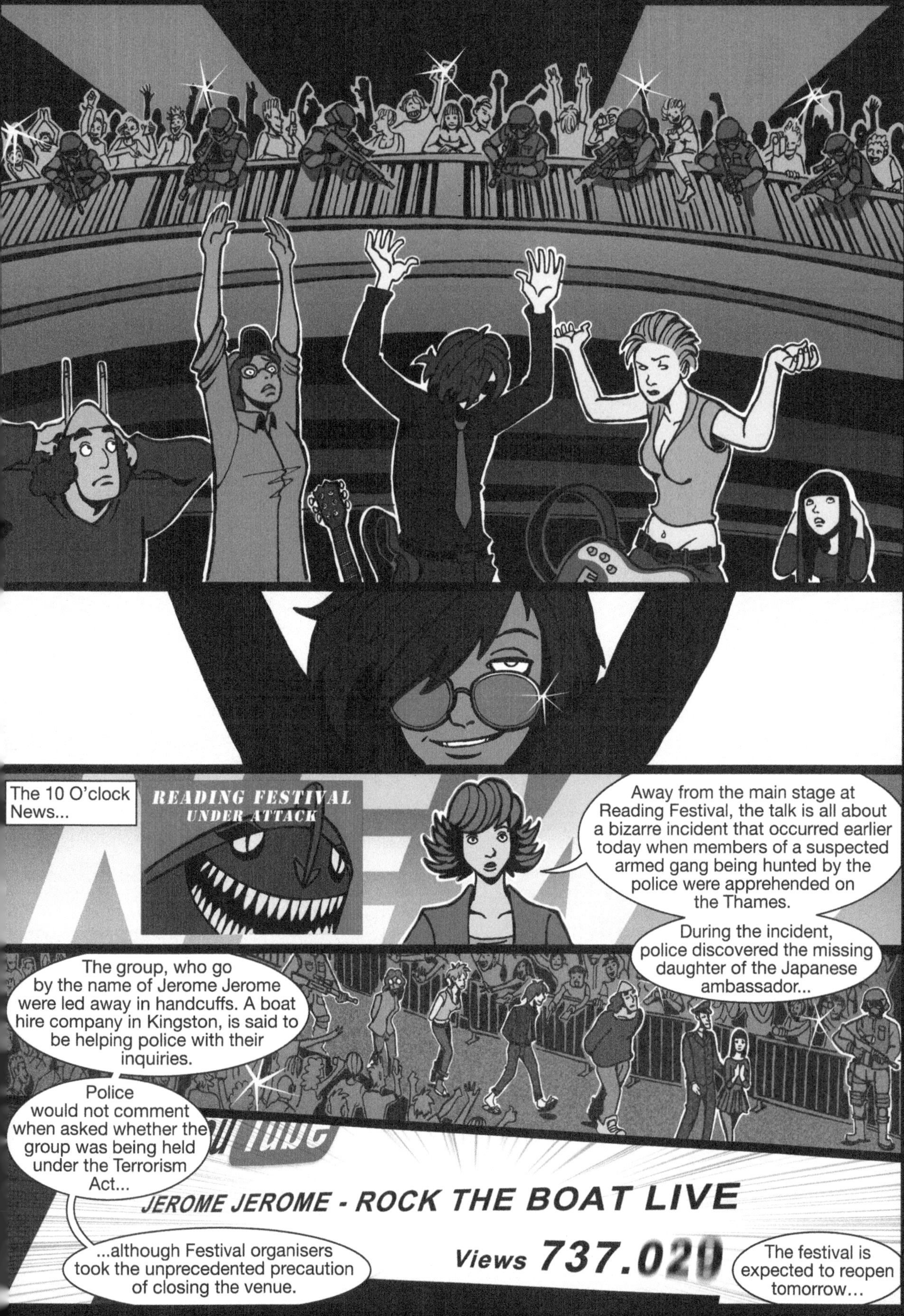
The 10 O'clock News...
READING FESTIVAL UNDER ATTACK
Away from the main stage at Reading Festival, the talk is all about a bizarre incident that occurred earlier today when members of a suspected armed gang being hunted by the police were apprehended on the Thames.
During the incident, police discovered the missing daughter of the Japanese ambassador...
The group, who go by the name of Jerome Jerome were led away in handcuffs. A boat hire company in Kingston, is said to be helping police with their inquiries.
Police would not comment when asked whether the group was being held under the Terrorism Act...
JEROME JEROME - ROCK THE BOAT LIVE
...although Festival organisers took the unprecedented precaution of closing the venue.
Views 737.020
The festival is expected to reopen tomorrow...

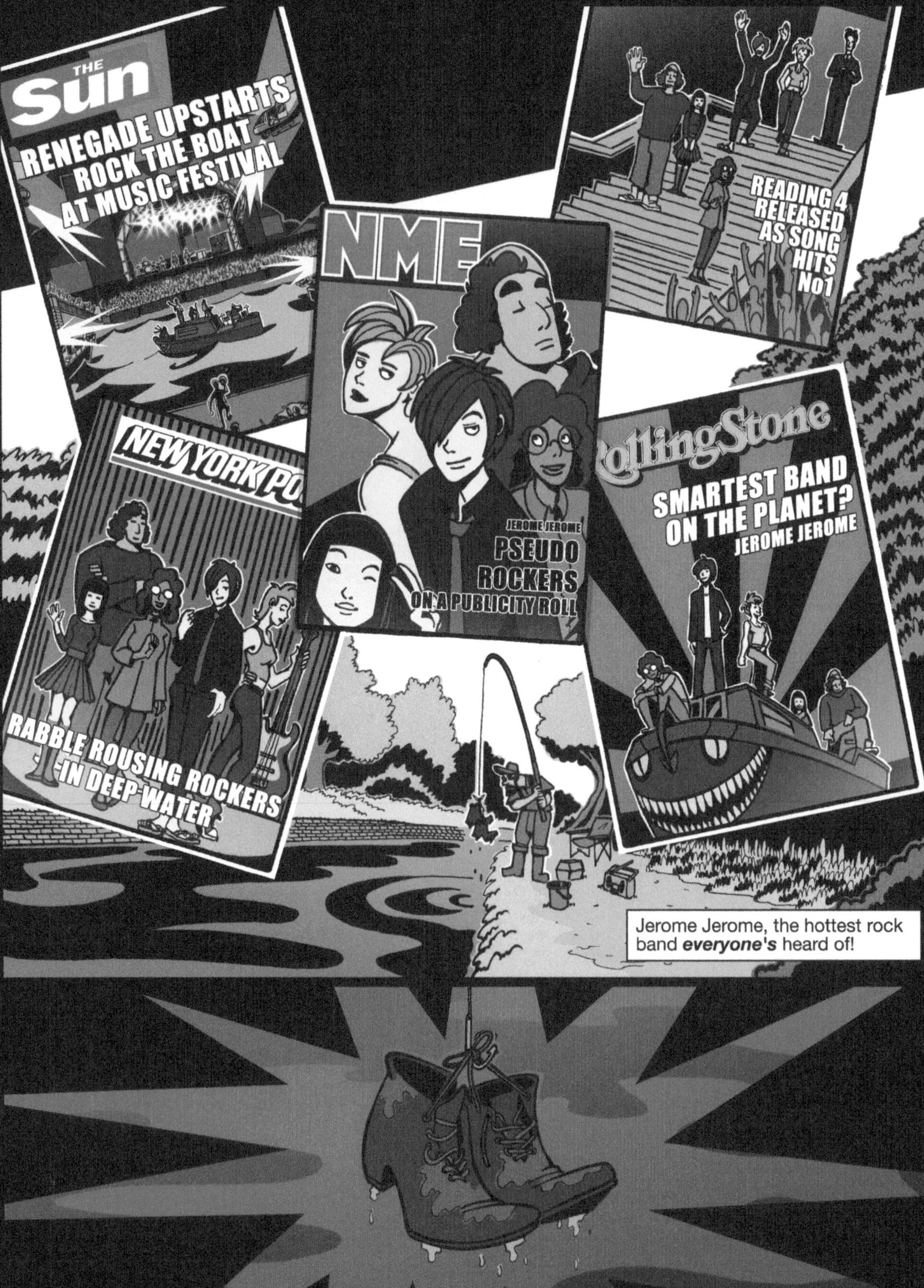
THE Sun
RENEGADE UPSTARTS ROCK THE BOAT AT MUSIC FESTIVAL
READING 4 RELEASED AS SONG HITS No1
NME
JEROME JEROME
PSEUDO ROCKERS ON A PUBLICITY ROLL
NEW YORK PO
RABBLE ROUSING ROCKERS IN DEEP WATER
RollingStone
SMARTEST BAND ON THE PLANET? JEROME JEROME
Jerome Jerome, the hottest rock band *everyone's* heard of!

BEHIND THE SCENES...

Biogs

Augustine Coll ...
is an artist with a background in film, animation and illustration. His artwork has been exhibited in galleries in London and Osaka. Originally from Barcelona, he now lives in London.

•

Tim Lay ...
is a writer and editor whose debut novel, The Sewerside Chronicles won the 2007 Undiscovered Authors prize. He has written and edited several books, writes scripts for films and graphic novels, promotes arts events and has invented card games. He divides his time between Devon and Brighton.

•

Paul Shinn...
is a London based illustrator and designer. His illustrations have been commissioned by magazines and charities, and his artwork has been exhibited in the UK and Japan.